REUNION AT THE MORGUE

I followed them into a room where we could see our breath. Dolan pulled a drawer out from the wall and uncovered the little old man. Ellis bent over the drawer and almost fell. Tears fell from his face onto the dead man's face.

"It's Nelson," he said in awe. "It's Nelson all right." He turned to Dolan. "But how did he get so old? He was just a young man when he went into the water off Okinawa."

"He was alive yesterday."

"No, you're mistaken. He was lost off the *Canaan Sound* over twenty-five years ago. And it was my fault." The awe was still in his voice. He turned to the dead man and touched his scarred face and said, "I'm sorry, Nelson." He got down on his knees, holding onto the edge of the drawers with his fingers. "Forgive me."

Half carrying him, we got him out of the cold room and sat him down on a chair. Dolan wet a towel and wiped his face. But he wouldn't look at us. He sat with his head hanging down in shame and sorrow.

Dolan drew me to the far side of the room and spoke in a low voice. "Do you think he's off his rocker?"

"He's drunk," I said.

SLEEPING BEAUTY
ROSS MACDONALD

BANTAM BOOKS

TORONTO • NEW YORK • LONDON • SYDNEY • AUCKLAND

SLEEPING BEAUTY
A Bantam Book / published by arrangement with
Alfred A. Knopf, Inc.

PRINTING HISTORY
Alfred A. Knopf edition published March 1973
2nd printing ..... May 1973   3rd printing ...... June 1973
4th printing . . . July 1973
Literary Guild edition published May 1973
Bantam edition / May 1974
2nd printing ..... May 1974   4th printing ... February 1980
3rd printing ...... June 1974   5th printing .. December 1984

ISBN 0-553-24593-7

Published simultaneously in the United States and Canada

PRINTED IN THE UNITED STATES OF AMERICA

H   14 13 12 11 10 9 8 7 6 5

To Eudora Welty

I

I flew home from Mazatlán on a Wednesday afternoon. As we approached Los Angeles, the Mexicana plane dropped low over the sea and I caught my first glimpse of the oil spill.

It lay on the blue water off Pacific Point in a freeform slick that seemed miles wide and many miles long. An offshore oil platform stood up out of its windward end like the metal handle of a dagger that had stabbed the world and made it spill black blood.

The flight steward came along the aisle, making sure that we were ready to land. I asked him what had happened to the ocean. His hands and shoulders made a south-of-the-border gesture which alluded to the carelessness of Anglos.

"She blew out Monday." He leaned across me and looked down past the wing. "She's worse today than she was yesterday. Fasten your seat belt, *Señor*. We'll be landing in five minutes."

I bought a paper at International Airport. The oil spill was front-page news. A vice-president of the oil company that owned the offshore platform, a man named Jack Lennox, predicted that the spill would be controlled within twenty-four hours. Jack Lennox was a good-looking man, if you could judge by his picture, but there was no way to know whether he was telling the truth.

Pacific Point was one of my favorite places on the coast. As I made my way out to the airport parking lot, the oil spill threatening the city's beaches floated like a depression just over the horizon of my mind.

Instead of driving home to West Los Angeles, I turned south along the coast to Pacific Point. The sun was low when I got there. From the hill above the harbor, I could see the enormous slick spreading like premature night across the sea.

At its nearest it was perhaps a thousand yards out,

well beyond the dark brown kelp beds which formed a natural barrier offshore. Workboats were moving back and forth, spraying the edges of the spill with chemicals. They were the only boats I could see on the water. A white plastic boom was strung across the harbor entrance, and gulls that looked like white plastic whirled above it.

I made my way down to the public beach and along it to the sandy point which partly enclosed the harbor. A few people, mostly women and girls, were standing at the edge of the water, facing out to sea. They looked as if they were waiting for the end of the world, or as if the end had come and they would never move again.

The surf was rising sluggishly. A black bird with a sharp beak was struggling in it. The bird had orange-red eyes, which seemed to be burning with anger, but it was so fouled with oil that at first I didn't recognize it as a western grebe.

A woman in a white shirt and slacks waded in thigh-deep and picked it up, holding its head so that it wouldn't peck her. I could see as she came back toward me that she was a handsome young woman with dark eyes as angry as the bird's. Her narrow feet left beautifully shaped prints in the wet sand.

I asked her what she was going to do with the grebe.

"Take it home and clean it."

"It probably won't survive, I'm afraid."

"No, but maybe I will."

She walked away, holding the black struggling thing against her white shirt. I walked along behind in her elegant footprints. She became aware of this, and turned to face me.

"What do you want?"

"I should apologize. I didn't mean to be discouraging."

"Forget it," she said. "It's true not many live once they've been oiled. But I saved some in the Santa Barbara spill."

"You must be quite a bird expert."

"I'm getting to be one in self-defense. My family is in the oil business."

She gestured with her head toward the offshore platform. Then she turned and left me abruptly. I stood and watched her hurrying southward along the beach, holding the damaged grebe as if it were her child.

I followed her as far as the wharf which formed the southern boundary of the harbor. One of the workboats had opened the boom and let the other boats in. They were coming alongside the wharf and tying up.

The wind had changed, and I began to smell the floating oil. It smelled like something that had died but would never go away.

There was a restaurant on the wharf, displaying on its roof a neon sign which spelled out "Blanche's Seafood." I was hungry, and went that way. On the far side of the sprawling restaurant building, the wharf was covered with chemical drums, machinery, stacks of oil-well casings. Men were debarking from the workboats at a landing stage.

I went up to an aging roustabout with a sun-cracked face under a red hard hat. I asked him what the situation was.

"We ain't supposed to talk about it. The company does the talking."

"Lennox?"

"I guess that's their name."

A burly straw boss intervened. He had black oil on his clothes, and his high-heeled Western boots were soaked with it.

"You from a media?"

"No. I'm just a citizen."

He looked me over suspiciously. "Local?"

"L.A."

"You're not supposed to be out here."

He nudged me with his belly. The men around him became suddenly still. They looked rough and tired and disappointed, ready to take their revenge on anything that moved.

I went back toward the restaurant. A man who looked like a fisherman was waiting just around the corner of the building. Under his ribbed wool cap, his face was young-eyed and hairy.

"Don't mess with them," he said.

"I wasn't planning to."

"Half of them came from Texas, inland Texas. They think water is a nuisance because they can't sell it for two or three dollars a barrel. All they care about is the oil they're losing. They don't give a damn about the things that live in the sea or the people that live in the town."

"Is the oil still running?"

"Sure it is. They thought they had it closed down Monday, the day she blew. Before that she was roaring wild, with drilling mud and hydrocarbon mist shooting a hundred feet in the air. They dropped the string in the hole and closed the blind rams over her, and they thought she was shut down. The main hole was. But then she started to boil up through the water, gas and oil emulsion all around the platform."

"You sound like an eyewitness."

The young man blinked and nodded. "That I was. I took a reporter out there in my boat—man from the local paper named Wilbur Cox. They were evacuating the platform when we got there, the fire hazard was so bad."

"Any lives lost?"

"No, sir. That's the one good thing about it." He squinted at me through his hair. "Would you be a reporter?"

"No. I'm just interested. What caused the blowout, do you know?"

He pointed with his thumb at the sky, then down at the sea. "There's quite a few different stories floating around. Inadequate casing is one of them. But there's something the matter with the structures down there. They're all broken up. It's like trying to make a clean hole in a piece of cake and hold water in it. They should never have tried to drill out there."

The oil men from the workboats went by, straggling like the remnants of a defeated army. The fisherman gave them an ironic salute, his teeth gleaming in his beard. They returned pitying looks, as if he was a madman who didn't understand what was important.

I went into the restaurant. There were voices in the bar, at the same time boisterous and lugubrious, but the dining room was almost deserted. It was done in a kind of landbound nautical style, with portholes instead of windows. Two men were waiting to pay at the cashier's desk.

I noticed them because they made a strange pair. One of them was young, the other was old and shaky. But they didn't give the impression of being father and son. They didn't even look as if they had come from the same world.

The old man was almost hairless, with livid head scars which ran down the side of his face and puckered it. He had on an old gray tweed suit which looked tailor-made. But his slight body was almost lost in it. I guessed that the suit had been made for another man, or perhaps for himself when he was younger and larger. He moved like a man lost in the world, lost in time.

The younger man wore Levis and a black turtleneck sweater which emphasized the breadth of his shoulders. They were so wide that they made his head seem small. He noticed that I was looking at him, and returned the look. His eyes reminded me of certain losers I had known. They peered out at the world through reinforced windows which kept them in and other people out.

A heavy blonde woman in an orange dress took their money and rang it up on the cash register. The young man paid, and picked up the change. The man in the tweed suit took hold of his arm, in the manner of a blind man or an invalid with his nurse.

The blonde woman opened the door for them and, as if in answer to a question, pointed south along the beach.

When she brought me a menu, I asked her who they were.

"Never saw them before in my life. They must be tourists—they don't know their way around the Point at all. We're getting a lot of sightseers the last couple of days." She gave me a sharp look. "You're new here yourself. You wouldn't be one of these troubleshooters they're bringing in for the oil?"

"No. I'm just another tourist."

"Well, you came to the right place." She looked around the room possessively. "I'm Blanche, in case you were wondering. Something to drink? I always serve doubles; that's the secret of my success."

I ordered bourbon on the rocks. Then I made the mistake of ordering fish. It seemed to taste of oil. I left my dinner half eaten and went outside.

II

The tide was coming in more strongly now, and I was afraid that the oil would come in with it. It might be on the beaches by tomorrow. I decided to go for a farewell walk southward along the shore. That happened to be the direction the woman with the grebe had taken.

The sunset spilled on the water and flared across the sky. The sky changed through several colors and became a soft crumbled gray. It was like walking under the roof of an enormous cave where hidden fires burned low.

I came to a kind of natural corner where the shoreline curved out and a cliff rose abruptly from the beach. A few late surfers were waiting on the water for a final big one.

I watched them until a big one rose out of the darkening sea and brought most of them in. A cormorant flew across the water like an urgent afterthought.

I walked on for another half-mile or so. The beach was narrow and getting narrower, encroached on by the waves and crowded by the cliff. The cliff was fifty or sixty feet high at this point. Rough paths and precarious wooden stairways climbed here and there to the houses on its top.

I told myself I couldn't get caught by the tide. But night was falling now, and the sea was rising to meet it.

A couple of hundred yards ahead of me, a scattering of boulders lay at the foot of the cliff and blocked the beach. I decided to walk that far and then turn back. There was something about the place that worried me. The cliff and the boulders at its base looked in the fading light like something seen for the last time.

A white object was lodged high among the boulders. When I got nearer, I could see that it was a woman and hear between the sounds of the surf that she was crying. She turned her face away from me, but not before I'd recognized her.

As I came near, she sat perfectly still, pretending to be an accidental object caught in a crevice.

"Is there something the matter?"

She stopped crying with a gulp, as though she had swallowed her tears, and turned her face away. "No. There's nothing the matter."

"Did the bird die?"

"Yes. It died." Her voice was high and tight. "Now are you satisfied?"

"It takes a lot to satisfy me. Don't you think you should find a safer place to sit?"

She didn't respond at first. Then her head turned slowly. Her wet eyes gleamed at me in the deep twilight.

"I like it here. I hope the tide comes and gets me."

"Because one grebe died? A lot of diving birds are going to die."

"Don't keep talking about death. Please." She struggled out of her crevice and got to her feet. "Who are you anyway? Did somebody send you here to find me?"

"I came of my own accord."

"You followed me?"

"Not exactly. I was taking a walk." A wave came in and splashed against the boulders. I could feel the cold spray on my face. "Don't you think we better get out of here?"

She looked around in a quick, desperate movement, then up at the cliff where a cantilevered house hung over her head like a threat. "I don't know where to go."

"I thought you lived in the neighborhood."

"No." She was silent for a moment. "Where do you live?"

"Los Angeles. West Los Angeles."

Her eyes shifted as if she had made a decision. "So do I."

I didn't quite believe in the coincidence, but I was willing to go along with it and see where it led. "Do you have transportation?"

"No."

"I'll take you home."

She came along without any argument. She told me that her name was Laurel Russo, Mrs. Thomas Russo. I said my name was Lew Archer. Something about the situation made me hold back the fact that I was a private detective.

Before we reached the end of the cliff where the beach curved, a high wave came up and soaked our feet and brought in the last surfer. He joined the others, who were squatting around a driftwood fire built under the brow of a natural cave. Their oiled faces and bodies gleamed in the firelight. They looked as if they had given up on civilization and were ready for anything or nothing.

There were other people on the beach, talking in low tones or waiting in silence. We stood with them for a little while in the semidarkness. The ocean and its shores were never entirely dark: the water gathered light like the mirror of a telescope.

The woman was standing so close to me I could feel her breath on my neck. Still she seemed a long way off, at a telescopic distance from me and the others. She seemed to feel it, too. She took hold of my hand. Her hand was cold.

The wide-shouldered young man in the black turtleneck whom I had seen in Blanche's Restaurant had appeared on the wharf again. He jumped down onto the sand and came toward us. His movements were rather clumsy and mechanical, as if somebody had activated them by pressing a button.

He stopped and looked at the woman with a kind of menacing excitement. Still holding on to my hand, she turned and pulled me toward the road. Her grip was tight and spasmodic, like a frightened child's. The young man stood and watched us go.

Under the streetlights, I got a good look at her. Her face seemed frozen, her eyes in deep dark shock. When we got into my car, I could smell her fear.

"Who is he?"

"I don't know. Honestly."

"Then why are you afraid of him?"

"I'm just afraid, period. Can't we leave it at that?"

"It wasn't Tom Russo, was it? Your husband?"

"Certainly not."

She was shivering. I kept an old raincoat in the trunk of my car, and I got it out and put it over her shoulders. She didn't look at me or thank me.

I drove up the ramp onto the freeway. The traffic going north with us wasn't heavy. But an unbroken stream of headlights poured toward us from Los Angeles, as if the city was leaking light through a hole in its side.

III

The woman rode in a silence so complete that I hesitated to break it. I glanced at her face from time to time. Her expression seemed to keep changing, from grief and fear and dismay to cold indifference. I wondered what caused the changes, or if my mind had conspired with the lights to half imagine them.

We left the freeway at my West Los Angeles turnoff.

She spoke in a small, tentative voice: "Where do you live, Mr.—?" She had forgotten my name.

"Archer," I said. "I have an apartment just a few blocks from here."

"Would you greatly mind if I phoned my husband from your apartment? He isn't expecting me. I've been staying with relatives."

I should have asked where her husband lived and driven her there. But I took her home to my place.

She stood barefooted in my living room with my old raincoat hanging on her, and looked around as if she was slumming. Her thoughtlessness of manner made me wonder what her background was. There was probably money there, possibly quite new money.

I showed her the phone on the desk and went into the bedroom to unpack my carry-on bag. When I went back into the living room, she was huddled over the phone. The black receiver was pressed to the inside of her head like a surgical device which had drained all the blood from her face.

I didn't realize that the line was dead until she laid the receiver down, very gently. Then she put her face down on her arms. Her hair fell across my desk like a heavy shadow.

I stood and watched her for a while, unwilling to intrude on her feelings, perhaps unwilling to share them. She was full of trouble. But somehow she looked quite natural in my room.

After a while, she lifted her head. Her face was as calm as a mask. "I'm sorry, I didn't know you were there."

"Don't be sorry."

"I have something to be sorry about. Tom won't come and get me. He has a woman with him. She answered the phone."

"What about the relatives you've been staying with?"

"Nothing about them."

She looked around the room as if her life had suddenly narrowed down.

"You mentioned you had a family. You said they were in the oil business."

"You must have misunderstood me. And I'm getting tired of being questioned, if you don't mind." Her mood was swinging like an erratic pendulum from being hurt to hurting. "You seem to be mortally afraid of getting stuck with me."

"On the contrary. You can stay here all night if you want to."

"With you?"

"You can have the bedroom. This chesterfield opens out into a sleeper."

"And what would it cost me?"

"Nothing."

"Do I look like an easy mark?"

She stood up, dropping my raincoat from her shoulders. It was an act of rejection. At the same time she was inadvertently showing me her body. It was deep in the breast, where the bird had left its dark stains on her shirt; narrow in the waist, deep in the hips, full-thighed. There was sand on the rug from her dirty elegant feet.

I caught an oblique glimpse of myself as a middle-aged man on the make. It was true that if she had been old or ugly I wouldn't have brought her home with me. She was neither. In spite of her discontent and fear, her head had a dark unchanging beauty.

"I don't want anything from you," I said, asking myself if I was telling her the truth.

"People always want something. Don't try to fool yourself. I should never have come here with you." She looked around like a child in a strange place. "I don't like it here."

"You're free to leave, Mrs. Russo."

She began to cry suddenly. The tears ran down her uncovered face, leaving shiny tracks. Moved by compunction or desire, I reached for her shoulders with my hands. She backed away and stood vibrating.

"Sit down," I said. "You're welcome to stay. Nobody's going to hurt you."

She didn't believe me. I guessed that she had been badly hurt already, perhaps damaged like the grebe beyond hope of recovery. She touched her grief-smeared face.

"Is there someplace where I can wash?"

I showed her the door to the bathroom. She locked it emphatically behind her. She was in there quite a long time. When she came out, her eyes were brighter and she moved with more confidence, like an alcoholic who has taken a secret drink.

"Well," she said, "I'll be on my way."

"Do you have any money?"

"I don't need money where I'm going."

"What is that supposed to mean?"

My voice was sharp, and she overreacted to it. "You expect me to pay you for the ride? And here I am breathing your valuable air."

"You want to pick a fight with someone. Why does it have to be me?"

She chose to take this as a final rejection. She opened the door abruptly and left the apartment. I had an urge to follow her, but I went no farther than the mailbox. I sat at my desk and began to go through the mail that had piled up during my week's vacation.

Most of it was bills. There was a three-hundred-dollar check from a man whose son I had found living with

five other teenagers in an apartment in Isla Vista. I had
gone to Mazatlán on the strength of it. There was a la-
boriously hand-printed letter from an inmate of a maxi-
mum security facility in central California. He said he
was innocent and wanted me to prove it. He added in a
postscript:

"Even if I am not innocent, why can't they let me go
now? I am an old man, I would not hurt nobody now.
What harm can I do if they let me go now?"

Like a long-distance call being placed, my mind made
an obscure series of connections. I got up, almost over-
turning the light chair, and went into the bathroom. The
door of the medicine cabinet was partly open. There had
been a vial of Nembutal in the cabinet, thirty-five or
forty capsules left over from a time when I had forgotten
how to sleep, and then had learned again. They weren't
there now.

IV

She had been gone ten or twelve minutes when I went
down to the empty street. I got into my car and drove
around the block. There were no pedestrians at all, no
trace of Laurel Russo.

I drove as far as Wilshire, then realized that I was
wasting my time. I went back to my apartment and
looked up Thomas Russo in the phone directory. His
address was on the border of Westwood, not more than
three or four miles from me. I made a note of his address and telephone number.

His phone rang a dozen times, rhythmic and raucous
as a death rattle, before the receiver was lifted. "Russo
residence, Tom Russo speaking."

"This is Lew Archer. You don't know me, but it's
about your wife."

"Laurel? Has something happened?"

"Not yet. But I'm concerned about her. She took
some sleeping pills from my apartment."

His voice became suspicious. "Are you her boy friend?"

"No, I'm not. You are."

"What was she doing in your apartment?"

"She wanted to phone you. When you turned her down, she left with my sleeping capsules."

"What kind of sleeping capsules?"

"Three-quarter-grain Nembutal."

"How many?"

"At least three dozen. Enough to kill her."

"I know that," Russo said. "I'm a pharmacist."

"Is she likely to take them?"

"I don't know." But there was a whisper of fear in his voice.

"Has she attempted suicide before?"

"I don't know who I'm talking to." Which meant she probably had. "Are you some kind of policeman?"

"I'm a private detective."

"I suppose her parents hired you."

"Nobody hired me. I met your wife on the beach at Pacific Point. Apparently the oil spill upset her, and she asked me to bring her to Los Angeles. When you turned her down—"

"Please don't keep saying that. I didn't turn her down. I told her I couldn't take her back unless she was ready to give it a good try. I couldn't stand another patch-up job and then another break. The last one nearly killed me."

"What about her?"

"She doesn't care about me the way I— Look, I'm telling you my family secrets."

"Tell me more, Mr. Russo. Who else would she be likely to call, or go to?"

"I'd need time to think about that, and I don't have the time. I have the night shift at the drugstore. I ought to be there now."

"Which store?"

"The Save-More, in Westwood."

"I'll come by there. Will you make me a list of the people she might try to get in touch with?"

Russo said he would try to.

I drove up Wilshire in the right-hand lane, looking for

Laurel among the people on the sidewalk. I parked in the Save-More lot and went into the drugstore through a turnstile. The fluorescent lighting made the atmosphere seem artificial and remote, like that of a space station.

A dozen or so young people were wandering around among the display shelves, boys with John-the-Baptist heads, girls dressed like Whistler's mother. The man in the glass-enclosed pharmacist's booth at the rear of the store was about midway between their age and mine.

His black hair was neither short nor long, and there were glints of premature gray in it. The clean white smock he was wearing had the effect of making his head seem detached from his body, floating free in the white fluorescent light. The flesh on his head was sparse, and I was conscious of the skull it contained, like a fine ancient bronze buried in his flesh.

"Mr. Russo?"

He glanced up sharply, then came to the open space between the glass partition and the cash register. "What can I do for you?"

"I'm Archer. You haven't heard from your wife again?"

"No, sir, I haven't. I left word at Hollywood Receiving and the other hospitals, just in case."

"You do think she's suicidal, then?"

"She's done some talking about it, I mean in the past. Laurel's never been a very happy girl."

"She said that when she called your house a woman answered the phone."

He looked at me with dark brown sorrowful eyes, the kind that faithful dogs are supposed to have. "That was my part-time cleaning woman."

"She comes at night?"

"As a matter of fact, she's my cousin. She stayed and made me some supper. I get tired of restaurant cooking."

"How long have you and Laurel been separated?"

"A couple of weeks this time. We're not separated, though, not legally."

"Where has she been living?"

"Mostly with friends. And with her father and mother and grandmother in Pacific Point."

"Did you make the list I asked you for, of her friends and relatives?"

"Yes, I did." He handed me a piece of paper, and our eyes met again. His seemed smaller and harder. "You're really going into this matter, eh?"

"With your permission."

"May I ask why?"

"Those were my pills she ran off with. I could have stopped her, but I was a little angry."

"I see." But his eyes were looking past me. "Do you know Laurel well?"

"Not really. I just met her this afternoon. But I have a strong sense of her, if you know what I mean."

"Yeah, everybody does." He took in a breath, and let it out audibly. "Those names I gave you are mainly relatives. Laurel never told me about her boy friends—I mean before she was married. And she only had the one real girl friend that I know of. Joyce Hampshire. They went to school together someplace down in Orange. A private school." His eyes came up to my face, defensive and thoughtful. "Joyce was at our wedding. And she was the only one of the bunch who thought Laurel ought to stay married. I mean, to me."

"How long have you been married?"

"Two years."

"Why did your wife leave you?"

"I don't know. She couldn't even tell me herself. Things broke down on us—the good feeling broke down on us." His gaze wandered away to the bottles and cartons on the shelves behind the partition, with their infinite variety of medicines.

"Where does Joyce Hampshire live?"

"She has an apartment not so far from here, in a place called Greenfield Manor. It's in Santa Monica."

"Will you give her a ring and tell her I may drop in on her?"

"I can do that. Do you think I ought to call the police?"

"It wouldn't do much good. We don't have enough to get action. But call them if you want to. And call the Suicide Center while you're at it."

While Russo used the phone, I studied his typed list of names:

Joyce Hampshire, Greenfield Manor.
William Lennox, El Rancho (grandfather).
Mrs. Sylvia Lennox, Seahorse Lane, Pacific Point (grandmother).
Mr. and Mrs. Jack Lennox, Cliffside, Pacific Point (Laurel's father and mother).
Captain and Mrs. Benjamin Somerville, Bel-Air (her aunt and uncle).

I tried to memorize the list.

Russo was saying on the phone, "I didn't have a fight with her. I didn't see her tonight or today. I had nothing to do with this at all; you can take my word for it." He set the phone down and came back to me. "You could talk to Joyce from here, I guess, but I'm not supposed to let anyone use this phone."

"I'd rather talk to her in person, anyway. I take it she hasn't heard from Laurel?"

Russo shook his head, his eyes staying on my face. "How is it you call her Laurel?"

"That's what you call her."

"But you said you didn't know her hardly at all." He was upset, in a quiet way.

"I don't."

"Then what makes you so interested? I'm not saying you don't have a right. But I just don't understand, if you hardly know her."

"I told you I feel a certain responsibility."

He hung his dark head. "So do I. I realize I made a mistake when she phoned tonight and wanted to come home. I should have told her to come ahead."

He was a man whose anger and suspicion easily turned inward on himself. His handsome face had a shut and disappointed look, as if he felt he had foreclosed his youth.

"Has she run out before, Mr. Russo?"

"We've been separated before, if that's what you mean. And she was always the one that did the leaving."

"Has she had any drug trouble?"

"Nothing serious."

"What about not so serious?"

"She uses barbiturates quite a bit. She's always had trouble sleeping, and calming down generally. But she never took an overdose." He looked at the possibility with half-closed eyes, and couldn't quite face it. "I think it's just a bluff. She's trying to scare me."

"She succeeded in scaring me. Did she say anything about suicide when she talked to you on the phone?"

Russo didn't answer right away, but the skull behind his thin-fleshed face became more prominent. "She said something."

"Can you remember exactly what she said?"

He took in a deep breath. "She said if I ever wanted to see her again in her life that I should let her come home. And be there waiting for her. But I couldn't do that, I had to get down here and—"

I interrupted him. "In *her* life?"

"That's what she said. I didn't take it too seriously at the time."

"I do. She's pretty disturbed. But I still think she wants me to find her."

His head came up. "What makes you think that?"

"She left the door of my medicine cabinet open. She wasn't trying very hard to get away with those capsules —at least not all the way." I picked up his list of names. "What about this family of hers? Bel-Air and El Rancho and Seahorse Lane are pretty expensive addresses."

Russo nodded solemnly. "They're rich." The droop of his shoulders added: And I'm poor.

"Is her father the same Jack Lennox who owns the oil well that's spilling?"

"Her grandfather owns it. William Lennox. His company owns quite a few oil wells."

"Do you know him?"

"I met him once. He invited me to a gathering at his home in El Rancho last year. Me and Laurel and the rest of the family. It broke up early, and I never did get to talk to him."

"Is Laurel close to her grandfather?"

"She used to be, before he got a new woman. Why?"

"I think this oil spill upset her pretty basically. She seems to feel very strongly for the birds."

"I know. It's because we have no children."

"Did she say so?"

"She didn't have to say so. I wanted children, but she didn't feel ready for motherhood. It was easier for her to care about the birds. I'm just as glad now that we don't have children."

There was a poignancy in his words, perhaps not wholly unconscious. He seemed to realize as we talked that the possibilities of his life were being cut off.

"Do you know Laurel's parents—Mr. and Mrs. Jack Lennox?"

"I know them. Her father's picture was on the front page of the *Times* this morning."

"I saw it. Would she go home to them, or to her grandmother Sylvia?"

"I don't know what she'd do. I spent the last couple of years trying to understand Laurel, but I never could predict which way she'd jump."

"Captain and Mrs. Somerville, in Bel-Air—is Laurel close to them?"

"They're her aunt and uncle. I guess she was close to them at one time, but not lately. I'm not the best source on this. I don't really *know* the family. But there's been quite a lot of pulling and hauling in the family since the old man changed his domestic arrangements. It caused Laurel a lot of grief."

"Why?"

"She couldn't stand trouble, any kind of trouble. It always tore her up to hear people fighting or arguing. She couldn't even stand an ordinary disagreement in the home."

"Did you have a lot of disagreements?"

"No. I wouldn't say that."

A woman with a prescription in her hand came up to the counter beside me. She had on high black boots and a yellow wig. Russo seemed relieved to see her. He took the prescription and started back into his booth.

"So long," I said.

He came back and leaned toward me, trying to make private what he had to say: "If you do see Laurel, tell her—ask her to come home. No conditions. I just want her home. Tell her I said that."

The phone in his cubicle started to ring. He picked up the receiver and listened and shook his head.

"I can't come there, you know that. And I don't want them coming here. This job is all I've got. Wait a minute."

Russo came back to me, looking quite pale and shaken. "Laurel's father and mother are at my house. I can't leave here, and I don't want them coming to the store. Anyway, I can't talk to those people. You'd be doing me a big favor, Mr. Archer, if you'd go and talk to them for me. You were the one who saw her last. It isn't far from here. And I'll be glad to pay you for your trouble, whatever you think is fair."

"All right. I'll take a hundred dollars from you."

His face lengthened. "Just for talking to them?"

"I expect to do more than that. A hundred is what I charge for a day's work."

"I don't have that much on me." He looked in his wallet. "I can give you fifty now."

"All right. I'll trust you for the rest."

The woman in the yellow wig said, "Do I get my prescription filled, or are you two going to go on talking all night?"

Russo said he was very sorry. He gave me a quick emphatic nod and returned to the phone.

I went out to my car, feeling slightly more legitimate now that I had Laurel's husband as a client. For a man of his apparent background, who had probably made his way into the professional class by way of pharmacy school, the transfer of money, even under pressure, was proof of real concern.

I asked myself as I drove across Westwood where my concern for his wife originated. The answer wasn't clear. She seemed to be one of those people to whom you attached your floating fears, your unexamined sorrows.

Her eyes appeared to be watching me out of the darkness like the ghost of a woman who had already died. Or the ghost of a bird.

V

It was a declining middle-class block. The flat-roofed stucco houses had been built in the twenties, and faced each other across the street like concrete strong points in a forgotten battlefield. Tom Russo's house was distinguished from the others by the new black Cadillac standing in front of it.

A big man got out of the driver's seat. "Are you Archer?"

I said I was.

"I'm Jack Lennox, Laurel's father."

"I recognized you."

"Oh? Have we met before?"

"I saw your picture in the morning paper."

"Good Lord, was that just this morning? It feels like a week ago." He wagged his head gloomily. "They say trouble always comes in bunches. Which certainly conforms with my experience."

Behind his casual complaining talk I could sense a questioning doubt which wasn't unexpected in Laurel's father. He moved toward me and spoke in a lower voice.

"I understand my son-in-law"—he pronounced the words with distaste—"doesn't want to see us. Believe me, the feeling is mutual. It's good of him to send an emissary. But I don't quite understand your position in this matter."

"I'm a private detective." I added, overstating the case a little: "Tom Russo hired me to look for your daughter."

"I didn't know he cared that much."

"He cares. But he couldn't leave the drugstore just now. Since I was the last one who saw her, I agreed to come here and talk to you."

Lennox took hold of my arm. As if he had closed a circuit, I could feel the tension running through him and into me.

"The last one who saw her? What do you mean by that?"

"She took off from my apartment with a vial of Nembutal capsules." I looked at my watch. "That was a bit over an hour ago."

"How did she get into your apartment?"

A hectoring note was entering his voice. His grip on my arm was tightening. I shook it off.

"I met her on the beach at Pacific Point. She asked me to give her a lift to West Los Angeles, and I did. Then she wanted to use my phone to call her husband."

"What happened between Laurel and her husband?"

"Nothing much. He was about to leave for work and couldn't come for her. He blames himself, of course, but I don't blame him. Your daughter was upset before she ever left Pacific Point."

"Upset about what?"

"The oil spill, for one thing. She rescued a bird, and it died on her hands."

"Don't give me that. People are blaming the spill for everything that happens. You'd think it was the end of the bloody world."

"Maybe it was for your daughter. She's a very sensitive person, and she seems to have been living close to the edge."

He shook his head. He seemed to be strained close to his own limit, and he didn't really want me to tell him about his daughter. I said:

"Has she often been suicidal before?"

"Not to my knowledge."

"Who would know?"

"You could ask her mother."

He took me into the house as if he owned it. We were close together for a moment in the lighted hallway, and we exchanged a quick look. He was weathered brown, with impervious blue eyes, and quite a lot of wavy brown hair growing not too high on his forehead. His eyes were a little overconfident, his mouth a little spoiled. And there was a touch of dismay in the eyes and on the mouth, as if he'd felt the first cold draft of age. He had to be at least fifty but looked younger.

His wife was waiting in the living room with Tom's

cousin, the one he had described to me at the drugstore. The two women sat on facing chairs in stiff-necked poses which meant that they had long since run out of things to say to each other.

Tom's cousin, the younger, had on a light blue pants suit which exaggerated the shape of her body. She looked trapped. But when I gave her a one-sided grin she gave it back to me.

"I'm Gloria," she said. "Gloria Flaherty."

The older woman looked the way Laurel might look in twenty years, if she lived. She still had some of her beauty, but there were lines of suffering connecting the wings of her nose and the corners of her mouth, and charcoal marks under her eyes as if she had been through fire. Her hair was streaked with white.

She lifted one of her black-gloved hands and placed it limply in mine. "Mr. Archer? We can't make any sense of this at all. Can you? Is it true as her husband says that Laurel is suicidal?"

"She may be."

"But why? Did something happen?"

"I was going to ask you that."

"But I haven't really talked to Laurel for several days. She's been staying at her grandmother's. She likes to use the tennis court there. She says it's good therapy for her."

"Does she need therapy, Mrs. Lennox?"

"I was using the term rather loosely." She turned and looked quite openly at the cousin, then back at me. "I really prefer not to discuss this matter under the circumstances."

Gloria got the message and stood up. "I'll finish cleaning up in the kitchen. Can I get anybody anything?"

Mr. and Mrs. Lennox grimaced and shook their heads. They seemed appalled by the idea of eating or drinking anything in Tom Russo's house. They were like astronauts artificially sustained on an alien planet, careful but contemptuous of the unfriendly environment and its unlikely inhabitants.

The cousin went into the kitchen. Mrs. Lennox got up and moved back and forth in the limited space in front of the fireless fireplace. She was tall and rather gaunt, but she moved with a certain nervous youthfulness. She flapped her gloved hands in front of her face.

"I wonder what perfume she uses. It smells like Midnight in Long Beach."

"That's an insult to Long Beach," her husband said. "Long Beach is a good oil town."

I supposed that they were trying to be light, but their words fell heavy as lead. Mrs. Lennox turned to me:

"Do you suppose she's living here with him?"

"I doubt it. Tom says she's his cousin. What's more important, he seems to be in love with your daughter."

"Then why doesn't he look after her?"

"I gather that she takes some looking after, Mrs. Lennox."

She went into a thoughtful silence. "That's true. She always has. Laurel's been an unpredictable girl. I was hoping that her marriage—"

"Forget about her marriage," Lennox said. "It's obviously on the rocks. They haven't been living together for weeks. Russo says he doesn't want a divorce; but he's just holding out in the hope of some moola. I know these types."

"You may be mistaken about him," I said. "He seems to care about her just as much as you do."

"Really? Bear in mind that I'm her father. And I resent being bracketed with that druggist."

He was in a mood to resent almost anything. His face had flushed up red, and then gone gray. His wife was watching the changes in its color as if they were familiar signals to her. There was a certain distance in her look, but she leaned over him and put both hands on his shoulders.

"Calm down, Jack. It may be a long night." She turned to me. "My husband suffers from tension. Under the circumstances, you can understand why."

I said, "I don't understand exactly why you came here, Mrs. Lennox."

"We thought Laurel might be here. Her grandmother said she's been talking about coming back to Tom."

"You must have been concerned about her."

"I've been concerned about her all my life—all *her* life."

"Do you want to tell me why?"

"I wish I could."

"Does that mean you can't, or you won't?"

She looked at her husband again, as if for a further signal. His face had turned a mottled pink. He pulled his hand across it in a wiping motion which left it quite unchanged. But his voice had changed when he spoke.

"Laurel is very important to us, Mr. Archer. She's an only child, the only child we'll ever have. If anything happened to her—" He shrugged and slumped in his chair.

"What do you think might happen to her?"

Lennox remained silent. His wife stood looking down at him as if she was trying to read the thoughts in his head. I asked them both:

"Has she attempted suicide before?"

"No," her father said.

But her mother said, "Yes. She has in a way."

"With drugs?"

"I don't know about that. I caught her once with her father's revolver. She was playing Russian roulette in his room."

Lennox moved from side to side in his chair as if he was strapped there. "You never told me any of that."

"There are a number of things I haven't told you. I never had to, till now."

"Hold them for the present, will you? This is a hell of a time to open the floodgates." He stood up, turning his back on me and towering over her. "What if the old man hears about it?"

"What if he does?"

"Dad's estate is hanging in the balance; you know that. All that woman needs is a good excuse to take it away from us. And we're not going to give it to her, are we?"

He raised his hand to the level of her face and brought the open palm against her cheek. It wasn't a blow, exactly, and it wasn't exactly a love pat. It made a small slapping noise, and it seemed to jar her.

It jarred me. They were one of those couples who

couldn't pull together. The energy of their marriage passed back and forth between them like an alternating current that shocked and paralyzed.

The woman had begun to cry, dry-eyed. Her husband tried to comfort her with little noises and touches of his hands. Her dry sobs continued like hiccups. She said between them:

"I'm sorry. I always do the wrong thing. I spoil your life for you."

"That's nonsense. Be quiet."

He took her out to their car, and then came back to the front door. "Archer?"

I was waiting in the hall. "What do you want?"

"If you have any sense and compunction at all, you won't spread this around."

"Spread what around?"

"The trouble with my daughter. I don't want you talking about it."

"I have to report to Russo."

"But you don't have to tell him everything that was said. Particularly what just passed between us."

"You mean about your father's estate?"

"That's right. I was indiscreet. I'm asking you to be discreet for me"

I said I would do my best.

VI

I went out to the kitchen. Cousin Gloria was drying dishes at the sink, her black hair tied up on each side with shoelaces. She gave me a quick bright glance over her shoulder. "You shouldn't come out here. This place is a mess."

"It looks all right to me. Everything's clean."

"I have been working on it," she admitted. "I'm practicing up for getting married again."

"Have you picked the lucky man?"

She turned to face me with a plate in one hand and

the dish-towel in the other. "As a matter of fact, I have. He's a beautiful person. *I'm* the one who's lucky."

She was polishing the plate as if it was a symbol of her future. There was something touching about her faith and energy.

"May I offer my congratulations?"

"Sure, and I accept. We'd be married now, but we want to do it right. That's why I took this little job with Tom on top of my regular job. I'd do it for nothing, but Tom can afford to pay me."

She was a lively, open girl, and in a mood to talk now that Laurel's parents were out of hearing.

"Where do you work?" I asked her.

"In the kitchen at the Medical Center. I'm studying to be a dietitian. Harry's in the food business, too, when he's working. Right now he isn't working. We have a dream that someday we'll open our own little restaurant."

"I hope you make it, Gloria."

"We'll make it. He's a smart man, and he has a nice touch with people. Even Tom likes him."

"What do you mean, 'even'?"

"Tom doesn't like too many people. He didn't like Flaherty—that was my first—at all. You could count the people he really likes on the fingers of one hand." She raised her left hand, with the fingers spread. "Losing his mother the way he did, when he was so terribly young, it made him kind of suspicious of other people. My mother often said that she's surprised Tom turned out as well as he did, considering the poor start he had. I think old Mr. Russo deserves a good deal of credit. Old Mr. Russo has his limitations, but he's a good father to Tom, and always has been."

She heard herself talking perhaps a little too much, and turned back to her dishes. I was content with a little silence while I took in what she'd said. Tom had lost his mother young, and now he was in danger of losing his wife. The two losses together didn't form a pattern but they suggested the possibility of one. It hung in the bright kitchen like a double shadow caused by a defect in the lighting.

"What happened to Tom's mother?"

Gloria said after a pause, "Aunt Allie died. It happened so long ago I don't remember it. I remember we lived here for a while, all of us together in this house." She looked around the kitchen nostalgically, possessively. "But everything comes to an end. Mother got an offer of a job, and Mr. Russo thought she ought to take it."

"Does Mr. Russo live here with Tom?"

"Not any more. Tom took over the house from him when Tom and Laurel got married. Mr. Russo moved into an old people's home in Inglewood. It was kind of rough on him, but he always wanted Tom to have the house."

"How did Tom and Laurel happen to meet?"

"She just walked into the drugstore one day, and he fell for her at first sight. When she said she'd marry him, he thought he was the luckiest man in the world."

"Didn't you think so?"

She shook her head, and her tied-up hair flopped like vestigial wings. "It's nothing against Laurel, though God knows she has her problems. But I sometimes think Tom took on too much when he married into that family. They're so rich, and we work for everything we get. All Tom really has is a job in somebody else's drugstore. And this old house which he's buying from his father."

"And Laurel."

"*If* he's got her."

"What was the trouble between them, do you know?"

"Tom never discussed it with me. He's very close-mouthed."

"But you know both of them. You've seen them together."

"Sure."

"How did they get along?"

"It's hard to say. They didn't talk much to each other. But each of them always knew the other one was there, if you know what I mean. I think they love each other. Harry thinks so, too."

"Does Harry know them?"

"Sure he does." Her face was open, ready to say more. Then she seemed to remember something, and fell silent for a while. She added, without apparent connection, "Tom is very jealous of Laurel. I think she's the only girl he ever looked at."

"How old is Tom?"

"Thirty-one. He's four years older than I am."

"And Laurel's the only girl he ever had?"

"So far as I know. I was his girl for a while. Not really—we were more like brother and sister—but he used to take me places. I taught him to dance, stuff like that, but we both knew it didn't amount to anything. He just wanted to find out how to conduct himself with a young lady."

"How did he conduct himself?"

"All right. He was kind of stiff and stand-offish, though. He still is. I don't think he ever kissed me once in his life." Her dark eyes came up to mine, sober and confiding. "He was waiting for Laurel, if you know what I mean. She was his fate, the only one for him."

"Then why did they break up?"

"They didn't really break up. She goes back to her folks from time to time, or she goes and lives with friends."

"Like Joyce Hampshire?"

"That's right. They're real old friends. I might do the same thing if I was married to Tom. He goes in for these long silences; he always has. And Laurel has troubles of her own—you don't need me to tell you that. But they'll be back together, I guarantee it."

"I hope so."

I thanked her, and left.

VII

Greenfield Manor, where Joyce Hampshire lived, was a row of two-story town houses surrounded by an imitation adobe wall. A thin young man dressed like a spy in a trench coat and turned-down hat came out through Joyce's gate as I went in.

The patio light was on, and I caught a glimpse of his face. It wasn't so young after all. It was grooved by time and trouble, like my own. He turned away from me as if he didn't want to be known or remembered.

I pressed Joyce's doorbell. She must have been waiting on the other side of the door, because she flung it open immediately. She opened her arms and said:

"Honey?"

She was a nice-looking woman, but everything about her was a trifle blurred. Her soft hair was blurred by the light behind it, her eyes were blurred by doubt, her figure by excess flesh.

"I'm sorry, I didn't mean to call you honey. I thought you were someone else."

"I don't mind."

"But it's so embarrassing."

"Not to me." I told her my name. "Tom Russo called you about me."

"Of course. Come in, Mr. Archer."

She led me into her living room. It was filled with heavy old furniture and what looked like the mementos of not very successful trips: a battered conch shell, a polished slab of redwood inscribed with verse, a liter stein bearing the Hofbrau emblem—disconnected memories that failed to add up to a life.

We sat side by side on a black leather settee. My presence continued to make her uncomfortable. She edged away from me and pulled her skirt down over her plump pink knees. "I don't know what I can do to help. I haven't seen Laurel for at least a week."

"I understood that she'd been staying with you."

"She did for a few days. But last week she went to stay with her grandmother. Have you talked to Sylvia Lennox?"

"Not yet."

"You should. She's very fond of Laurel, and she probably knows her better than anybody. Laurel's her only grandchild."

"Where does Sylvia Lennox live?"

"On the beach at Pacific Point, not too far from Laurel's parents."

"But Laurel chooses to stay with her grandmother?"

"Part of the time, anyway. Laurel isn't too wildly crazy about her parents. And she's been quite a headache to *them*."

"I gather you've known Laurel a long time."

"Practically ever since I can remember. We went to the same school together, starting with the first grade."

"What school was that?"

"River Valley. It's a private school in El Rancho. That's where her grandmother Sylvia used to live, before she left her husband."

"I gathered there was some kind of split-up in the family."

"There certainly is. Sylvia moved out on her husband, and another woman—a much younger woman—moved in. It's terribly hard on Laurel to see her grandparents dissolving their marriage. She's fond of them both, and they're both fond of her, which puts her very much in the middle. The rest of the family think the old man's crazy to take up with a younger woman at his age. But they don't dare to say so, of course."

"Because he owns the oil company."

She nodded. "Laurel's father and mother have spent practically their whole lives waiting to inherit."

"Has Laurel?"

"Not really. She doesn't care about the money. She isn't a self-seeking person. Maybe she'd be better off if she were."

"What kind of a person is she? That isn't clear."

"It depends on who you're talking to. She was never a very happy girl, and she wasn't very popular with her teachers. You know how teachers are. They get a down on somebody and after that they blame her for everything that goes wrong."

"What sort of thing went wrong?"

"Nothing very much, in the early days. Talking in class, refusing to do her work—little things like that. Sometimes she played hooky."

"What about the later days?"

"Things got worse. I don't want to talk about it, really. I'd be giving you the wrong impression of Laurel. She had a real sweetness underneath it all, and she was a serious girl, too, and a good friend. We used to have these long talks; that was really the basis of our friendship. And we used to have some pretty good laughs together."

"You're putting all this in the past tense, Miss Hampshire."

She was slightly appalled. "Am I? I didn't mean to. But it's true we haven't seen so much of each other since we've grown up—especially since she married Tom Russo. He seemed to want to keep her pretty much to himself. And of course I have my own affairs." The word embarrassed her, and she added quickly, "I do a lot of traveling, for example."

"But Laurel was here with you last week."

"Part of last week."

"Did she say why she moved out on Tom?"

She shook her blond head. "Not really. In fact, she intended to go back to him. But first she said she had to get her nerves under control."

"What was the matter with her nerves?"

"She said it made her nervous living in that house. She said it gave her nightmares. I told her she was probably blaming the house for problems that were caused by other things."

"What other things?"

"Tom wanted children; she didn't. She said she didn't want to bring children into this world."

"What did she mean?"

"I don't know. All the violence and cruelty in the world, I guess." She lifted her hands and made karate chops at the air, like a soft embodiment of the world's violence. "Laurel used to talk about it all the time."

"Did Tom Russo treat her badly?"

"Not to my knowledge. He treated her quite well, according to his lights. I'd say he put her on a pedestal."

"That isn't always doing a woman a favor."

"I know that," she said with a self-referring smile. "They put you on a pedestal and leave you there to gather dust. But that wasn't how it was with Laurel. Tom Russo really worshipped her."

"Then why did Laurel leave him? Because the house made her nervous?"

Joyce stood up and faced me. "I'll tell you what I really think. I think Laurel left him on account of Laurel. It's hard for her to stay with anything or anybody. She has no real self-confidence; in fact, she doesn't like herself very much at all. She seems to consider herself unworthy."

"Unworthy of Tom?"

"Unworthy of having any kind of a life. She's a really decent girl, with really deep feelings." For the first time, Joyce's own feelings were coming up from their artesian depths, and her impression was no longer blurred. "I think she's a fine person in spite of everything. But the way she talks about herself, you'd think she was the worst sinner in the world."

"Is she?"

"She's made her mistakes. But it isn't for me to judge her. We all make mistakes." She looked around her living room as if it was crowded with the ghosts of her own.

"Can you give me an example of Laurel's mistakes?"

She was embarrassed. "Well, she ran away to Vegas with a boy when she was at River Valley School. The two of them ran out of money, and actually made a ransom demand on Laurel's parents."

"A ransom demand?"

"They pretended she had been kidnapped, and asked her parents for a thousand dollars for her return. They collected it, too, I heard, and lost every cent of it on the tables. Then Laurel's father brought her home."

"How old was she at the time?"

"About fifteen. She was a junior at River Valley that year."

"Do you remember who the boy was?"

"I think his last name was Sherry. He was a senior, and I never really knew him. He never came back to the school. Neither did Laurel. Her parents kept her at home with private tutoring until she was ready to go away to college."

"No more boy friends?"

"She had boy friends in college and afterward. But none of them stuck with her. Laurel's difficult, as I said. She needed someone steady and faithful, like Tom."

"I heard they met in the drugstore."

"That's true. I happened to be with her that day.

Laurel went in to get a prescription filled. Tom got so excited and nervous when he saw her it must have taken him fifteen minutes to fill it. When we finally got away, he followed Laurel right out through the drugstore to the parking lot. It was really funny, except that he took it so seriously. He was so pale and intense in his white coat, he looked like some kind of medieval fanatic. Laurel told me that after that he called her every day—he had her name and address from the prescription—and they were married just a few months later."

"Are you certain that was the first time they met?"

"Of course. Laurel didn't know him at all. And she told me she'd never been in that drugstore before. It was the Save-More in Westwood."

"What was the prescription she got filled?"

"I think it was sleeping pills—some kind of barbiturates."

"Does she use a lot of them?"

"Yes, I'm afraid she does. Just last week we had a bit of an argument about it. She was eating Seconals as if they were salted peanuts. And then she'd sleep like the dead."

"Is she self-destructive, would you say?"

The woman considered the question, her face inert in thought. "I'd say she is, in a way. But I don't know exactly what you're getting at."

"I'll be specific, since you're a good friend of hers—"

"I try to be. Sometimes it's hard. I'm not too happy about some of the things I just told you."

"I'd say you were doing her a favor. Earlier tonight, Laurel took a tube of Nembutal capsules from the medicine cabinet in my apartment. I don't know where she went with them or what she's likely to do with them."

The woman's eyes darkened and enlarged. "Did something happen to upset her?"

"A couple of things. One was the oil spill off Pacific Point. She seemed to take it personally—probably because her family's involved. She was trying to rescue an oiled bird, and it died on her. She asked me to bring her here—"

"To me?" Joyce said in pleased surprise.

"To her husband. But when she phoned him from my

apartment, he wouldn't pick her up. Apparently he had to go to work, but she took it as a major rebuff. Right after that, she grabbed my pills and took off. And I'm afraid."

"So am I afraid," she said quietly.

"Has she ever attempted suicide?"

"No. I don't think so. She's talked about it, though."

"As something she might do?"

"Yes. I believe so."

"Did she say how?"

"She mentioned pills, I think, but that was some time ago, before she was married. She told me more than once that it would be nice to go to sleep and never wake up again."

"Did she say why?"

"The way Laurel's mind worked, she didn't have to have a good reason. She wasn't a happy girl." The woman's voice deepened. "There was a part of her that always wanted to die."

"That almost sounds like an epitaph."

"I didn't mean it that way." She clenched her fists and made an exaggerated shivering movement as if she was shedding the cold thought. "I'm sure she's alive. I'm sure she took your sleeping pills just to get a good night's sleep."

"They'd give her a very good night's sleep. Where should I look for her, Joyce?"

"I really don't know. Does she have much money with her?"

"I doubt it. I thought of trying her uncle's place in Bel-Air. What's his name—Somerville?"

"Captain Benjamin Somerville. He's a retired Navy captain who married her father's sister. His phone number is unlisted, but I can give you his address."

She copied it out of an address book and followed me to the door. "Have you known Laurel long?"

"We met on the beach this afternoon."

She didn't ask me how, which was just as well. I might have had to tell her that I had followed Laurel, just as Tom Russo had followed her out of the drugstore in his white coat.

VIII

The darkness in Bel-Air was almost thick enough to lean on. I drove around in it for a while and eventually found a mailbox with "Capt. Benjamin Somerville USN (ret.)" printed on it in white. There were several bullet holes in the mailbox.

I went up the asphalt driveway. The house and its outbuildings sat on the hilltop under an unobstructed sky. I could see stars overhead, and below them the night fields of the city looking as if they had been fenced with light and seeded with more stars.

There was no visible light in the large one-storied house. I knocked and waited, and after a while knocked again. The hushed sound of feet approached the other side of the door. In the overhang above me and all around the house, lights went on. The door was opened about five inches on a chain.

Dark eyes looked out at me from a dark face. "What is it you want?"

"I'd like to see Captain Somerville."

"There's nobody home." The black man's voice was flat and toneless.

"You are."

"That's true. But I don't know you."

And he didn't particularly want to. I started to give him a fairly detailed account of who I was and how I had happened to come there. He interrupted me and asked to see my license. I showed it to him through the five-inch opening.

Even then he didn't let me in. He unhooked the chain and stepped outside, closing the door behind him, then testing it to see if it was locked. He had keys in his hand, and he dropped them into his pocket. His other pocket sagged with the weight of what looked like a gun.

He was a big man about my age. His face was unreadable. He had on a faded blue shirt and pants which resembled a uniform. His left arm appeared to be crippled, and I noticed that the hand remained half closed. His voice was low and impersonal.

"Captain Somerville's niece hasn't been here tonight. I've been here all night, and I can guarantee it. I understand she's staying with her grandmother in Pacific Point."

"She left there earlier today. Would she be likely to come here?"

"She used to come here often enough when she was younger. But not so much any more."

"What about Captain Somerville?"

"This is where he lives, man. He's lived here nearly thirty years."

"I mean where is he now?"

"I'm not supposed to say. We've had some bad calls in the last couple of days."

"About the oil spill?"

"That was the idea. The Captain's the executive vice-president of the company. Naturally he gets the blame, even if he's clean as the driven snow."

"I noticed bullet holes in the mailbox."

"That's right. Some people just aren't happy unless they're shooting up other people's property."

"Was that another protest against the oil spill?"

"They didn't stop to say. They came here on motorcycles. I think they were just trigger-happy, looking for something to shoot at." He peered down at the road, then turned and gave me a long appraising look. "But you didn't come out here to talk to me about the motorbike boys."

"They interest me. When were they here?"

"Last night. They roared up the hill and fired a few rounds and roared away again. Captain Somerville wasn't here at the time. Fact is, I was in the house watching him on TV when it happened. The Captain and young Mr. Lennox—Laurel's father—were on the ten o'clock news explaining the oil spill to the people."

"How did they explain it?"

"They said it was an act of God, mainly." There may have been some irony in his voice but I could detect no trace of it in his face. "They said that every now and

then nature lets them down and all they can do is clean
up after her."

"Isn't that a little rough on nature?"

"I wouldn't know about that." He took a deep breath
of the sweet-smelling night air. "I look after the Captain's place for him and that's about all I know."

He looked and talked like a man who knew a good
deal more.

"Have you worked here long, Mr.—?"

"Smith. My name is Smith. I've worked for him over
twenty-five years, ever since me and the Captain retired
from the Navy, and before that. I was his special steward when he had his last sea duty. We were at Okinawa
together. That's where the Captain lost his ship. And
where I got this." He touched his crippled left hand with
his right.

He seemed ready to unload his war reminiscences. I
warded them off: "So you've known Laurel since she
was a little girl?"

"Off and on, I guess you could say that. I knew her
better when she was a little girl than I have since. After
the war, her parents used to live in the Palisades." He
pointed downhill toward the sea. "And they used to
drop her off here when they needed a baby-sitter. She
was a sweet little thing, but also a handful sometimes."

"What did she do?"

"She used to run away, just like she did on you.
Sometimes I'd spend a couple of hours looking for her.
If she'd been doing it for fun, it wouldn't have been so
bad. But she wasn't. She used to be really scared. You'd
think I spent a lot of time beating on her. But I never
raised a hand to the little tyke. I was fond of her." His
voice and eyes had softened.

"What was she scared of?"

"Just about everything. She couldn't stand any kind
of trouble—anybody lifting his hand or raising his voice
in anger. If a bird flew into the window glass and got
killed, it used to shake her up for half a day. I remember once I threw a stone at a cat that didn't belong here.
I wasn't aiming to hit him, just scare him off. But I hit
him and he let out a yowl and Miss Laurel saw it hap-

pen. She went and hid for the rest of the afternoon."

"Where would she hide?"

"She had several places. She kept changing them on me. The room back of the garage. The pool house. The storage shed. Those were some of them."

"Show me the places, will you?"

"Tonight?"

"She may not last till morning."

He looked closely into my face. "You honestly think she could be holed up around here?"

"It's a possibility. Sometimes when people are badly shaken they go back to childish patterns."

He nodded. "I know what you mean. I've done it myself."

He led me around the house to the garage and unlocked the door. The building contained three cars—a middle-aged Continental, a new Ford, a half-ton GMC pickup—and there was no space for another car. That made me wonder if Captain Somerville wasn't at home after all.

Laurel wasn't in any of the cars, or in the toolroom or the half-bathroom behind the garage. Smith picked up a flashlight in the toolroom. We went down the hillside through trees, bumping our heads on unripe oranges. He opened the door of the storage shed.

It was built of roughly finished redwood, now weathered light, and filled with the random accumulations of years: old furniture, shelves of fading books, dusty luggage covered with foreign labels, a rusted filing cabinet, garden tools and insecticides and rat poison. No Laurel. Smith's flashlight beam probed the dark corners for her.

He let the beam rest for a moment on a wooden sea chest painted blue and stenciled in red with the Captain's name and rank and the name of a U.S. Navy vessel, *Canaan Sound*. Then he raised the light to a picture that hung on the rough wall above the chest. The picture had a twisted black frame out of which a man in a captain's hat smiled through cracked dusty glass.

"That was the Captain before he lost his ship," Smith said.

He kept his light on the picture while I studied it. The Captain had been handsome and confident, though his half-smiling mouth could hardly support the boldness of his eyes.

When we went outside, I said, "Are you sure the Captain isn't home tonight?"

"What makes you think he is?"

"You're showing me everything but the inside of the house."

"Those are my orders. Nobody is allowed in the house."

We went along a flagstone path to the pool house. The pump inside was breathing like a marathon runner. Under that noise I could hear the scurrying sounds of a small animal.

Smith handed me the flashlight and took the gun from his pocket. It looked like a .38 with a two-inch barrel.

"What are you going to do with that?"

"I hear a rat in there. Try and get the light on him."

He pulled the door open with his crippled hand. The pool house was full of faint moving lights from the heater. I turned the flashlight on the cement floor, fearful for an instant that Laurel might be in there and be accidentally shot.

A bright-eyed rat was caught in the light. He ran for the drainage hole. Before he got there, the gun went off beside me. The rat fell in a red blur, twitched, and lay still.

IX

As if the sound of Smith's gun had been a prearranged signal, a phone began to ring somewhere uphill from us. It rang three times, and stopped. By that time, Smith was at the top of the hill and I was close behind him.

We paused on the concrete pool deck at the side of the house. I could hear a man's voice, hoarse and strained, talking inside.

"The Captain's at home, isn't he?" I said.

"That's right. I had orders not to disturb him."

"Now that he's been disturbed, will you let me see him?"

"What about?"

"Laurel."

"She isn't here. You saw that for yourself."

"That could be Laurel on the phone now."

"I'll ask him."

He unlocked a sliding glass door and went into the house, leaving me outside. I walked up and down on the deck, trying to lose my feeling of frustration. All I had to show for my evening's work was a dead rat and a persistent vision of Laurel lying somewhere with an empty vial beside her.

Inside the house, the Captain's intermittent voice continued like a voice in a dream, just beyond the range of comprehension. Then I heard Smith's voice. He came to the sliding glass door and opened it exactly wide enough to admit me.

"The Captain says he'll see you. Don't keep him too long. He hasn't had any real sleep for two nights."

The Captain was sitting in pajamas at the desk in his study. He was gray and haggard. In the collapsing structures of his face I could barely recognize the younger man whose picture hung in the storage shed. There were no pictures at all on the walls of his study.

He stood up and gave me a brisk handshake which failed to convey an impression of energy. "I understand you're a private detective, Mr. Archer. It isn't clear to me who you're working for."

"Tom Russo, your niece's husband."

"Where is my niece?"

"I don't know. She took off with a tube of Nembutal capsules—"

His voice cut in on mine: "Where and when?"

"From my apartment in West Los Angeles, sometime before eight tonight."

"Who did she leave with?"

"She was alone."

"Are you sure?" His eyes probed at me from his sun-scarred face.

"She may have been picked up on the street," I said.

"Are you telling me somebody picked her up?"

"I'm saying it could have happened."

"Who picked her up?"

"I don't know. I don't know that she was picked up."

He turned and walked the short distance to the end of the room. His bare feet made no sound at all on the carpet. He turned and came back toward me with his finger pointing at me like a prosecutor's.

"Why did you come here?"

"I've been trying various places she might be. Her husband's house. Her friend Joyce Hampshire's place. I've talked to her parents."

"How long ago?"

I looked at my watch. It was past eleven o'clock. "Within the last couple of hours. I don't get the point of all these questions you're asking."

"Don't you?"

The Captain raised himself on his toes. He was the shortest man of the three of us. Smith towered over him but held himself quite still and silent, frozen in a wartime hierarchy which should have dissolved in history long since.

"You're being rather mysterious, Captain."

"Then I'll be plain. Before I talk to you any further, I want the name of someone who will vouch for you. Someone known to me personally or by reputation."

"That's a little tough at this time of night."

"This is a tough situation," he said.

"All right. Do you know John Truttwell in Pacific Point?"

"Yes. I know him slightly. I know his former associate Emerson Little better. Little happens to be my mother-in-law's attorney."

"Ask him about me."

The Captain sat down at his desk, made the call, and got Emerson Little at home. After a few preliminaries, he asked Little for his opinion of me. He listened to what Little had to say without any visible change in his expression. Then he thanked him and hung up.

"He gives you a clean bill of health. I hope he knows what he's talking about."

"I hope he does."

"My niece's life may be in danger."

"I've been working on that assumption."

His face closed up like a fist, which he thrust at me. "Did you know that she's been abducted?"

"No."

"She has been. Her father received a ransom demand shortly after he got home tonight."

"In writing or by phone?"

"I understand by phone. The amount is quite large —a good deal more than he has available."

"How much?"

"A hundred thousand dollars, in cash. Since Jack and Marian don't have the money themselves, they appealed to his mother. It was his mother—Laurel's grandmother—who phoned me just a few minutes ago. Jack asked her not to tell anyone, but she decided that she'd better consult with me. I'm the active head of the family, you might say, though I'm only a member by marriage."

There was a streak of vanity in him, I noticed, which went a little strangely with his concern for his niece. His niece by marriage. I said:

"How soon does the money have to be available?"

"They asked for it tonight. But of course that isn't possible, since they're demanding cash. They've got to give us more time."

"Are they going to call back?"

"I understand they are, sometime in the course of the night. Jack will try to put them off until tomorrow noon at least."

"Is he going to call the police?"

"I don't think so; they warned him not to. You understand I haven't talked to Jack. I've only heard from my mother-in-law. Sylvia's naturally very upset and not too coherent."

"Is she willing to provide the money?"

"Of course she is. Sylvia is extremely fond of Laurel. We all are. There's no problem about the money."

"There may be other problems. Before the family pays it, make sure that the person or persons paid actually have her. And make sure that she's alive."

Somerville looked at me in alarm. "I can't assume that responsibility myself. I have my hands full with the blowout."

"Do you think the blowout had anything to do with what's happened to your niece?"

"I don't quite understand. You mean some environmentalist maniac is responsible?"

"I wasn't suggesting that. I'm a bit of an environmentalist myself. So was—" I realized as I caught myself that I half believed Laurel was dead. "Your niece is, too."

"Then what exactly did you mean?" he said.

"The family's been getting a lot of publicity this week, some good, some bad. You and her father were on television last night. His picture was in the paper."

"But not Laurel's."

"No, but she's the vulnerable one. And she's the one who got taken."

A woman's voice said from the hall, "Who got taken?"

She brushed past Smith in the doorway, a well-made woman who looked as if she had dressed in a hurry and hadn't brushed her blond hair. Captain Somerville got to his feet.

"Laurel was kidnapped tonight." He gave her a few of the details: the amount of the ransom, the fact that Sylvia was willing to pay it. Then he turned to me. "Mr. Archer here is a private detective. I was about to ask him if he could help us in this matter. He saw Laurel earlier this evening."

The woman gave me a long look, then her hand. "I'm Elizabeth Somerville, Laurel's aunt."

I could see a resemblance to her brother Jack in the handsome bones of her face. But her eyes were different, and they were her best feature. They were blue and candid, with depths behind them hollowed out by human feelings including pain.

"How did you happen to see Laurel?"

I told her, not omitting the sleeping pills.

"Poor Laurel. Can you help her, Mr. Archer? And help us?"

"I can try. I'll need your brother's cooperation."

"I'm sure you'll have that."

She was wrong. When Somerville called her brother's house in Pacific Point, Jack Lennox refused to listen to him. The rest of us in the study could hear Jack shouting over the line. Somerville slammed the receiver down.

"Jack won't talk to me. He said he's got to keep his house line open. He doesn't want any interference."

"He's going to get it, though," Elizabeth Somerville said. "I don't trust Jack to handle this by himself. He's terribly upset—I could hear it in his voice—and when my brother gets that way he makes wrong decisions."

"*I* can't go down there now." Somerville's voice was querulous. "I've had less than two hours' sleep in the last forty-eight, and tomorrow is going to be a really tough day. We're going to try and plug the leak tomorrow."

His wife was watching him with a mixed expression on her handsome face, part pity and part impatience, which made me realize that she was much younger than he was.

"What about your company's security people?" I said. "Can't you use them?"

"It's a possibility," the Captain said.

But his wife said, "No. It isn't a good idea."

I asked her why it wasn't.

"Because my father's still the head of the company. The kidnapping would get back to him within a couple of hours, and I think it's really important that it shouldn't. At least until it's over and Laurel's back safe."

"Is your father very old?"

"He won't admit it, but he is. And he's already had one heart attack, a bad one. Will you drive me down to Pacific Point, Mr. Archer? Jack will listen to me, and I'm sure that he'll cooperate with you."

I wasn't so sure, after what I had seen of Jack, but I said that I'd go with her.

"What about me?" Captain Somerville said.

"Go back to bed," his wife told him. "Smith will look after you. Won't you, Smith?"

The black man in the doorway broke his silence. "Certainly will, Mrs. Somerville."

She looked at him intently. "What was that shot that woke me up?"

"There was a rat in the pool house," he said with some embarrassment.

"But I told you not to shoot them. Trap them if you have to."

"All right, Ma'am. I'll try that."

"*Do* it," she said.

The Captain cleared his throat and produced a heavier voice than he had been using. "I give the orders to Smith. Remember that, Elizabeth."

She offered no sign that she had heard him. The two men looked past her at each other. Each of them smiled faintly. I got the impression that their relationship was deeper and stronger than the marriage, and that it shut her out.

Before we left, I tried to call Tom Russo. There was no answer at his house, and the drugstore was closed.

X

Elizabeth Somerville came to the front door in a tourmaline mink which almost matched her blond head. It seemed to me she was overdressed, considering her errand. She may have caught my look, because she went back into the house and put on a plain dark coat.

"My family," she said in the car, "has a fatal gift for ostentation."

"You look even better in that coat."

"Thank you—thank you very much." Her voice was serious, as if she hadn't had a compliment for some time.

We rode in unstrained silence down the dark hill. I had liked the woman at first sight, just as I had liked Laurel, and for some of the same reasons: their honesty and passionate directness, their concern. But Laurel was a troubled girl, and the woman beside me seemed to have everything under control.

Except perhaps her marriage, which seemed to be on her mind: "I'm not about to explain or apologize for anything. But you must have gotten a rather odd view of us. This dreadful oil spill has thrown the family into a crisis. And now with what's happened to Laurel—" She took in a deep breath and let it out.

I turned onto the lighted boulevard, heading for the San Diego Freeway. "I know how you feel."

"How could you possibly?"

"In a situation like this, people get to know each other in a hurry. That is, if the components are present."

"The nuclear components?"

I glanced sideways at her face. She was smiling in a slightly feline way. I said:

"I don't think you and I are going to have an explosion. Don't misunderstand me—I'm sure you're highly explosive, just as Laurel is."

"Really? You think I'm like Laurel?" She sounded both complimented and dismayed. "They do say an aunt and a niece have about thirty percent of the same genes —almost as close a relation as mother and daughter. And I *feel* that way about her." She leaned toward me. "What happened to Laurel?"

"I don't know. I think she was ready for almost anything, and very close to the edge of emotional breakdown. I'm not offering this as a theory, just an idea, but I wouldn't be surprised if the kidnapping was a spur-of-the-moment thing. Perhaps somebody recognized her and saw she was vulnerable and picked her up on the street. It may have been someone she knew. She may even have gone along willingly."

"You're not suggesting that she's a party to the extortion attempt?"

"No, but it's not impossible." I was thinking of what Joyce Hampshire had told me about the Las Vegas incident when Laurel was fifteen. I decided not to mention it to Elizabeth.

She said, "But she'd have no reason. Laurel doesn't care about money. And if she did, she could always get it from my parents."

"Not her own?"

"Jack and Marian don't have much money in the here and now. The company pays him a good salary, of course, but they live right up to it, and beyond. I don't mean that they couldn't or wouldn't raise money for Laurel if they had to."

"Money isn't always the main thing in these extortion attempts. The extortioner may think it is. But what he's really after is some kind of emotional satisfaction. Some kind of revenge on life. Would Laurel do something like that to her parents?"

"I don't know. They've certainly had a lot of trouble with her. And she with them," Elizabeth added carefully. "Jack and Marian have had a troubled marriage. But all three of them really care about each other. I suppose it's what they call a love-hate relationship. *Odi et amo. Excrucior.*"

"What does that mean?"

" 'I hate you and I love you. And it hurts.' That's my own translation from Catullus. They printed it in the annual at River Valley School."

"The same school Laurel went to."

"Yes. You know quite a lot about her."

"Not nearly enough. I didn't have much of a chance to question her husband. He was at work."

"He wouldn't be able to tell you much, anyway," she said with faint contempt.

"Why do you say that?"

"He doesn't really know Laurel. How could he, with his background? I've spent some time with them, and if ever I saw an unreal marriage—"

"Tom seems to be in love with her."

"Whatever that means," she said. "As far as Tom is concerned, she's a creature of romantic fantasy. He treats her as if she were a fairy princess. Laurel really deserved something better than that."

Her voice was surprisingly bitter. I wondered if she was talking about her own marriage as well as Laurel's.

"How did—how does Laurel feel about him?" And how do you feel about your husband, Mrs. Somerville?

"I think she loved him, in a way, and she was grateful to him. It isn't easy for Laurel to be intimate with anyone, certainly not with a man. But she really should have had something more than Tom Russo. She's a remarkable young woman. If she had met her match in life, this dreadful thing wouldn't have happened."

"What do you think happened?"

"I don't know." She shook her head. Her hair fluffed

out, and caught the light of a car coming up behind us. "After what you said about her possible complicity, I don't think I ought to speculate about it."

"I was speculating."

"You certainly were."

"But I thought the question ought to be raised. I'm not suggesting that Laurel originated the idea. At worst, she simply went along with it."

"Why would she?"

"She wanted out, and she was so desperate that any out would do. Assume she did go with someone, and that someone made the extortion call to her parents, with or without her knowledge—it doesn't follow that Laurel is out of danger. In fact, it works the other way around."

"You mean if she knows who she's with, he's just as likely to kill her?"

"That's what I mean. He or they."

"But you're simply imagining all this," she said with synthetic scorn.

"What else can I do? I said I wasn't offering you a theory, just some possibilities. You seem to take them seriously. So do I. Remember, I spent some time with Laurel just before she took off. She was wide open to possibility, ready for anything to happen. And if she ran into someone else in the same condition—"

"The nuclear components would come together?"

Her voice was sober. We climbed the ramp onto the midnight freeway. I was keenly aware that I'd brought Laurel this way a few hours before.

"Speaking of nuclear bombs," Elizabeth said, in the tone of someone hoping to change the subject, "this isn't the first time tonight that they've come up. My husband was talking about bombing earlier this evening, before I persuaded him to go to bed. I know men aren't supposed to have hysterics, but he was pretty close to it. Of course, he's been through a lot more than I have, particularly in the last couple of days. I have to make allowances for that, and for the fact that he's older."

She seemed to be having a quiet debate with herself on the subject of her husband's manhood.

"What did he have to tell you about bombing?"

"Nothing worth hearing, really. If anyone but Ben had said it, I would have laughed in his face. He had the wild idea that perhaps our oil well started leaking because some enemy had planted a small nuclear device in the sea floor. Of course, he was very tired, and he can't drink—"

"Some enemy of the United States?"

"He didn't go quite that far. Some personal enemy, or enemy of the company. Or someone trying to make the oil industry look bad."

"It isn't possible, is it?"

"No." Her voice was definite. "I think my husband may be getting a bit paranoid. It's understandable. He's a sensitive man, and I know he feels terribly guilty. He told me once himself that he was too emotional to be a naval combat officer. He said he realized it when he saw the official photographs of the fire-bombing of Tokyo. He was appalled by them."

"Did he have something to do with the Tokyo bombings?"

"No. I didn't mean that. But this oil thing isn't his first disaster. It's the second one that he—that he was made to feel responsible for. His ship the *Canaan Sound* was disabled by fire at Okinawa, and some of his men were lost."

"Was it his fault?"

"He was the Captain. He naturally assumed responsibility. But Ben has never talked about it. Neither has Jack. I don't think either of them knows how the fire started."

"Was your brother Jack aboard the *Canaan Sound?*"

"Yes. Jack was a young officer just out of Communications School. Ben arranged to take him aboard, so Jack would be under his wing. It wasn't a very protective wing, I'm afraid. Jack wasn't on the carrier for more than a week or two when it was ordered to Okinawa, and then burned. That was the end of Jack's sea duty, and the end of my husband's naval career."

"You mean they fired him out of the Navy?"

"Not exactly. They gave him shore duty at Great Lakes. Ben hated it. So did I. But it was much harder on him than it was on me. When I married him, he was terribly ambitious. He used to talk about someday becoming CINCPAC. The job at Great Lakes led nowhere, and wasn't intended to. As soon as the war was over, Ben resigned from the Navy. Fortunately he was married to me, and my father took him into the company."

Her voice had dropped into the half-conscious rhythm of memory. She was aware of my presence, which made speech possible, but she wasn't just talking to me. She was telling herself about her life, and finding out how it sounded.

"Is this the end of your husband's career in the oil business?"

"I don't know. It feels like the end of a lot of things to me." Her voice dropped out of hearing, but I sensed its quiet rhythms continuing in her mind. Then it was audible again: "I'm afraid my father has turned his back on us. We disappointed him by having no children. Now he's got himself a woman named Connie Hapgood. She used to be a teacher at River Valley School, and she's actually younger than I am. Younger than I ever was," she added in a flash of wry and angry wit. "Father is in his seventies, but he plans to marry her as soon as his marriage to Mother is dissolved. He's even talking about having another family."

"Talking will do no harm."

"He means it, though. He's got himself persuaded, with that woman's help, that he can have a second life. And of course she'll do her best to get Ben fired and put her own people in. There were rumors of it even before the blowout, and now that it's happened I'm afraid Ben's finished."

"But the blowout was pure accident, wasn't it?"

"It must have been. Of course. But Father will blame Ben. Father has always had to have someone to blame." The sentence came out heavy and cold, like a capsule history of her early life. After a while, she added:

"One of the planets—I forget which one—takes something like a hundred and sixty-five years to revolve around the sun. It makes for a long long year. And that's the kind of a year our family seems to be having."

"Neptune?"

"It may be Neptune. He's the god of the sea, isn't he?

Maybe *he* got mad and blew up our oil well. But please don't suggest that possibility to my husband. He'd be only too willing to believe it."

XI

We rode in silence, like companions on a journey to inner space, until we left the freeway at Pacific Point. Elizabeth told me how to find her brother's house, just south of the city limits in the suburb of Montevista.

As we turned down the driveway, the night sky was blacked out by overarching trees. Then it opened out ahead of us, flooded by moonlight, floored by the glittering sea. In that perspective, the house which clung to the edge of the cliff looked small and low. All its windows were lit.

I parked by a masonry wall on the left side of the driveway.

"Let me do the talking," Elizabeth said.

"All right. But I want to come in."

She looked into my face. "Why? It will be easier for me to talk to Jack and Marian alone."

"We didn't come here to make it easier for you. And I didn't come along for the ride."

"Very well. Come in if you like."

"I don't like. I'd rather be home in bed. But I will if you insist."

She drew in her breath in a little gasp of irritation, which she controlled. Her gloved hand pressed my arm.

"Don't get angry, Mr. Archer. Jack is about all I can handle at any one time."

As if to demonstrate the truth of this, Jack Lennox came out through a gateway in the stone wall. He carried a rifle with a telescopic sight, and before I guessed his intention he was beside the car and pointing it at my head.

I froze, half out of the car. The fear of death thrilled through me. I said carefully:

"Put it down, Mr. Lennox. Don't you recognize me?"

He glared along the barrel for an instant. He didn't seem to care who I was. Then he raised the gun so that it was no longer pointed at me. I straightened up.

Cold fear and anger boiled up in my head like liquid air. I wanted to take the rifle out of his hands and throw it cartwheeling over his house, far out over the cliff, into the sea.

His sister felt the violent possibility of the scene. She hurried around the car and came between us, speaking to him in a voice that adults use on children.

"Give me that, Jack. You don't need it. Mr. Archer came here to help you."

"I don't want his bloody help." His voice was thick with alcohol and passion.

"Come on, Jack. Straighten up now. I know you're under bad strain but the rifle just makes it worse."

He was holding it pointed approximately at the moon, which floated low like a target balloon. The woman reached for the gun. They wrestled for a second, more with their wills than their muscles. Her will won. She lifted the gun away from him, and he let her.

Without it he looked strangely empty-handed. He was one of those men who need a gun to complete themselves.

The three of us moved awkwardly to the house.

Marian Lennox was waiting just inside the front door, as if she had been afraid to come out.

"I told you it was Elizabeth," she said to her husband.

Her voice was monotonous and her movements limp, as if her nerves had been strained too far and gone slack. But she took the rifle from her sister-in-law and stood it in a corner of the hallway. Jack Lennox scowled at the two women, and turned the same face on me:

"You had no right to come here. You'll ruin everything."

He was full of grief and anger, and spoiling for a fight. I wasn't. I said: "Your sister asked me to come. I think it was a good idea. People shouldn't try to handle these things by themselves."

"We're doing all right," he said without conviction.

"Have you had a second call yet from the kidnappers?"

"No."

"Exactly what was said in the first call?"

He looked at me with suspicion. "What do you want to know for?"

"I'd like to get some idea of who we're dealing with —whether they're amateur or pro—"

"You're not doing the dealing. We are."

"I understand that. I'm not trying to interfere."

"Of course you're trying to interfere. You walked into my house uninvited and unwanted. You don't give a damn about us, or about what happens to my daughter."

"I do, though. That's why I'm here."

He shook his head. "You're spying for Tom Russo, aren't you? How do I know he isn't involved in this? And maybe you are, too, for all I know."

He had worked himself up into another rage and was letting it talk for him. I didn't know how seriously to take him. The gun was still resting upright in the corner. The two women were standing, as if by design, between the gun and him.

It seemed to me that I had already spent a long time in the hallway with Jack Lennox and his sister and his wife and his bloody gun. It was an ugly cold dark room without any furniture, like a holding cell for prisoners waiting for paroles that never came.

His wife approached him with one hand stretched out. She was pale and enormous-eyed and awkward in her movements, as if she had been in solitary for years. Her hand paused in the air before it touched him.

"You mustn't get so excited, Jack. You said that yourself. We've got to keep a clear head or the family will never get through this alive. He's liable to phone now any time."

"Has he threatened to kill your daughter?" I said, unwisely.

Lennox turned on me with clenched fists. His wife took hold of his raised right arm. He flung her away from him, and she almost fell.

"For God's sake, Jack," Elizabeth said, "calm down."

"Then take this spying bastard out of here."

She moved past him to the door and opened it. "Out, Mr. Archer, please."

The heavy door clicked shut behind me. The air was cool on my face. The moon soared above the sea. In the middle distance, a screech owl made small weird grouchy noises like nature talking back to the world of men.

But I wasn't interested. I wanted to be inside the house, in the cell with the prisoners, waiting for the second telephone call.

I waited for nearly an hour. It seemed to stretch out like time on the planet Neptune. The screech owl spoke occasionally. I had nothing to say in return.

Then the telephone rang in the house, once. It required an effort of will to stay in the car. I felt partly responsible for the danger Laurel was in, and I didn't trust her father to get her out of it.

I reached for a cigarette. I hadn't smoked a cigarette in several years, but I felt defrauded when I couldn't find one. I sat and bit my lips and listened to the slow ponderous clock of the waves at the foot of the cliff.

Elizabeth came out alone. She walked very slowly toward my car, as if the house behind her exerted a magnetic influence. I got out and opened the car door for her. In the light of the moon, she looked pale and subdued.

"Did the kidnappers phone again?"

"Yes. Jack talked to one of them. A man."

"What did the man say?"

"Jack asked me not to discuss it with you. He wants to handle it alone. That's his way, especially where Laurel is concerned."

"He's making a mistake."

"I told him that. But I might as well have been talking to that wall." She pointed toward the stone wall that enclosed the house. "I'm afraid he doesn't trust you. He doesn't trust anyone, not even me."

"Has he always been like that?"

"Not really. I think he's breaking down under the strain." She was silent for a moment; then she shook her head in denial. "That's really unfair to Jack. He's terribly eager to do the right thing and do it all by himself.

He hasn't been the best and most understanding father in the world, and there's been a lot of trouble between him and Laurel. I'm sure he feels that if he can save her now, and show her how much he loves her—" Her voice dropped again, as if she couldn't imagine the sequel to this.

"It's a poor time for grandstanding. Her life is in danger. She may be dead now. What assurance has he been given that she isn't?"

"I don't know."

"Did he ask to talk to her?"

"I don't know," she repeated. "He took the call in his study, and kept the door closed. He promised to deliver the hundred thousand tomorrow. That was all he told me about the conversation."

"When tomorrow?"

"Early in the afternoon, I gather. Jack said he'd need the money around noon."

"Would there be any point in trying to talk to him now?"

"For you to try?"

"Either of us. Or both."

She considered the idea. "I'm afraid not, Mr. Archer. It's better not to press Jack when he's feeling like this. Perhaps tomorrow—"

I turned the key and started the car. As I was backing away from the wall, the front door opened. Marian Lennox came toward us, stumbling on the flagstone walk and waving. She looked like a disoriented bird blundering into the headlights.

We both got out to meet her. Elizabeth said in a slightly bedside manner:

"What is it, Marian?"

"Jack had a dizzy spell. I got him to lie down."

"He hasn't had a heart attack?"

"No. He'll be all right."

"Do you think we should call a doctor?"

"I'm afraid that would only upset him."

Elizabeth put her arm around the other woman's shoulders. "I'll stay with you if you like."

"No. You're awfully kind. But Jack and I have to do this by ourselves. It's the way Jack wants it."

"What about you?"

"I'm willing to do whatever Jack says. He's the strong one."

"I think you're showing a lot of strength, Marian." Marian shook her head and drew away, ending their moment of affection.

"I'm only doing what I have to do," she said. "Just make sure that Sylvia gets hold of the money by noon. That's all we're asking of you."

"Don't worry, dear."

Marian Lennox turned to me before she went inside. Her face was like a clay mask in the moonlight:

"I'm sorry, Mr. Archer. After coming all this way, you should have been given a better reception."

"That's all right."

"You will let us know if you find out anything?"

I said I would. She moved back toward the house as if she dreaded both what was ahead of her and what was behind her. She let herself in at the front door.

"Poor Marian," Elizabeth said. "Poor both of them. I wish I could help them."

"Has your brother ever had a heart attack?"

"No, but my father almost died of one a few years ago." She added after a thinking pause, "That was the real beginning of the trouble in the family. Father suddenly realized that he was mortal, and he decided to make the most of the life he had left. So when he was physically able he took up with Connie Hapgood.

"Mother's a proud woman. Also she has some money of her own. She moved out of the old house in El Rancho and bought a house on the beach here."

"Is that where we're going now?"

"Yes. It's only a mile or so from Jack's house." She gestured toward the south. "Which was the big attraction for Sylvia, I suppose. Jack was always her favorite." Her voice was cold without being bitter. "She should have stayed and fought it out with Connie. She could have held on to Dad if she'd wanted to. But she didn't care. She left him to that woman. And now she's letting him dissolve the marriage without even putting up a fight."

"Why does it matter so much?"

"Dad is in his seventies. He's not going to live forever.

And if Connie inherits the company, or even a major part of it, that will be the end of the Lennox family. Money is the glue that holds us all together—money and oil."

I turned south along a dark tree-lined road which paralleled the shore. A barn owl flew across the space of sky between the trees, moving as silently as a fish under water.

The woman was almost as quiet for a while. Finally she said in an unwilling voice, "Dad loves Laurel, you know. She's his only grandchild. And if Jack is covering up for her in some way, you can understand why. Laurel is his ace in the hole."

"Are you telling me that you think Laurel may not have been kidnapped after all?"

"I guess I am. At least I'm admitting the possibility."

"What made you change your mind about it?"

"I don't really know." She considered the question in silence. "I have a feeling there's something funny going on. There's a queer atmosphere in Jack and Marian's house tonight—what you might call an atmosphere of complicity."

"You think they know that Laurel's trying to take them?"

"I think they know something like that, or at least Jack does. It wouldn't be the first time that he's covered up for Laurel."

"Tell me about the other times."

"I don't think I'd better," she said. "You wouldn't see them in context, and I don't want to turn you against her. She may need your help. We all may."

"Good. What was the context?"

She thought about the question, and answered in general terms: "When there's trouble in a family, it tends to show up in the weakest member. And the other members of the family know that. They make allowances for the one in trouble, try to protect her and so on, because they know they're implicated themselves. Do you follow me?"

"I learned it long ago in the course of my work. Where did you learn it, Elizabeth?"

"From my family. Yes, do call me Elizabeth, please."

XII

We turned right on Seahorse Lane, which dipped toward the sea, and turned again at Mrs. Lennox's mailbox. Her name was painted on it in new black lettering: "SYLVIA LENNOX." The house at the end of the cypress-haunted lane was single-storied, and sprawled like a stucco labyrinth along the edge of the sea.

A young man came out across the lighted courtyard to meet us. He was of normal size but he gave the impression of being dwarfed by his surroundings. He walked on his toes like a dancer, ready to move in any direction. His moist brown eyes looked rather eager to please.

"How are *you,* Mrs. Somerville?"

"I'm fine," she said in a tone that denied it, and turned to me. "Mr. Archer, this is Tony Lashman, my mother's secretary."

We shook hands. He told Elizabeth that her mother was waiting in her room to see her, and she excused herself.

From the window of the front room where Lashman took me, I could look out across the beach and the water and see the lighted oil platform. I couldn't tell how close the oil had come to shore, but I could sense its odor invading the house.

The young man sniffed. "Filthy stuff."

"How does Mrs. Lennox feel about it?"

"She's pretty ambivalent." He gave me a quick sharp look to see if I understood what he was saying. "After all, she's been married to an oilman most of her life."

"Do you know old Mr. Lennox?"

"As a matter of fact, I've never met him. I've only been with Mrs. Lennox since she and her husband agreed to separate." He ran his fingers through his wavy black hair. "This is very much a temporary thing for me. I'm going back to college in the fall. Or else to photography school. I haven't decided. I only took this job to help Mrs. Lennox out."

"I understand her granddaughter has been staying here."

"That's right, she's been using the guesthouse." He turned to face me. "I heard she's missing."

"Yes."

"I'm not surprised. She wasn't too happy here. Or anywhere else, for that matter. I did my best to cheer her up, but it didn't do too much good."

His eyes reflected a facile sympathy, but it soon faded. There seemed to be a restless movement behind them, a constant turning in his head like an occulting light.

"How did you cheer her up?"

"We played a lot of tennis—she plays a fairly good game of tennis. And we had some good old heart-to-heart talks, you know? She wants to do something with her life. I'm the same way myself—creative. Laurel and I have quite a lot in common. I went through a marriage that didn't work out myself."

"Her marriage didn't work out?"

"I didn't mean to say that, exactly." He touched his mouth with his fingers. "Laurel hadn't really made up her mind about it, but I could tell which way it was likely to go. It's hard to imagine her married to a druggist."

"Why?" I said.

"*You* know, a girl with all that charm and class. And all that money in the background."

He made an inclusive gesture toward the contents of the room. The heavy dark furniture, devoid of charm, failed to support him. There was money there, I thought, but it hadn't been wholly humanized.

"How much money is there in the background?"

"Millions and millions."

The thought of the money seemed to excite him momentarily. I wondered if money was his unrequited passion. I doubted that Laurel was.

He became aware that Elizabeth had come into the room. As if the light had altered, embarrassment changed his face and made it almost ugly. But if she had overheard him talking about her family's money, she gave no sign.

"My mother would like to see you," she said to me.

She led me through another wing of the house, to a closed white door which she opened.

"Mr. Archer is here, Mother."

Sylvia Lennox was a thin elegant woman sitting on a canopied bed. A round bedside table held a pink telephone, a glass of water, and two red pills. She lifted her head at a consciously attractive angle. But in spite of her silk cap and robe, and the room that surrounded her like the interior of a pink cloud, she looked rather like an aging boy.

"My lawyer, Emerson Little, tells me that you know John Truttwell."

"I worked with him on a case once."

"He seems to have a high opinion of you."

"I'm glad to hear that. I'm also glad you've been in touch with your lawyer."

"Yes. Emerson will make the arrangements in the morning." She turned to her daughter. "May I talk to Mr. Archer alone for a minute?"

"Certainly, Mother." Elizabeth was a little awkward in her presence.

"Could you possibly not call me Mother, dear? I've asked you to call me Sylvia."

"Yes, Sylvia."

Elizabeth went out, shutting the door a little harder than necessary, but not quite hard enough to upset the wary balance between her and her mother. Mrs. Lennox waved me into a chair beside her bed.

"I love my daughter dearly," she said without heat, "but she's terribly conscious of the generations. I suppose a woman gets that way when she marries an older man. When Elizabeth met Captain Somerville, he was already old enough to be her father. In 1944, when they were married, she was just out of Vassar and barely twenty-one. She thought it would be romantic to be married to a Navy captain, and my husband arranged the marriage. Of course he was thinking of the future of the company—he always had two reasons for doing any one thing he did." There was acid in her voice, and it etched lines in her face. "But," she added a little belatedly, "you're not interested in our family history."

"I am, though. You and your daughter are very candid."

"I taught her that, if not much else. She was her father's daughter." Her experienced blue eyes came up to the level of mine and rested there coolly. "What did Elizabeth have to say about me?"

I decided to match her candor. "That you'd left your husband, for cause. That you had money of your own. That you were very fond of Laurel."

"I love her better than myself. She's my only grandchild." A fine nest of wrinkles had formed around her eyes, and her look was partly quizzical, partly wincing. "You sound as if you're interested in my money. I don't mean that as an accusation. Most people are."

"I'm not particularly. Older people's money can be expensive to buy."

Her head came up as if I had insulted her. But she seemed to see in my face that that hadn't been my intention, and she subsided.

"I'm interested in your money to this extent," I said. "I understand you're putting up the ransom for Laurel."

"Yes. I can't afford it, but I'm willing. If Laurel needed it, she could have everything of mine." She moved her thin arm in a gesture which seemed to take in the house and everything it contained.

"You're very generous."

"Not really. I wouldn't offer up my worldly goods for anyone else but Laurel. But if she were gone permanently, I wouldn't have much reason to go on living." She leaned toward me with restrained eagerness. "Elizabeth mentioned that you saw her tonight."

"Yes." I told her quickly what had happened between Laurel and me. "I shouldn't have let her get away from me. I knew she needed help, but I didn't want to admit it to myself. I wasn't prepared to give it, I suppose."

She reached for me with her narrow brown hand and touched me on the knee. "You're fond of her, too, aren't you?"

"Fond isn't quite the word. She made a deep impression on me, and I'm concerned about her."

"What sort of an impression?"

"Dark and troubled," I said. "At the same time quite strong, in her way, and valuable, even beautiful. I never met a girl who cared so much. What's happening out on the ocean here seemed to affect her as if it was happening to her own body."

The old woman nodded. "You put it very well. She has so much empathy it's virtually psychotic. And I think it was this oil spill, with her own family involved in it, that set her off."

"*Is* she psychotic?"

"One or two doctors have thought she had psychotic tendencies. One of them came up with the opinion—this was several years ago, some time before Laurel got married, and she was going through a particularly bad spell —I was afraid she might kill herself, in fact—" Her blue eyes widened and filled up with fear which turned inward, away from me. After a blank time, she said, "What was I saying?"

"You were going to tell me about the doctor's opinion."

"Yes, I remember now. He thought that Laurel had been frightened or shocked when she was a small child, and that it had left her permanently shaken. He couldn't get at the source of it—her memory had blanked out."

"Was he a psychiatrist?"

"Yes. Laurel has seen several psychiatrists. But she didn't stay with any of them long. This may seem a strange thing to say about a girl who has suffered as much as Laurel and made so many mistakes. But I don't think she wants to be any different. And of course she's had her good times. She seemed quite content this last week here with me."

"I'd like to look at her room."

"Of course. Elizabeth will show it to you. Laurel spent her nights in the guesthouse. Apparently she liked the isolation."

"What did she do in the daytime?"

"Her days were quite full, actually. She read, listened to music, walked on the beach—"

"Alone?"

"So far as I know. She played some tennis with Tony,

but she has no personal interest in him, I'm sure. She's still in love with her husband; she told me so herself."

"Then why did she leave him?"

"He got on her nerves, she told me. She couldn't bear to live in such intimacy, especially in that dreary little house. I would have been glad to help them buy another house, but her husband wouldn't hear of it. He's very much attached to that awful house of his. Apparently he's lived in it all his life."

"He's very independent."

"Yes. I suppose it's a virtue in a man."

"Not in a woman?"

"I don't know. I've always been a little too independent myself. And I've ended up quite alone in the world." The wincing, quizzical look was pinching her eyes again. "Now I'm starting to complain about my lot, and that means it's time to go to sleep. I wake up very early in the morning. Would you be good enough to hand me my sleeping pills?"

"In a minute. Was Laurel on barbiturates?"

"No."

"Has she ever been?"

"Not to my knowledge."

"What about other drugs?"

"She's always been quite careful about drugs. I taught her that. I've never believed in them. I only started taking Seconal because I was waking up so terribly early. I'd wake up long before dawn and listen to the seconds of my life ticking away and wonder what I could do for Laurel." She moved restlessly. "Well, now there is something I can do."

"You mean the money."

"Yes. I mean the money. I want you to see that Jack delivers it properly. My son has many good points, but he does tend to get excited in emergencies."

"I've noticed that."

"Will you go along with him when he delivers the money?"

"You're asking me to take quite a responsibility, Mrs. Lennox."

"Elizabeth says that you're a responsible man."

"Jack may not think so."

"I'll talk to him in the morning. I'll make it a condition that you go along. We don't want any slip-ups. Are you willing?"

I said I was, but I added, "Before we go any further, there's one thing we ought to consider."

"About Jack?"

"About Laurel. I've been told that when she was fifteen or so, she went to Las Vegas with a boy. They ran out of money and faked a kidnapping situation. I understand they collected a thousand dollars from her parents."

Her face hardened. "Did Jack and Marian tell you this?"

"No. I got it from another source."

"I don't believe it."

"I do, Mrs. Lennox."

"Who was your source?"

"It doesn't matter. What does matter is the possibility that the same trick is being repeated now, on a larger scale."

She looked at me with distaste. "My granddaughter is not a criminal."

"No, but sometimes people do things to their families that they wouldn't think of doing to anyone else. Especially a young woman who's under the influence of a man."

"What man? There is no man."

"It was a man who called your son tonight and asked for the money."

She lay back against her pillows and absorbed the implications. They seemed to shrink her body and her face. She said in a diminished voice:

"I simply don't believe it. Laurel wouldn't do such a thing to me."

"She doesn't know you're involved."

"Laurel wouldn't do it to her parents either."

"She did once."

Mrs. Lennox waved the fact away. "If what you heard is true—which I seriously doubt. Even if it is true, she was just a young girl at the time. She's grown up since, and she's really quite fond of her parents. Why, she went to visit them this very day."

She was tired and hurt and suddenly quite old. I rose to go. She stretched out a hand toward me:

"Give me my pills, will you, please? And a sip of water? It must be terribly late, and I wake up so early."

I offered her the red pills in the palm of my hand. Her fingers pecked them up and placed them on her pale tongue. She drank the water as if it was hemlock.

"Anyway," she said, "I don't care what she's done, I want her back. I'm willing to pay the money for her, sight unseen."

XIII

I found Elizabeth in the big front room.

"How did you get along with Mother?" she said.

"All right. She answered my questions."

"Don't you ever get tired of asking questions?"

There was a slight edge on her voice. I wondered if she was self-conscious about telling me so much about her life.

"I'm tired now," I said. "But I'd rather ask questions than have to answer them."

She looked at me with bright interest, as if I'd revealed a weakness in myself. "I'll remember that. Now, what about tomorrow?"

I told her what the plans were.

"Jack won't want you to go along. You know that."

"Jack may have to put up with me," I said. "Right now, I'd like to have a look at the guesthouse where Laurel was staying."

She looked at the watch on her wrist. "It's nearly two o'clock."

"I know that. It's the only time I have."

She turned on an outside light and led me out through a sliding door onto a breezeway which deserved its name. A cold wind laden with the scent of oil poured over us from the sea. Several miles offshore, the platform that marked the source of the oil blazed like a Christmas tree.

The guesthouse was a new-looking flat-roofed build-ing which projected on pilings over part of the beach. The tide had gone out, and at the foot of the beach I could see the surf breaking white and sliding back into darkness. It looked as if the oil hadn't reached shore yet.

Elizabeth turned on the lights as we went in. The in-terior of the guesthouse was divided into living and sleeping quarters. The bed was unmade; the twisted sheets looked like something that a prisoner had escaped from. Some dresses and a coat hung in the closet above a single empty pair of shoes. There was a sweater and some stockings and panty hose in the chest of drawers. Neither here nor in the bathroom could I find any drugs, legitimate or illegitimate.

The only personal thing I found was a letter folded into a book of stories entitled *Permanent Errors*. The letter was typed on Save-More stationery and signed "Tom." I stood under the light and read it through while Elizabeth watched me.

Dearest Laurel:

Business is good at the drugstore. It keeps me busy. I do not have much reason to go home these nights, and I have been taking over some of their night shifts from the other pharmacists. I would just as soon work at night than go home to an empty house. The days are not so bad, it is the night that gets me down. After we got married and you were with me, I used to lie beside you when you were sleeping and feel like the luckiest man in the world. I used to lie there and count your breathing. I felt like a king.

But sometimes I thought your breathing stopped and I would go into a panic until I could hear it again. Just for you to go on breathing was the most important thing in my life.

It still is, Laurel. If you can't live in this house, all right, we'll sell it. I'll put it on the market today, just say the word. We'll move into an apartment or buy wherever you say. We do not have to go on living in L.A. if you do not want to. With my record of employ-ment here at Save-More, I can get a job someplace else. And I will do it if you come back to me. You do not

*have to give me an answer right away, Laurel. Take
your time. All I want is for things to work out for you.
If you include me, I will be the luckiest man in the
world. I will feel like a king again.*

All my love,
Tom

I handed the letter to Elizabeth. She read it through.
There were tears in her eyes when she had finished. She
wiped at them ineffectively with her fingers, and turned
away.

"What's the matter?"

"I feel so sorry for them."

"I thought you didn't approve of Tom."

"As a husband for Laurel, I don't. He's so simple,
and Laurel is so complex."

"That combination can make a match."

"I know it can. But in this case it hasn't been working. He thinks he can bring her back, and close the gap
between them, by moving to another house, or getting a
job somewhere else."

"He's a willing man," I said, "more willing than I realized. If I had been half as willing, I could have held on
to my own wife."

She gave me a direct bright look which went strangely
with her tears. It passed through me like a laser beam
assaying an unidentified object. My heart accelerated a
little, and I wondered if her tears had been for herself as
well as for Tom.

She turned the letter over. "There's something written
on the back. It's Laurel's handwriting."

She read aloud: " 'You're a sweet boy, and I do love
you. I think I always have. Nobody else. And I will
come back. And we will get another house. Or an apartment if we can't afford a house. And maybe we'll have
a child, after all. But you have to give me some time,
Tom. I get these terrible dark depressions and then I
don't want to live in the world at all. Even with you. But
I'm fighting it.' "

Elizabeth's voice broke. Her eyes were wet again.

"I haven't cried for years," she said. "What's the matter with me?"

"You're turning out to be human, after all."

She shook her head in short quick arcs like a child. "Don't laugh at me."

"It's better than crying."

"Not always. Not if you've got something to cry about."

She turned her back on me and went to the window. Touched by emotion, her back was beautiful. The narrow waist blossomed out into strong hips, which narrowed down again into a fine pair of legs.

Beyond her on the water, the lights of the platform blazed cold.

"It looks like a burning ship." She sounded like a child recognizing something for the first time. Later she said in a colder, adult voice, "It's a recurring theme. Other people burn their bridges behind them. We do things on a grander scale in our family. We burn ships and spill oil. It's the all-American way."

She was losing the feeling stirred in her by Tom's letter and Laurel's unsent answer, dissipating it in irony. I moved up close behind her, not close enough to touch.

"You're taking this oil spill very hard."

"I suppose I am."

"Laurel did, too."

"I know that." But it wasn't Laurel she wanted to talk about. "It's really made me take a look at my life. I was brought up to think in terms of gain. Not just financial gain—we didn't need that—but gaining points, the way you do in tennis. Make good grades in school, have more friends than anyone, marry the most eligible man, and so on. But it really doesn't work out too well if your gain has to be someone else's loss. Or if the rules of the game turn out to be different from what you thought."

"I don't quite follow that."

"I mean you might think you're gaining, and be a loser. I am, and I knew it long ago, but I didn't have the courage to act on the knowledge. I'd given up a boy I met in New York who probably would have married me if I'd waited. But there were no points to be gained there —we were merely in love with each other. I married Ben because there was a war on—he was Captain War himself, going to be Commander-in-Chief Pacific someday. Also because my father wanted me to. He was in the oil business, after all, and at that time he was supplying oil to the Navy. It was what they used to call a dynastic marriage, based on mutual gain. But I was the one who lost."

"What did you lose?"

"My life. I stayed with Ben and let it slip away from me. I should have left him in the first year of our marriage. But I was ashamed to admit that I was a loser. I was afraid that my father would turn against me. Now my father has turned around and done what I should have done."

"What happened in the first year of your marriage? Do you mean the loss of your husband's ship?"

"It was part of it, but the crucial thing happened before that. I lost Ben, or knew I'd lost him, before he lost his ship. I never had him, really. He had a mistress at the same time that he was courting me, and he didn't even break with her when he married me. I suppose she was a pretty little thing from the masculine point of view, but I was appalled by her. She couldn't even speak grammatical English."

"You knew her?"

"I met her once. She came to see me in our new house in Bel-Air. Ben was at sea, and I was living there by myself. She came to the door one day, with her little boy, and told me she needed money—just like that. When I asked her who she was, she explained to me that she was Ben's girl. She was so matter-of-fact about it I couldn't be angry with her—at least not with the little boy there. I gave her some money and she drove away in her old-beat-up car.

"It was afterwards that I had the bad reaction. I couldn't bear to live in the house any more. I wanted to burn it down. One night, I took a can of gasoline into Ben's study. I intended to sprinkle it on the floor and furniture and on his books, and then set fire to it. At the last minute, I changed my mind.

"But I decided I couldn't go on living there. I went home to live with my parents and lent the house to Jack and Marian. Jack had just graduated from Communications School in the East, and he was waiting on the West

Coast to join Ben's ship. Everything happened so quickly in those days. The ship came into Long Beach Harbor in a few weeks, stayed for a night or two, and then went out again, with both my husband and my brother aboard. And then the ship caught fire off Okinawa, and that was the end of Ben's career in the Navy. It was hardly more than a month between the time I carried the gasoline can into his study and the time his ship caught fire. I used to make a connection between the two things."

"You mean you imagined that you set fire to the ship?"

"Not exactly," she said. "But something like that. From the time that woman came to see me, with her little boy, I think I must have been a little out of touch. For all I knew, he was Ben's illegitimate son, though she said he wasn't."

She was gazing at the lighted platform as if its cold blaze on the contaminated sea might be a symbol of her life and its meaning.

She moved back against me. Then she stood very still as if she had frightened herself. I put my hands on her.

"Don't do that," she whispered urgently.

"Why not? It's better than burning ships and spilling oil. Or setting fire to houses."

XIV

I dreamed I was sleeping with Laurel, and woke up guilty and sweating in her bed. Dawn was at the window, and so was Beth. Leaning into the cold marine morning, her unclothed body looked like a carved figurehead.

I threw off the blanket she had covered me with. She turned with a start, her breasts swinging.

"There's a man out there."

"What's he doing?"

"Floating in the water."

I knotted a bath towel around my waist and went out.

The man was spread-eagled on the surface beyond the place where the waves were breaking. He lay face down as if he was studying the bottom, and moved as the waves moved under him. I waded in through the surf. It rose like liquid pain around my body. It was bitterly cold and tinged with brown. Farther out, the oil lay on the water like a blotched undulating skin.

I swam with my head and face held out of the water. When I got close to the floating man, I seemed to enter a special zone of cold. I tried to grasp him by the hair, but my hand slid off his scalp. It was dark with oil and almost hairless.

Facing him and kicking hard, I took hold of him by the arms and turned him over. One of his arms flopped like a broken wing. His face was damaged—I couldn't tell how badly, because he was in blackface from the oil.

I got hold of him by the shirt collar and towed him in toward shore. A wave broke over us and sucked him out of my grasp. He slid away from me in the brown surf, turned as he struck the sand, and rolled over and over.

Beth was waiting for him just above the farthest reach of the waves, fully clothed except for her bare feet. She ran and held the dead man until I could reach him. Each of us took an arm, and we dragged him up the beach onto dry sand, as if either water or oil could do any further damage to him or his soaked tweed suit.

I wiped his face with a corner of my towel. It was badly damaged: one eye socket was caved in. There were crinkled marks that looked like burn scars on one side of his face and on his scalp. The scars were not recent.

"What do you suppose happened to him?" Beth said. "Could he have fallen off the oil platform?"

"It's possible. But the platform's quite a long way out —three or four miles. I don't think he's been in the water that long. And he isn't wearing working clothes. He may have fallen off a boat, or been caught and rolled by a high wave on the beach. He looks pretty frail."

As I said that, I remembered him in life. He was the bald uncertain little man I'd seen with the younger man in Blanche's Seafood Restaurant on the wharf.

"Do you know him, Beth?"

She leaned over to look at him. "No. I never saw him before. He has nothing to do with us."

She straightened up, and turned. Her mother had come out of the house and started down the steps to the beach. Beth said to me in a low monotone, "Don't call me Beth in front of Mother, please. Nobody calls me Beth."

"Okay, Liz."

"Not that, either. *Please.* Call me Mrs. Somerville if you have to call me anything."

Sylvia came up beside us, wrapped in a heavy wool robe which made her look androgynous and monklike. "Where did *he* come from?"

"Mr. Archer was in the guesthouse. He saw the man in the water and swam out and brought him in."

Sylvia looked from her daughter to me, her eyes bright and dubious in her wrinkled boy's face. "What do you suggest we do with him?"

"We'd better call the police," I said.

"I really hate to do that, unless we know who he is, and what killed him. You know what the press and the news programs will make of this. Look at the fuss they've been making about a few dead birds."

She bent over, her hands on her knees, and looked down at the ruined man as if he was a harbinger of her own fate. She glanced up with the image of death in her eyes.

"Look. He's got oil in his nostrils, oil in his mouth. That's all they'll need to ruin us."

"We can't just leave him lying here," I said.

"No. We'll take him inside, into the guesthouse."

"Then you'll really have trouble. It isn't a good idea, Mrs. Lennox."

She gave me a sharp look. "I didn't ask you for your opinion."

"But you're getting it. Call the police."

"I think we'd better, Mother. I'll do it if you like."

They went toward the main house, the older woman's feet dragging in the sand. There was a fresh morning wind blowing across the beach, and I was shivering so hard that I couldn't see straight. The wet towel hung like a cold lead apron around my loins. I was lobster red in the trunk, fish blue in the extremities, and not thinking too clearly.

I searched the dead man's clothes. The pockets of his tweed suit were empty. But inside the right breast pocket of the jacket, a label had been sewn by the tailor who made it:

TAILORED FOR RALPH P. MUNGAN
JOSEPH SPERLING
SANTA MONICA, CALIF. DEC. 1955

Tony Lashman came out of the house and crossed the slanting beach. He was fully dressed but his hair was uncombed and he was blinking in the morning light.

He stopped blinking when he saw the dead man. Approaching with a kind of unwilling fascination, he leaned above him and studied his damaged face.

"Do you know him?" I said.

Lashman seemed to be startled by my question. He straightened up as if I'd caught him in a compromising position:

"No, I never saw him before. Who is he, anyway?"

"I don't know. I just pulled him out of the water."

"What happened to his face?" Lashman touched his own face, as if he suspected that it could happen to him.

"He may have been struck with a blunt instrument. Or he may have gotten banged up on the rocks."

"You think he was murdered?"

"It's a strong possibility. Are you sure you've never seen him before?"

"Of course I'm sure."

He backed away from the body as if death was a contagion. But he lingered not far away, and after a little time he spoke again.

"You're a private detective, isn't that right?"

"I work at it."

"What kind of money do you make?"

"A hundred a day and expenses. Why? Does Mrs. Lennox want to know?"

"I was asking on my own account. I've sometimes thought of going into the detective business myself. But I understood there was more money in it."

"There is for a few. But it's not a way to get rich quick, if that's what you're looking for. Besides, you need some background."

"What kind of background?"

"Most private detectives come out of police work. I used to be on the Long Beach force myself."

"I see." He gave me a discouraged look, and went back into the house.

I stayed with the man's body until the Sheriff's deputies arrived. I told them I had seen him alive in Blanche's Restaurant, but I didn't mention the tailor's label sewn into the pocket of his suit. They could find it themselves if they looked.

I went back into the guesthouse and took a hot shower. It failed to free me of the smell of oil or the chill that the dead man had left on me.

I had more than one reason to take his death personally. I had pulled him out of the water; and he was connected with the young man in the turtleneck who had frightened Laurel off the beach.

XV

Before I got on the freeway to Santa Monica, I stopped at the harbor. The plastic boom across the harbor mouth had broken during the night. The floating oil had surged in with the morning tide and covered the surface of the enclosed water, coating the hulls of the boats lying at anchor and splashing the rocks and walls that lined the inner harbor. The black scene was barely relieved by a few white gulls with dirty feet.

It was too early, and the front door of Blanche's place was locked. There were violent noises somewhere in the back which sounded to my recently sensitized ears like somebody beating somebody else to death.

It turned out to be a man in the kitchen pounding abalone with a wooden mallet. I asked him through the screen door if Blanche was there.

"Blanche never comes in this time in the a.m. She's generally here by ten."

"Where does she live?"

He lifted his shoulders. "Don't ask me. She likes to keep it a secret. She doesn't give out her telephone number, either. Is it important?"

I didn't know. It had looked from where I sat the night before as if the younger man accompanying the man in the tweed suit had asked Blanche a question, and she had pointed south along the beach. Possibly she could tell me where they had intended to go.

I thanked the man and turned back toward land. Two cars had stopped in the restaurant parking lot, and several men got out. They wore business suits and hard hats, and they looked like engineers, or like publicity men trying to look like engineers.

One of them was Captain Somerville. His face was closed and harried. I lifted my hand to him, but he didn't notice me, let alone recognize me. The Captain and his entourage headed past the restaurant to the landing area, where a truck was unloading heavy drums.

On the way to Santa Monica, I listened to the morning news and learned that Lennox Oil was bringing in a wild-well team from Houston and preparing a major attempt to stop the spill. I switched off the radio and enjoyed the silence, broken only by the sounds of my own and other cars.

Traffic was still fairly light, and the day was clear enough to see the mountains rising in the east like the boundaries of an undiscovered country. I lapsed for a while into my freeway daydream: I was mobile and unencumbered, young enough to go where I had never been and clever enough to do new things when I got there.

The fantasy snapped in my face when I got to Santa Monica. It was just another part of the megalopolis which stretched from San Diego to Ventura, and I was a citizen of the endless city.

I found Joseph Sperling's tailor shop in a side street off Lincoln Boulevard. I remembered it as a pleasant street of shops, but the flow of time and traffic had eroded it. A real-estate office next to the tailor shop was standing empty, with photographs of unsold houses gathering dust in the window.

The door of Joseph Sperling's shop was locked. A cardboard clock with a movable hand hung inside the window and indicated that he would be in at eight. It was a few minutes before eight. I locked my car and went to a drive-in around the corner for breakfast. With the second cup of coffee, I finally warmed up and stopped shivering.

When I went back to the tailor shop, Joseph Sperling was there. He was a small gentle-looking man with curly gray hair and bright eyes behind rimless spectacles. He looked at me as if he was estimating my measurements and planning a suit.

"What can I do for you, sir?"

"Do you know Ralph P. Mungan?"

His eyes widened as if to register trouble, and narrowed down again in defense against it. "I used to know him quite well. Is Ralph in some kind of a jam?"

"The worst kind."

He leaned on a table, supporting himself on a bolt of fabric. "What does that mean, the worst kind?"

"He's dead."

"I'm sorry to hear it, very sorry."

"Were you close to him, Mr. Sperling?"

He was shocked into reminiscence. "We haven't been close in a long time—not really what you could call close. But I knew Ralph in Fresno, where we grew up. I was a few years older than Ralph and Martha, and I came down here to the big city first. By the time they made the move, I owned the building next door as well as this one, and I rented it to them." He looked a little afraid that I might not believe him.

"Was this recently?"

"Not recently, no. It was over twenty years ago that they first came here. And nearly ten years since they left. What on earth happened to Ralph?"

"He drowned in the sea off Pacific Point."

Sperling's face lost its color. "Are you from the police?"

"I'm a private detective."

"Was it suicide?"

"I doubt it. Would you say Ralph was suicidal?"

"He talked about it sometimes, especially when he was drinking. Ralph was bitterly disappointed in his life —it hadn't worked out the way he hoped. I don't mean to insult the memory of a dead man, but Ralph did a lot of drinking in his day. He and his wife, Martha, used to drink and fight, fight and drink. Sometimes when I was sewing in the back"—he waved his hand toward an area behind a hanging green curtain—"I could hear them through two thicknesses of wall."

"I'd like to talk to his wife. Have you seen her recently?"

"I'm afraid I haven't. I haven't seen either of them in years. Anyway, I heard they went their separate ways."

"Divorced?"

"So I heard. Still, Martha will have to be told about this. I'd rather you told her than have to do it myself. Or does she know?"

"I doubt it. It just happened last night or early this morning. I pulled him out of the water myself."

He gave me a sympathetic look. "I noticed you were a little blue around the gills. Why don't you sit down? I'll see if I can find her number for you."

He pulled out a chair for me and left the room. The green curtain fell into place behind him. I sat and listened to the whisper and whir and stutter and roar of the boulevard.

Sperling came back after a while with a memo pad in his hand. He tore off the top sheet and handed it to me.

"Martha's phone isn't listed, and neither is Ralph's. But I got his number and address from a mutual friend in the real-estate business. Ralph lives in Beverly Hills now —I mean he did live there. It looks as if he finally made it, after all."

I doubted it. The little old hairless man in Blanche's Restaurant had looked as if he had never made it anywhere. But the address on the slip of paper was Bottlebrush Drive, an expensive street in a very expensive city.

"I suppose you could call his house," Sperling said. "There may be somebody there who should be told. For all I know, Ralph may have married again. Some of us do and some of us don't. But Ralph was the type who would, if you want my opinion."

Still I hesitated to place the phone call. I had the feeling that I had made a mistake, or was about to make one.

"Can you tell me a little more about Ralph, Mr. Sperling?"

"What sort of thing do you mean?"

"Well, you made him a suit in 1955."

"That's right, I did. He couldn't really afford it, but I gave it to him at cost for a birthday present." He fell silent, and his sensitive eyes registered the implications of what I had said. "Was he wearing my suit when you found him?"

"Yes, he was."

"He must have lost weight. The last time I set eyes on him, he was much too large in the waistline to get into that suit. We had a little joke about it at the time. He was too fat for his own good, but he still was a fine-looking man."

"Fine-looking?"

"I always thought so. So did Mrs. Sperling, when she was alive."

"How did he get the burns on his face and head?"

"Burns?"

"Yes. He was pretty badly disfigured."

"That must have happened since I saw him."

"How long ago was that?"

"A couple of years at least, more like three. I ran into him in Century Plaza. He was in a hurry, and we didn't spend much time together. But he certainly had no burn marks on his head. I noticed what a fine head of hair he still had."

"Can you describe him for me, Mr. Sperling?"

"Well, he's—he was middle-aged—he'd be about fifty or so, with a tendency to stoutness, but Ralph was always light and fast on his feet. And always cheerful, except when he was drinking and down in the dumps." He looked past me at the light coming through the front window. "It's hard to believe that Ralph is dead."

I didn't believe it myself. It was clear that there had been a mistake. I asked Sperling to let me use his phone.

He took me into his back room, where suits in various stages of completion hung like the makings of artificial men; then he delicately withdrew as I dialed the Beverly Hills number.

A sedate woman's voice answered: "This is the Mungan residence."

"May I speak to Mr. Mungan, please?"

"Who shall I tell him is calling?"

I gave her my name and occupation. After a minute's wait, he came to the phone. "Ralph Mungan speaking. My wife's housekeeper says you're a detective."

"A private detective cooperating with the Orange County police. The body of a man came in with the tide this morning off Pacific Point."

"What man?"

"He was wearing a suit with your name sewn into it."

Mungan was silent for a moment. "I don't like that. It makes me feel as if somebody walked on my grave. How could a thing like that happen?"

"I don't know. I'd like to come and discuss it with you."

"Why? Is it somebody I know?"

"That's possible. In any case, you may be able to help me identify him. May I come over, Mr. Mungan? I won't take much of your time."

Reluctantly, he agreed. I left Sperling looking more cheerful.

XVI

Ralph Mungan lived in a handsome Spanish house dating from prewar days. The lawn in front of it was green and smooth. There were waxwings on the pyracantha bushes like beige-and-yellow ornaments fastened among the red berries they were eating.

I knocked on the front door and waited. I could see the tower of the city hall standing feudally against the sky.

Mungan came to the door with his wife behind him.

His fine dark head of hair was turning gray. He was short and heavy—so heavy that it was hard to imagine him wearing the same suit as the floating man.

Mrs. Mungan had a face like ivory, smooth and hard, and a coil of black hair that probably wasn't her own. The figure under her pink morning gown wasn't all her own, either. In spite, or because, of these artifices, she looked a few years older than her husband.

But her eyes were bright and interested. She led us into a sitting room where the three of us sat equidistant from each other on formal chairs.

I could feel the lines of tension stretching like taut wires across the room. Without moving, Mungan gave the impression of squirming.

"Well," Mrs. Mungan said to me, "what's the excitement about?"

I told them about the man in the water.

She leaned toward me, baring part of her rib cage. "And it's your theory, is it, that he was wearing Ralph's suit?"

"It isn't my suit," he said. "There's some mistake. I never had a suit like that and I don't know any man like that."

"Sperling the tailor said he made it for you."

His face swelled and darkened like a ripening plum. His wife looked at him, smiling rather intensely, and said in mock raillery:

"What deep dark secret are you trying to cover up, dear?"

Mungan didn't respond right away. His gaze was inward, looking down the tunnel of the past. He made an effort which shook him to his foundations, and answered her smile with an equally ghastly one.

"Okay, I confess. I murdered him myself. Now are you satisfied?"

"What was your motive, dear?"

"Jealousy," he said. "What else? He threatened to take you away from me, so I took him down and drowned him in the ocean."

Mrs. Mungan made a show of laughter, but she wasn't happy with his answer. She gave him a quick insulted look, as if he had expressed a wish that she should be taken away from him, or drowned. She said:

"We can't very well go to Palm Springs with this hanging over your head. Can we, Ralph?"

"There's nothing hanging over my head. I was only kidding." He grinned widely, toothlessly, mirthlessly. "I *want* to go to Palm Springs. I've got golfing dates and business commitments."

"What business commitments?"

"We have an offer for the Palm Springs building, don't forget."

"I've decided I don't want to sell it. And I don't want to go to Palm Springs. Go by yourself."

"I wouldn't do that," he said. "I wouldn't enjoy it."

"I would. Sometimes I think we see too much of each other."

He seemed appalled by the idea, as if she had suddenly proposed a divorce. "Okay, we'll give up the Palm Springs idea. I can call off my golf dates. As for the building, it's bound to appreciate anyway."

"That doesn't mean you can't go to Palm Springs. Go ahead. Don't let me stop you."

"I don't want to go to Palm Springs. I'd be lonely. Lonely for you."

He gave her a lonely look which was still on his face when he turned in my direction. But he wasn't lonely for either of us.

I was getting impatient. "Didn't you own a real-estate office in Santa Monica?"

"I didn't own it. I rented the building."

"And Joseph Sperling had a tailor shop next door?"

"Yeah, I remember Joe." His face went through the motions of remembering, eyes widening and brightening with false pleasure. "Come to think of it, he did make me a suit at one time. That was way back in the fifties."

"A gray tweed suit?"

"That's right."

"What happened to it?"

"I'm sorry, I haven't the foggiest. I think I gave it to the Salvation Army."

"When?"

"Just before we got married last year. I put on weight since that suit was made, and I realized I'd never be able to wear it again. So I gave it to the Salvation Army."

I didn't believe him. Neither did his wife. She said gaily, "Are you sure you didn't drown the man, after all?"

"How could I? I was home in bed with you."

Her eyes narrowed, as if he had offered her a further insult or threat. It wasn't a happy marriage, even from where I sat on the outside.

I stood up. "If you remember anything else, let me know. I'll leave you a number to call."

"All right."

I gave Mungan the number of my answering service. He wrote it down. Then he followed me to the door, and stepped outside. As soon as the door closed, he looked once behind him and moved along beside me, talking in a changed low anxious voice.

"I remember something else. I don't know whether I ought to tell you or not. I mean, can you promise it won't get back to my wife?"

"I can't promise that. It depends on what it is."

"You're really putting me in a bind."

"I'm sorry, but it isn't me doing it. The regular police should be here before long. And if you think you can avoid publicity by covering up evidence—it's the surest way to get your picture in the paper."

Mungan covered his face with both hands and looked at me between his fingers. "Don't say that. It would really wreck my marriage."

"If your marriage is important to you, you better level with your wife *and* me."

He nodded heavily, and his head stayed down. "Yeah. I know. Sometimes it isn't so easy."

"Did you have anything to do with the man's death?"

"Of course not. Of course I didn't. What do you think I am?"

"I'll tell you when I know more about you," I said.

He dropped his hands, spreading them wide. He was a salesman, or an ex-salesman, who couldn't bear to be disliked.

"Look," he said. "Could you and I take a ride around

the block? I don't know what I'll tell Ethel, but I'll think of something."

"Why not tell her the truth?"

"I can't. You see, there's something in my life that Ethel doesn't know about."

"Isn't it about time you told her?"

He turned beside the open door of my car and looked at me as if I had just offered to push him down an elevator shaft. "No! It isn't possible."

"Get in and tell me about it."

He climbed in and I slammed the door on him. We were halfway around the block before he spoke:

"I've been married before. Ethel doesn't know about it."

"I do. Her name was Martha."

He made a miserable face at me. "Did somebody hire you to investigate me?"

"Somebody will if you go on like this."

"That sounds like a threat."

"It's more of a prediction."

I parked at the curb in front of a house with a mansard roof which had an old black Rolls parked in the driveway.

"Tell me this, Mr. Mungan. What has your former wife got to do with the man I found in the ocean?"

"I don't know. Maybe she can tell you. I'm pretty sure I left the suit in the house when I took off."

"How long ago?"

"Let's see, it'll be four years next month."

"And where does your ex-wife live?"

"The last I heard, she was managing an apartment house in Hollywood. The Excalibur Arms."

I knew where it was.

"Just keep my name out of it, will you?" Mungan said.

"Why is that so important?"

"Because I tell you it is. I'm cooperating with you. You should be willing to cooperate with me."

"It won't be easy. It doesn't matter what I do, your name is on that suit. The police will find it, if they haven't already. And they'll be beating a path to your door."

He slumped in the seat as if I had shot him. "I'm in a bind."

"Because you've been married before? That's common enough."

"You don't know Ethel. She can be very vindictive. So can Martie. If the two of them ever get together, I'm finished."

"There must be more to this than you're telling me."

"Yeah. There is." He looked apprehensively up and down the street. "I wouldn't be surprised if Martie did this to me. She's never forgiven me for leaving her, I know that."

"You mean she killed a man and put your suit on him just to get back at you?"

"No." He looked rather sheepish. "I guess even Martie wouldn't do that."

"Then what's the rest of it, Mungan?"

"There is no rest of it."

"There has to be. What is it?"

He answered a question I hadn't asked, in a high emotional voice I hadn't heard before. "A man should be able to change wives without living in hell for the rest of his life. Martie gave me good reason to leave her. She was drunk most of the time towards the end. I had a problem, too, I admit that. But I wanted to quit, and get out of that life."

And you met an older woman with some money.

Almost as if he had heard me, Mungan went on: "A man has a right to a second chance. I proved that when I quit drinking. And Ethel helped me. We have our troubles like any other couple. But Ethel's been good for me. She turned my footsteps onto the higher path." That sounded like a quotation, perhaps from Ethel. "And now you want to drag me back into that rotten life."

All I really wanted, by this time, was to get away from him. Even if he had quit drinking, he had slightly drunken emotions, with a tremolo of self-pity running through them.

I started the car. He took it as a rejection, and cast about for some way to stop me.

"There's something I haven't told you."

"Tell me now." I raced the engine a little.

"I got a Mexican divorce from Martie. I'm not absolutely certain that it's legal."

"You mean you know darn well it isn't legal?"

"That's right. I paid a lawyer in Tijuana two hundred and fifty dollars, but I found out later that the divorce didn't take. I was already married to Ethel by that time."

"So to speak."

"Yeah, so to speak. But Ethel watches me like a hawk, and it's tied my hands. So now you know the bind I'm in. All I'm asking you to do is not tell Martie where I'm living and who I'm living with. I got the divorce in good faith. How was I to know that Tijuana lawyer was a crook? And Ethel and I were married by a minister in Vegas. So all I'm really worried about is Martie and *her* vindictiveness." His fingers scratched lightly at my elbow. "Don't tell Martie, eh?"

I said I wouldn't. When I dropped him off at his house, Ethel was waiting for him out in front.

XVII

The Excalibur Arms was on a side street off Sunset Boulevard, not very far from my office. It had been there as long as I could remember. Its four-story façade stood in the diluted sunlight like an old woman with a powder-caked face surprised by morning.

I found the manager's apartment, Number 1 on the ground floor, and rang the bell. A middle-aged man in his shirt sleeves came to the door chewing. The look in his eyes suggested that what he was chewing was bitter.

"We have no vacancies," he said around his cud.

"Thanks, but I'm looking for Mrs. Mungan."

He ruminated and swallowed. "She left here a long time ago."

"Do you have a forwarding address?"

"We might have." He turned and shouted into his apartment, "Do we have an address for Martha Mungan?"

A woman's voice answered, "I'll see."

The man leaned on the doorframe. "You wouldn't be a bill collector, would you?"

"No. I simply want to talk to her."

He looked at me as if he didn't believe me, hadn't believed anyone for a number of years. He shouted back into his apartment again:

"What's the holdup, anyway?"

"Wait a minute, can't you? It took me a while to find the address book."

The woman appeared behind him. She had a face matching his, with wary eyes and lines of discontent running down from the sides of her nose.

"The last we heard of Mrs. Mungan, she was managing a place called Topanga Court." She gave me an address on the Coast Highway. "I can't swear she's still there. She drinks, you know."

"Don't tell her who told you," the man added. "We have enough enemies as it is."

I didn't go directly to Topanga Court. It was several days since I had been in my office, and time I paid it a visit.

It was on the second floor of a two-story building on Sunset. I parked in my slot behind it and went up the back stairs. Girls were twittering in the modeling agency next door.

The name and occupation on my door, "Lew Archer: Private Investigator," looked rather strange to me, and I understood how they might look to a client. There was no sign of any. The scattering of mail under the slot in the outer office was mostly advertisements and bills.

I took the mail into the inner office, discarded the advertisements, and mentally added up the bills. The total came to about three hundred dollars, which was the amount of the check in my pocket. I still had a couple of hundred in my checking account, but that was earmarked for the rent.

I wasn't anxious, though the traffic below the window seemed to have a slightly anxious sound, as if it couldn't wait to get where it was going. I told myself I was better off than usual. I was in the middle of a case, dealing with people who had plenty of money.

But I didn't want to have to depend on those people. I decided to call Tom Russo and see where we stood.

The cousin answered, "This is the Russo residence."

"Archer speaking."

She dropped her formal tone. "Hello, Mr. Archer. Are you having any luck?"

"I think I'm making some progress. How are you, Gloria?"

"I'm all right. I guess you want to talk to Tom, don't you?"

"It's what I had in mind."

"I really hate to wake him up. After he got off work last night, he was out on the streets driving around for hours. It was nearly dawn when he got home, and he was in poor shape. He was talking about death and destruction."

"Exactly what was he saying?"

"I wouldn't want to repeat it over the phone. You never know who's listening these days. Anyway, it didn't make too much sense."

I decided I still had a client, and it was time I paid him another visit.

Gloria answered the door. Her dark hair was damp and spread to dry on her shoulders, which she had protected with a thick towel.

"You didn't say you were coming or I wouldn't have washed my hair."

"I decided I better talk to Tom in person."

"He's still asleep. Do you want me to wake him up?"

"I'll wake him." I wanted an intimate look at Tom.

Gloria showed me his room and opened the door for me. The old wooden Venetian blinds were closed, and Tom was snoring in the gloom. I opened the blinds, and the light sliced in, but it didn't disturb the sleeper. The back yard outside the window was a jungle of pittosporum dotted with red geraniums which had grown up through it toward the light.

Tom was huddled like a fetus under a light blanket, one fist against his chest, the other under his cheek. The lower part of his face was peppered with beard. The pillow crushed under his head was the only one on the bed, and I couldn't see any signs of lipstick stains.

I looked around at Gloria. As if she could read my thoughts, she said from the doorway:

"I haven't been sleeping with him, if that's what you think." Her voice was quite matter-of-fact. "Laurel's the only girl he can see, and anyway I have a boy friend of my own."

"Where do you sleep?"

"Last night? In the spare room. It was too late to go home. Anyway, my boy friend has the car."

Tom groaned and turned onto his back, using his fists to shield his eyes from the light. I took him by the wrists and shook him a little. His half-awakened face was full of grief, and there were tears in the hollows of his eyes. He sobbed very loudly and pulled away from me.

"I tried to make her warm again," he said. "But she was cold. Mummy was cold."

Gloria said, "He's having another bad spell. You just have to wait it out."

"Shut the door, will you please?"

She gave me an insulted look, but she did as I asked her to. I stayed with Tom.

"What made Mummy cold?" I said.

"I pushed her and she fell down." His voice seemed to mimic the voice of a child. "I didn't mean to make her fall when I pushed her. I didn't mean to die her. But the back of her head was all sticky." He peered at his clean pharmacist's hands. "And she was cold. I couldn't warm her up."

"People don't turn cold right away when they die, Tom."

"Mummy did." He rocked his head from side to side. "She wouldn't let me get in bed with them. She said I had to stay in the room with the little girl. She got out of bed and said she was going to spank me. The man said don't, just get him out of here, but she said spank. She spanked me and I pushed her and she fell down on the floor and I couldn't wake her up even by singing."

"What did you sing?"

" 'Jingle Bells.' The bed made a noise like Jingle Bells. She called him that sometimes, and then they laughed."

"What did he look like?"

"He was just a man."

"Old or young?"

"I don't know."

"What kind of clothes was he wearing?"

"I don't know." Tom looked at me anxiously, clutching at the bedclothes as if the strata of time were shifting under him and might bury him. "He said he'd come back and fix me if I told on him."

"He won't be coming back, Tom. That was a long time ago."

He heard me, and seemed to understand me. I waited for him to come out of his half-waking dream. New tears formed like protective lenses in his eyes. Gradually they cleared, and he recognized me.

"Archer? Is Laurel dead? I dreamed that she was dead."

"That doesn't make it so, Tom. As far as I know she's alive."

"Where is she, then?" His voice was still distraught.

"Apparently she's been kidnapped."

"What do you mean?"

"There's been a ransom demand made on her parents. And they're prepared to pay it. But there's some indication that it may be a phony and Laurel may be making a play for the money herself. Do you think that's possible?"

"But Laurel has plenty of money."

"Her family has. She doesn't get on too well with them. And I understand she took them for some money with a fake kidnapping when she was in her teens."

He regarded me with such loathing that it silenced me. His eyes narrowed down to dark slits, his lower lip pushed out. There were flecks of premature gray in his beard, like the first seeds of age beginning to sprout in him. He was just about young enough to be my son, and just about the age that I had been when I lost my wife.

"I read your letter to Laurel," I said.

"Which one?"

"The one you sent to her grandmother's house on Seahorse Lane. Laurel wrote you an answer on the back of it. But I guess she never got around to sending it."

"What did she say?"

"The general idea was that she cared about you. I think she means to come back to you, if she can."

"I hope she does."

But he spoke without real hope. He sat on the bed with his legs dangling, like a man who had been invalided in combat with nightmares. I left him barely holding the ground he had won.

Gloria was waiting in the narrow hallway. I couldn't help wondering if she hoped to inherit Tom, or if it might happen without her consciously wishing it. And I asked myself if my own unconscious wish might be to inherit Laurel.

We moved into the kitchen, where it had been easy to talk the night before.

"What happened to Tom's mother, Gloria?"

She clasped her upper arms in her fingers and hugged herself as if she could feel a chill. "I don't want to talk about it. Tom gets very upset when anybody talks about it."

"He doesn't have to know."

"You expect me to talk behind his back?" she said unreasonably.

"Tom hired me to work for him, which probably means he trusts me."

"Maybe he does. He trusts a lot of people. That doesn't mean I should tell them the family secrets."

"I think you better tell me, though. It could have some bearing on what happened to Laurel."

"What *did* happen to Laurel?"

"I don't know that either. Was Tom's mother killed?"

"Yes, she was shot." The young woman's eyes were dark with feeling. "I don't think Tom remembers except when he's dreaming—he has these nightmares."

"Does he have them often?"

"I don't know how often. I don't spend that much time here. I think he gets them in cycles, if you know what I mean. Whenever something comes up that sets him back."

"Like Laurel's taking off?"

She nodded. "And there was another thing that probably got him started. My mother brought up the subject of the killing again."

"In front of Tom?"

She nodded. "I couldn't stop her. Mother gets pretty emotional sometimes, and she still thinks if she could get Tom to remember the shooting, *really* remember it, she might find out who did it. She hasn't given up hope of finding the murderer, even after all these years."

"How many years?"

"Over twenty-five. It happened when I was just a tiny baby."

"Why didn't you tell me about this last night?"

"I couldn't. We don't even talk about it in the family, let alone outside the family."

"Who shot her?"

"Nobody knows. The killer was never brought to justice, anyway. I don't know why I'm telling you these things. Mother would *kill* me if she heard me." She caught her breath. "I don't really mean that. Mother wouldn't hurt anybody, let alone me. She's her own worst enemy. She wouldn't hurt a hair on anyone's head." Gloria stroked her damp hair absently.

"What was her relation to Tom's mother?"

"They were sisters, almost the same age, and very close at one time. I used to wonder why Mother was always so sad, until I found out she had a reason."

"Would she discuss it with me, do you think?"

"I doubt it. I certainly wouldn't want to ask her."

"Where is your mother?"

"I'm not going to tell you." There was a sudden note of obstinacy in her voice which made me wonder what she was covering up.

"Aren't you interested in what happened to your aunt? What was her name?"

"Aunt Allie. Alison Russo. Sure I'm interested. But I don't want to put my mother through it again. She has enough on her mind."

"So has Tom," I said. "It might be a way of getting it off both their minds."

She shook her head. "It wouldn't work that way. I said the same thing to my boy friend when he got gung ho on the subject. In our family, the only way to do is let things lie, keep things quiet."

"You can't, though. Look at Tom. He's having night-mares about his mother's death."

"It's better than daymares."

"How do you know?"

"I've tried them both," she said.

"Has Tom ever talked to a psychiatrist?"

"Of course not. There's nothing the matter with his head."

I looked at my watch. The morning was wasting, and I was due back in Seahorse Lane at noon. I thanked Gloria and started out. She followed me to the front door.

"I hope there's no hard feelings because I wouldn't tell you certain things."

"No hard feelings," I said. "Take care of Tom."

I was out of the house before I realized that I hadn't asked him to pay me anything more. Perhaps I didn't want to take his money.

XVIII

Topanga Court, where Martha Mungan lived, was a long step down from the Excalibur Arms. It was a collection of peeling stucco buildings huddled between the Pacific Coast Highway and the eroding cliff. An earth slide leaned against the cliff like sand in the bottom of an hourglass which had almost run out.

I parked in front of the central building. A sign offered family accommodations by the day or week, some with kitchen. A bell jingled over the door when I opened it.

Behind the archway which contained the desk there were television voices in a darkened room. A woman called out:

"Who is that?"

An empty registration card lay on the desk. Mentally I filled it in: Lew Archer, thief catcher, corpse finder, ear to anyone. I said:

"Do you know Joseph Sperling?"

"Joe? You bet I do. How are you, Joe?"

I didn't answer her. I stood and listened to her slow footsteps as they approached the archway. Her face was closed and blind as she came through, a middle-aged woman wearing a harsh red wig and a kimono spilling colors down her front. She blinked against the light like a nocturnal animal.

"You're not Joe Sperling. Who are you trying to kid?"

"I didn't say I was." I gave her my name. "Joe and I had a little talk this morning."

"How is Joe, anyway? I haven't seen him in years."

"He seems to be all right. But I guess he's getting older."

"Aren't we all?" Her eyes came up to mine, surprisingly bright in her drooping face. "You say you had a talk with Joe. About me?"

"About you and your husband."

A sluggish ripple of alarm moved across her face, leaving wrinkles behind it. "I don't have a husband—not any more." She took a deep sighing breath. "Is Ralph Mungan in some kind of trouble?"

"He may be."

"I've been wondering. He dropped out of sight so completely, it made me wonder if he's in jail or something."

"Something," I said, to keep her interest alive.

A loose and empty smile took over the lower half of her face. She let it talk for her while her experienced eyes studied me. "Would you be a copsie-wopsie by any chancie-wancie?"

"A private one."

"And you want some info on Ralph?"

I nodded. In the shadow world behind the archway, the daytime television voices were telling their obvious secrets. I'd love you but I have a fractured libido and nobody ever set it. I'd love you back but you resemble my father, who treated me rotten.

"Where is Ralph?"

"I don't know," I lied.

"What do you want him for?"

"Nothing very important. At least, I hope it isn't important."

She leaned across the counter, resting the burden of her breast on it. "Don't play games with me, eh? I want to know what it's all about. And what does Joe Sperling have to do with it?"

"Remember a tweed suit Joe made for Ralph's birthday one year?"

Her eyes sharpened. "That was a long time ago. What about the suit?"

"It turned up in the ocean this morning."

"So? It was just an old suit."

"Have you seen it lately, Mrs. Mungan?"

"I don't know. After Ralph left, I threw out most of his things. I've moved a lot since then."

"So you don't know who was wearing it?"

With her fingers clenched on the edge of the counter, she pushed herself upright. Something that looked like a wedding band was sunk in the flesh of the appropriate finger like a deep scar.

"Somebody was wearing it?" she said.

"A little old man with burn marks on his head and face. Do you know him, Mrs. Mungan?"

Her face went blank, as if the impact of my question had knocked all sentience from her head.

"I don't know who it could be," she said without force. "Did you say the tweed suit was in the ocean?"

"That's right. I found it myself."

"Right off here?" She gestured across the Coast Highway.

"A few miles south of here, off Pacific Point."

She was silent, while slow thought worked at her face. "What about the man?" she said finally.

"The man?"

"The little man with the burn marks. The one you were just telling me about."

"What about him?"

"Is he all right?"

"Why?" I said. "Do you know him?"

"I wouldn't say I know him. But I may have given him that suit."

"When?"

"Answer my question first," she said sharply. "Is he all right?"

"I'm afraid not. He was in the suit when I found it in the water. And he was dead."

I was watching her face for signs of shock or grief, or possibly remorse. But it seemed empty of feeling. Her eyes were the color of the low city skies under which she had moved a lot.

"How did you happen to give him the suit?" I said.

She was slow in answering. "I don't remember too well. I do quite a lot of drinking, if you want the truth, and it washes everything out, if you know what I mean. He came to the door one day when I was slightly plastered. He was just an old bum, practically in rags. I wanted to give him something to keep him warm, and that old suit of Ralph Mungan's was all I had."

I studied her face, trying to decide among three main possibilities: either she was leveling, or she was one of those natural liars who lied more convincingly than they told the truth, or her story had been carefully prepared.

"He came here, did he, Mrs. Mungan?"

"That's right. He was standing where you're standing now."

"Where did he come from?"

"He didn't say. I guess he was working his way along the beach. The last I saw of him, he was heading south."

"How long ago was this?"

"I don't even remember."

"You must have some idea, though."

"A couple of weeks, maybe longer."

"Did he have a younger man with him? A broad-shouldered man of thirty or so, about my height?"

"I didn't see any younger man." But her look was defensive, and her voice had a whine in it. "Why are you asking me all those questions? I was just being a good Samaritan to him. You can't blame a woman for being a good Samaritan."

"But you didn't remember about it at first. You thought you threw the suit out with Ralph Mungan's other things. And then you remembered that you gave it to the dead man."

"That's just the way my mind works. Anyway, he wasn't dead when I gave it to him."

"He's dead now."

"I know that."

We faced each other across the counter. Behind her in the darkened room, the shadow voices went on telling the city's parables: Daddy wasn't the only one who treated me rotten. I know that, love, and my libido wasn't my only fractured part.

The woman was long past her prime, her mind leached out by drinking, her body swollen. But I rather liked her. I didn't think she was capable of murder. No doubt she was capable of covering for it, though, if she had a guilty lover or a son.

I left, intending to pay her another visit.

XIX

It was nearly noon when I got back to Pacific Point. The harbor was even blacker than it had been in the morning. Men wearing oilskins and hip boots were cleaning its rock walls with live steam.

Other workers in small skiffs were scattering straw on the floating oil, then picking up the oil-soaked straw with pitchforks. Hundreds of bales of fresh straw had been trucked in from somewhere and were piled on the beach like barriers against a possible invasion.

There were further changes on the wharf. A couple of dozen picketers were walking back and forth across its entrance. They carried homemade signs: "Do Not Patronize: Oil Facilities," "Oil Spoils," "Pollution!" Most of the picketers were middle-aged, though there were several long-haired youths among them.

I recognized the hairy-faced young fisherman I had talked to the previous evening. He shook his sign at me —"Consider the Poor Fish"—and yelled good-naturedly as I drove past him onto the wharf.

Blanche was watching the picketers from the almost

empty parking lot of her restaurant. She recognized me as a customer and raised her voice in complaint.

"They're trying to put me out of business. I want to know, did they use any force on you? Or threaten you?"

"No, they didn't."

"Too bad." She shook her frizzy head. "The police said unless they use force or threats it's legal and there's nothing I can do. But it doesn't look legal to me. I'd like to toss 'em over the railing and give 'em a little taste of that oily water. They've got their nerve, trying to take over my wharf."

"Is it really your wharf?"

"It is to all intents and purposes. I've got it on long-term lease, and it gives me the right to rent space to the oil company. I intend to make a personal appeal to the Governor."

Blanche was flushed and breathing hard. She ran out of breath.

"I had dinner in your restaurant last night."

"Sure, I remember. You didn't finish your red snapper. I hope it was all right."

"It was fine. I wasn't too hungry. I noticed a couple of other customers while I was here—an older man with a young one. The old man was wearing a tweed suit, and he had burn scars on his head—"

"I remember them. What about them?"

"I'd like to get in touch with them. Do you have any idea where they belong?"

She shook her head. "I never saw them before. They didn't come from these parts."

"How do you know?"

"They asked me for directions. They wanted to know how to get to Seahorse Lane." She pointed south along the beach in the direction of Sylvia Lennox's house.

"Did they say who they wanted to visit on Seahorse Lane?"

"No, but I wondered at the time. It's a very high-priced development, right on the beach. And they were strictly from hunger—at least the old one was. I mean literally. You should have seen him eat."

I thanked her and started back to my car. A gray-haired man climbed out of another car and casually intercepted me. He had sensitive blue eyes which wore, like a transparent shield, the detachment of an observer.

"You're not a local man, are you?" he said to me.

"No. It's a free country."

His face wrinkled in a self-deprecating smile which was almost a look of pain. "I'd be the last to deny that. Are you with Lennox Oil?"

"No. I'm a free lance."

"Exactly what does that mean?" He was still smiling.

"I'm a private investigator. My name is Archer."

"Mine is Wilbur Cox. I write for the local paper. What crime are you investigating, Mr. Archer? The crime of pollution?"

"I'd certainly like to know what caused this oil spill."

He seemed happy to oblige. "The oil people say it was an act of God, and in the long run there's some truth in that. The undersea formations here are naturally porous, delicate to fool with. You might say the area is blowout-prone. But in the short run the oil people are to blame. They didn't take the danger of a spill fully into account, and they didn't use the right preventive measures for drilling at this depth. The result is what you see." He flung out his arm toward the platform which stood against the horizon.

"Why didn't they take the right preventive measures?"

"It costs money," he said. "Oilmen are gamblers, most of them, and they'd rather take a little chance than spend a lot of money. Or wait for technology to catch up." He added after a moment, "They're not the only gamblers. We're all in the game. We all drive cars, and we're all hooked on oil. The question is how we can get unhooked before we drown in the stuff."

I nodded in agreement and started to move away toward my car. He drifted after me:

"Are you the man who pulled a body out of the water this morning?"

I said I was.

"Can you identify the victim?"

"Not yet. I'm working on it."

"Do you want to give me a quote?"

"I'm afraid I can't, Mr. Cox. Any publicity would interfere with my investigation."

"Was the man murdered?" Through his mask of detachment, the newsman's eyes burned cold.

"I honestly don't know. I'll see you later."

I didn't get far. The entrance to the wharf was blocked by a line of picketers facing landward. Beyond them was a big semitrailer loaded with tanks of drilling mud. The driver glared down at the picketers from his high seat and inched the truck forward.

One of the young sign carriers sat down in front of the wheels. His face was pale and scared, as if he knew what a poor brake his body was to the heavy movements of the world. But he sat without moving as the double wheels turned almost on top of him.

The driver spat an inaudible word and slammed on his brakes. He climbed down out of the cab, swinging a tire iron in his hand. I got out of my car at the same time and pushed through the line of picketers to face him. He was a flat-nosed young man with angry eyes.

"Get back," he said to me, "I'm making a delivery."

"Sorry, we don't need a tire iron."

"You look as if you need one, right across the face."

"It wouldn't be a good idea," I said. "Put it down, eh?"

"When you get out of the way. I'm on legitimate business."

"You don't look so legitimate with that thing in your hand."

The driver glanced down at his weapon with some surprise. Perhaps he recognized that he was a threatening figure, and that he was a minority of one. The picketers were beginning to move around me. The driver climbed back into the cab of his truck and sat there glaring. Thirty or forty feet ahead of him, the newsman Wilbur Cox was leaning on the railing and taking notes.

At the outer end of the wharf, beyond Blanche's Restaurant, a large black car appeared and moved slowly toward us. It stopped just behind my car. Captain Somerville got out, followed by a younger man who moved like the Captain's shadow. Both men looked rather haggard, as if they had had a rough morning.

It was threatening to get rougher. The picketers surged around the car, forcing the two men back against its side. Somerville looked grim. His companion was pale and frightened.

"Stand back," he said in an uncertain voice. "This is Captain Somerville. He's the executive v.p. of Lennox Oil."

"We know that," the young fisherman said. "When are you going to cap the oil spill, Cap?"

Somerville answered: "As soon as we possibly can. We made an attempt this morning. I'm sorry to say it didn't succeed. We have to stockpile more drilling mud, and bring in some experts, and we'll make another attempt by the end of the week. In the meantime I'm asking you for your patience and cooperation."

The picketers groaned. One of them called out: "When are you going to take your platform out of here? We don't need it."

"The platform is there legally," Somerville said in an unbending tone, "with the approval of the U.S. Geological Survey. And when you stop our deliveries—which is what you're doing now—you're interfering with our attempts to stop the spill."

The crowd began to get noisier, its groan deteriorating into a growl. The driver sitting up in the cab of the truck had a restless look in his eye. I decided I had better make a move before he did.

I inched through the crowd to Somerville. "You better get out of here, Captain. Get back in the car and follow my car, eh?"

Somerville and his aide climbed into the front seat, the white-faced younger man behind the wheel. I said to the picketers:

"Let them move out. Nobody wants any trouble."

"That's right," a middle-aged woman said. "We don't want trouble."

"We don't want oil on our beaches, either," a young man said.

I said, "It's better than blood."

The crowd made assenting noises. They moved back slowly, away from Somerville's car. I got into mine, eased it past the semitrailer, and turned toward Seahorse Lane, with Somerville behind me.

I was sweating with relief. Twice in no more than ten minutes, the threat of violence in the air had come very near to being actualized. There were sirens in the distance like the sound of a further threat.

XX

Several cars were already parked under the cypresses in Sylvia Lennox's courtyard. Captain Somerville's car pulled up behind mine. He got out and shook my hand, quite heartily, though his eyes were looking past me.

"I have to thank you for your intervention. This is Leroy Ellis, of our public-relations department. Let's see, your name is Archer, isn't it?"

The younger man climbed out from behind the wheel and gave me a limp handshake. He wasn't really young —he was close to my age—but was one of those middle-aging men who have never lost the mannerisms of youth. His eyes were damp and emotional. He smelled as if he had somehow managed to get hold of some whisky.

"Leroy's an old shipmate of mine." Somerville spoke with rather forced nostalgia. "He was with me at Okinawa. Today was the most excitement we've had since, wasn't it, Leroy?"

Leroy said that it was. He seemed upset and embarrassed, and I got the impression that the Captain, with a kind of affectionate sadism, was subtly needling him. The two men went inside, Leroy trailing behind. I waited a moment, listening to the pigeons talking in the cypresses.

Tony Lashman appeared beside the garages. His face was pale and intent, and he moved like a man with a grievance. He gestured toward the house.

"What's going on in there?"

"I was going to ask you. I just arrived."

"They're having one of their family conferences. I'm

supposed to be Mrs. Lennox's confidential secretary, but she told me to stay out. Are they letting you in?"

"I hope so."

I started toward the house, but Lashman stepped in front of me. He was beginning to turn into a nuisance.

"Look," he said. "I want to know what goes on in there. If you can give me the info, I'll pay you for it."

"How much?"

"I don't know how much. But it could be quite a lot —a lot more than a hundred dollars a day."

"And where would the money come from?"

He saw that I was trying to pump him, and it made him angry:

"All right. I'll handle it myself."

He turned on his heel and walked away from me.

Emerson Little, the lawyer, was waiting for me at the door. He was a bald-headed man with a funereal taste in clothes and an undertaker's exaggerated poise.

He gave me a soft hand and a hard look. "You're a bit late, Mr. Archer."

"I know that. I'm sorry."

"I had quite a time holding Jack Lennox in place. He's a headstrong man."

"Where is he?"

"Inside with his mother. Sylvia Lennox is my client. She wouldn't release the hundred thousand until you got here, and I supported her in that. The essential point of this operation is to get her granddaughter back safely. The money is quite secondary. Still, we don't want it wasted on a wild-goose chase."

"What form is the money in?"

"Unmarked twenties in a plain cardboard carton, as requested."

"And where's the drop?"

"Jack Lennox won't divulge that." Little's bland face was moved by a spasm of irritation. "Well. We have to do our best with what we have."

He went ahead of me into the front room. Sylvia was there with her family. Captain Somerville sat by Elizabeth, his eyes distracted and remote.

Elizabeth gave me a faint smile. Jack Lennox refused

to look at me, and his wife Marian looked at me without appearing to see me.

There were spatterings of oil on the windows. A brown cardboard box on the floor beside Sylvia's chair drew attention like a ticking bomb.

The old woman lifted her hand. "Come and sit down beside me for a minute, Mr. Archer."

Lennox said, "We're wasting time, Mother."

"Please try to be patient, Jack." She turned to me. "My husband—my ex-husband wants to see you and Jack in El Rancho after you've delivered the money. I'm afraid I needed some help from him in raising it this morning. It gives William an interest in it, and he isn't one to let such an interest go unused."

"It's a natural interest, Mother," Elizabeth said. "Laurel's his only grandchild."

Somerville turned and looked at Elizabeth as if perhaps she was criticizing his potency.

"I'm not suggesting that William's interest in Laurel is unnatural," Sylvia said dryly. "I'm sure he has his hands full with that young woman of his. And I'm afraid this business won't improve his feelings toward the rest of us. It's too bad he had to find out about it."

"It doesn't really matter," Marian Lennox said. "What matters is getting my daughter back. Everything else is unimportant." Her tormented gaze moved around the room as if daring anyone to contradict her.

"I quite agree," Emerson Little said.

Jack Lennox rose half out of his chair. "Then why don't we get moving?"

It was a nervous meeting, buzzing with unspoken thoughts. Before it broke up, I asked Sylvia Lennox if she had seen the man in the tweed suit or his companion the night before.

"What time were they here?"

"I'm not sure they were here. But if they were, it was probably around eight last night."

"I was out for dinner. Perhaps Tony Lashman saw them. You'll probably find him sulking in his room."

"Sulking?"

"I had to put him in his place. He's becoming much too inquisitive about my affairs." She gave me a bright look. "You're rather inquisitive yourself, aren't you?"

I didn't have to answer her. Jack Lennox stood up and looked at his watch dramatically:

"Let's get this show on the road, shall we?"

He was wearing a brown suede jacket, and the gun in his side pocket was obvious. He turned and strode out toward the courtyard. I followed him, carrying the box of money. The man in the tweed suit would have to wait.

"We'll take my car," Lennox said. "It has a telephone in it, which could turn out to be handy. And I'll do the driving."

"All right."

He said impatiently, "I wasn't asking your permission, I was stating my intention. I'd prefer to go alone. But for some reason my mother insists that I take you along. Against my wishes. Is that clear?"

Under his impatience I could sense his deep fatigue. I was determined to go along with him. "You make it very clear."

I put the money on the seat between us. Lennox drove out of the courtyard on whining tires which seemed intended to let his family know that nobody cared as much as he did.

I didn't speak until we were on the old highway heading south. "Where are we going, Mr. Lennox?"

"Sandhill Lake. It's between the Point and El Rancho."

"Isn't there a hunting club on the lake?"

"There used to be. My father was one of the members in the old days." He drove for a mile or so before he added, "That's where I learned to shoot."

"Who picked Sandhill Lake?"

After another silence, he said, "I don't understand your question."

"Did you or the kidnapper pick Sandhill Lake for the money drop?"

"He did, of course."

"That's quite a coincidence, isn't it?"

"Where's the coincidence?"

He sounded genuinely puzzled. I wondered how much

drinking he had done in the course of the night, and how little sleeping. I said:

"That he should pick a place you know. A club your father belonged to."

He answered after a while. "I see what you mean."

"It suggests he knows your family." Or at least knows Laurel, I thought. "I take it you talked to him on the phone yourself."

"When?"

"Last night."

"Yes. I did."

"Did you know him?"

"Of course not. What are you getting at?"

He gave me an angry questioning look, and the black Cadillac swerved onto the shoulder. Lennox pulled it back onto the road without slackening speed. We were going about eighty.

I didn't quite dare to answer him directly, that I suspected his daughter of conning him and the rest of the family. He had some of Laurel's wildness in him—or she had some of his—and he was capable of going into a black rage and wrecking the car.

"I'm only speculating, trying to get a lead on the people involved."

"There's only the one, so far as I know."

"A man?"

"That's right."

"But you didn't recognize his voice on the phone?"

"No, I did not. And while we're on the subject, I don't give a damn about nailing him, is that clear? It isn't my money, anyway. It belongs to my father and mother, and they've got more than they're ever going to need."

"I realize the money isn't important."

"I'm glad you do," he said. "At least we've got that straight."

"But even after the money is delivered, there's still the question of getting Laurel back. Did he give you any idea of where she is?"

"Of course not. But there's no problem. He gets the money, we get Laurel."

"What if you don't get her?"

"We will, though," he said. "I'm sure of it."

"Do you think he's got Laurel with him at Sandhill Lake?"

He turned on me, his face suffused with blood. "How the hell do I know?" The Cadillac had wandered out of its lane again, as Lennox's attention swerved to me. I took hold of the wheel with both hands, found the brake with my foot, and brought the heavy car to a screeching stop on the shoulder of the highway.

"What do you think you're trying to do?" he said.

"Not get killed."

"Then get out and walk."

"My orders are to go along with you."

"I'm changing the orders. Get out."

I went on sitting where I was, beside the money. Lennox thrust his hand into his jacket pocket and pointed the pocket at me.

"Out," he said.

I didn't think he'd shoot me deliberately. But he seemed accident-prone, and his hand was hidden. All I needed was a bullet in the kidneys. I opened the door and climbed out and watched him drive away.

Then I followed along on foot. The Cadillac climbed a long rise and disappeared over its crest. There were few cars on the old highway, and none of them stopped to pick me up. But it was a clear bright day, and I felt a certain pleasure in being alone and on foot, listening to the meadowlarks in the fields.

Eventually I reached the top of the rise. Beyond it was a series of dunes which marched in giant rhythm along the shore. Sandhill Lake lay on their landward side, an irregular oval which looked like a spattering of sky.

On its near side I could see the green buildings of the hunting club, with Lennox's black Cadillac parked beside them. Farther away, at the end of the lake, was a wooden lookout tower with gray shingled sides. A dirt road ran from the main buildings to the tower.

Jack Lennox was walking away from me along the dirt road, carrying the carton of money in his hands. He reached the tower and went inside. I heard a muffled explosion, and then another. Ducks rose from the lake, pintails and shovelers. They moved like visible echoes in wide expanding circles. Lennox came out empty-handed and ran along the road and fell down and crawled and lay still.

Another man emerged from the tower, carrying the brown carton of money in his hands. He paused beside Lennox. Then he turned in the other direction and began to run, limping, toward a eucalyptus grove that stood between the tower and the highway.

He moved like a young man, in spite of his limp, and he could have been the one I had seen at Blanche's with the man in the tweed suit. He was too far away for me to be sure. I started to run down the highway, regretting the fact that I had no gun with me, and no binoculars.

It was a long run. Before I reached the foot of the hill, the ducks had circled out over the sea and were coming back and dropping down to the lake again. As if to preserve some kind of natural balance which required live things to be in the air at all times, a flock of band-tailed pigeons exploded out of the eucalyptus grove.

Then a small green car shot out of its far end and turned down the highway away from me. It was too far away for me to catch the license number, but it looked like an old Falcon two-door.

XXI

Lennox was lying where he had fallen, unconscious but breathing. A .32 revolver was clenched in his hand, and its muzzle smelled as though it had been recently fired. A bullet had grooved the side of his head and snipped off the upper tip of his left ear. It didn't look like a fatal wound, but thick worms of blood ran down from it and coiled in the dust.

I tied a handkerchief around his head to stanch the flow of blood. Then I left him where he lay and used the phone in his car to call an ambulance and the Sheriff's men.

I went back and waited with Lennox. But a funny irrational feeling grew on me that the lookout tower was watching us. I went to the half-open door and looked in. There was nothing inside but a drift of sand marked with footprints. A dilapidated ladder went up to the observation platform.

I didn't climb the ladder, or even go in. There might be fingerprints on the rungs; the footprints in the sand might be identifiable. Anyway, the feeling of being watched had been dispelled. I leaned in the sun against the outside wall and watched the ducks fly up again when the ambulance and the Sheriff's radio car arrived together.

They strapped Lennox onto a stretcher and took him away. Two Sheriff's officers remained with me, and I told them how Lennox had put me out on the road, and what I had seen and heard from the hilltop.

The officers' names were Dolan and Shantz. Dolan was a straight-backed captain with a clipped gray mustache and probing eyes. Shantz was a heavy-shouldered young sergeant who looked like a football player going to seed.

Captain Dolan picked up Lennox's revolver and spun the chamber. Only one shot had been fired from it. He let me see that, but made no comment. The three of us walked along a dirt lane toward the eucalyptus grove, avoiding the footprints left by the running man.

Dolan bent over to examine one of the footprints. "He was losing blood. There's blood in his right footprints, like maybe his shoe filled up with it and slopped over." He turned to Shantz and me. "Take a look for yourselves."

We leaned over beside him. There was a paste of blood and sand in the footprint, and more in the footprints farther on.

"You did say you heard two shots, didn't you?" Dolan looked at me as if there might be some hope for me, after all. "It looks like a double shooting that we have here."

"I think it was. Each man shot the other."

Following the bloody footprints, we walked in under the gray-green eucalyptus trees. The pigeons hadn't come back, but there were warblers busy in the treetops.

I caught myself wishing that we could live like the birds and move through nature without hurting it or ourselves.

A pool of blood stood beside the deep tracks where the car had stood. I described the Falcon, and what I had seen of the man who had driven it away. Sergeant Shantz made some notes.

"Too bad you didn't get his license number," Dolan said. "We better get the mobile lab out here and take some casts, and check the tower for prints. You want to call 'em, Shantzie?"

The younger man went back along the lane. Dolan leaned on a peeling eucalyptus trunk and folded his arms. His eyes were bleak and intent, and they looked at me like the eyes of a rifleman getting ready to fire.

"This is an important case, you know," he said quietly. "A double shooting, for starters. And then it's got the Lennox name in it. They've been all over the newspapers the last few days. and this will blow the headlines even bigger. It could make and break some reputations in this county. Including mine," he added. "Let's face it."

"It's important, all right."

"You know it is. You know it better than I do. The question is this, Archer. When are you going to let down your inhibitions and tell me what it's all about?"

"I wish I knew."

"Don't give me that. I wish I knew what you know. This morning you pulled a body out of the water in front of Mrs. William Lennox's beach house. Six or seven hours later, you turn up here at the scene of another crime. How do you account for that?"

"Just lucky, I guess."

Dolan frowned and bit his mustache. "I want a serious answer. Did you know that this shooting, or these shootings, were going to happen?"

"Certainly not."

"Okay, what brought you here?"

"Jack Lennox came here on private business. His family asked me to accompany him."

"Private business with the man who shot him?"

"I think so."

"What was the nature of the business?"

I would have liked to tell him, but I hesitated. If Laurel was guiltily involved, I had to try to protect her. Even if she was an innocent victim, it wouldn't do her any good to blow the case wide open at this point.

"I can't tell you that," I said.

"You mean you can't or you won't?"

"I'd have to take it up with the Lennox family first."

"Maybe you better do that as soon as possible." Dolan looked down at the ground between us. "It wouldn't be a blackmail payment, by any chance?"

"No."

"It doesn't have anything to do with that body you hauled out of the sea this morning?"

"It may. I don't know what the connection is."

"Then how do you know there is one?"

"I don't. But I saw two men together last night at Blanche's on the wharf. One of them was the little man I pulled out of the water this morning. I think it was probably a coincidence that he was floating off Sylvia Lennox's beach."

"That could be," Dolan said. "He was in the water for eight or ten hours, and there's a southward current that probably brought him from the direction of town. You say you saw him with another man on the wharf?"

"In Blanche's Restaurant, last night about seven o'clock. The other man was young, about thirty or so. Medium to tall in height, exceptionally broad shoulders. Dark hair and eyes. Dark turtleneck sweater."

Dolan stepped away from his tree. "Sounds like the man who drove away in the Falcon—the one with the blood in his shoe."

"I think it was."

XXII

The keys were in Jack Lennox's Cadillac, and I took it. Instead of turning north toward Pacific Point, I went south to El Rancho, where his father lived.

Since I had last seen the place, an electronic gate had

been installed at the entrance. The armed guard on duty refused to let me in until he had phoned William Lennox at his house. He came out of his kiosk wearing a respectful expression.

"It's okay, Mr. Archer. Mr. Lennox says you can come right out. Know where to find his place?"

"I'm afraid I don't."

He showed me a large-scale map attached to the wall of his office. "Turn left at the far end of the golf course. That will take you past River Valley School. Then turn sharp right up the hill, and you'll see Mr. Lennox's mailbox at the top."

I followed his directions, paying special attention to River Valley School. It was a scattering of weathered redwood buildings dwarfed by the great native oak trees that surrounded it. Though I'd never been inside it, the school had associations for me. Both Laurel and Elizabeth had been students there. I wondered what it had been like to grow up in the protective shadow of those trees.

William Lennox's mailbox was made of stone and attached to a stone wall which ran parallel with the ocean in both directions as far as I could see. In the fields beyond it, on either side of the lane that led to the house, there were horses grazing. They looked like racing stock, and one of them, a sorrel mare, was running in irregular circles, apparently for the fun of it. She came to an uncertain stop near the wall, about a hundred feet from me.

Then I noticed the woman standing inside the wall. She was wearing a riding costume topped off with a Mexican hat, and held a long-handled whip upright in her hand. She flicked it harmlessly in the air. The mare started off on another circuit, arching her neck and swinging her head like a hammer from side to side.

I got out and approached the woman. "Nice-looking horse."

She regarded me coolly over the stone wall. "She isn't bad."

She was a nice-looking woman, probably in her early forties, but holding hard to what she had left of her youth. Her waist, cinched in by a wide Western belt, looked as if I could span it with my two hands. Her dark eyes looked at me as if that might be a dangerous thing to try.

"My name is Archer. I'd like to see Mr. Lennox." Her voice sharpened. "Is he expecting you?"

"Yes."

"Are you the detective?"

I said I was.

She looked along the fence at the Cadillac. "Is that Jack Lennox's car?"

"Yes."

"What happened to him?"

"He got shot."

"Fatally?"

"I don't know. I doubt it."

She looked at me so impassively that I couldn't tell if she was disappointed or relieved. Her eyes softened as the mare came running up to her, hoofs drumming. The woman leaned her whip against the wall and stroked the mare on the nose, then sent her trotting away into the field.

The woman turned back to me. "Did someone in the family shoot Jack?"

"No."

Her eyes hardened. "You don't have to answer me in monosyllables. I'm Mrs. Hapgood, and I have a serious interest in what's happened. I'm trying to protect my hus —Mr. Lennox."

"Your husband?"

"That was a slip of the tongue," she said. "We're not married yet. But I take my responsibility seriously. Believe it or not, I'm trying to keep this family together."

"Why?"

"Because William wants it that way," she said. "So what happened to Jack?"

I told her over the stone wall as we walked back toward the car. She climbed on a stile into the lane and got into the front seat beside me.

"Jack's always been wild and impulsive. He shouldn't have been the one to go."

"I know that. But he was determined. And Laurel's his daughter."

"Is she not."

"Have you known Laurel for a long time?"

"A very long time indeed, yes. But please don't try to interrogate me."

"I wasn't."

"Weren't you? I think you were. But I'm not your problem, or any part of it."

"Then maybe you're part of the solution."

She gave me a flashing smile, like a knife gleaming briefly from concealment. "As a matter of fact, I think I am. Let's get one thing straight. I love William Lennox. That's more than you can say for the members of his family—certainly more than you can say for his wife."

I drove down the long lane, which was almost blocked at one point by a bulldozer pulled to the side. I maneuvered the Cadillac around it.

The house stood on a rise above the beach. It was two-storied, white with a red tiled roof, and it stretched out for a hundred feet on either side of the entrance. Mrs. Hapgood took me into an oak-beamed room furnished like a medieval castle, with highbacked chairs and massive tables and couches too large for ordinary human use. She left me there and went to find Lennox.

I stood by one of the great windows and looked out over the ocean. It was a clear day and I could see, almost halfway to the horizon, a flight of shearwaters like a scrap of dark chiffon blowing along the blue surface. Off to the north, the color seemed to change from blue to brownish, and the sea seemed flat and inert. The oil slick was moving south with the current from Pacific Point.

William Lennox and Mrs. Hapgood came into the room. They weren't touching, or even close, but they seemed to be very conscious of each other. They moved together with a certain pride.

Lennox wasn't a big man like his son, but he was one you would notice anywhere. He was wearing a white shirt with a green stone at the throat. He walked upright, with his white head held high, and came across the room with his hand outstretched to greet me.

His hand was thin and frail, scrolled with enormous

blue veins. His eyes peered at me from their wrinkles like blue lights shining through a screen.

"Mr. Archer? How are you?" His handshake was firm. "Can I get you a drink?"

"Not when I'm working, thank you."

"You're very austere," the woman said dryly.

The old man cleared his throat. "Connie tells me that my son has been shot. Is it bad?"

"A bullet creased him just above the ear. It didn't look as if it penetrated the skull. I called an ambulance right away, and they took him back to the hospital in Pacific Point. The other man was shot, too, but he got away with the money."

"Jack shot him?"

"In the leg, apparently."

"Where were you when it happened?" His voice was quiet and even, but his blue gaze stayed on my face like a palpable force.

"About half a mile up the road." I explained why.

Lennox's face reddened slightly, and then grew pale. "The whole thing's been bungled. I'm not blaming you, Mr. Archer. I blame my wife and that stupid lawyer of hers. I should have gone there myself."

"And been shot?" Connie Hapgood said.

"I would have shot first. I would have blown his head off."

The woman touched his arm, reminding him that he was getting excited. He took a deep breath and turned away. He walked to the end of the room, stood facing the wall for a moment, and then came back.

"Have the F.B.I. been called in?"

"No."

"Why not? What's Sylvia doing?"

"Trying to protect your granddaughter, I believe."

"This is a hell of a way to protect her." He gave me a hot and narrow look. "Did you recommend this?"

"I was in favor of keeping them out, yes. I still haven't told the whole story to the police."

"Why not?"

"Don't get excited, William," the woman said. "Why don't we all sit down and relax a bit?"

"I prefer to stand." He turned to me. "I don't understand your purpose in concealing evidence from the police and the F.B.I."

"You may not want to hear my reason."

"On the contrary, I insist on hearing it."

"Whatever you say. Do you want me to talk in front of Mrs. Hapgood?"

"Yes. Quit stalling, man."

"This may not be a kidnapping in the ordinary sense. It doesn't feel like a kidnapping to me."

"What in hell does it feel like?"

"I can't say. But I found out last night that Laurel has been involved in a similar case before. When she was fifteen or sixteen, she ran off to Las Vegas with a boy. The two of them asked Laurel's parents for ransom money—a thousand dollars, I believe. And apparently they collected."

He squinted at me from a network of wrinkles. "I knew that she'd run off that time, of course. But Jack never told me about the money angle."

"He wouldn't," Connie Hapgood said. "He wasn't going to tell you this time either. But Sylvia couldn't raise the hundred thousand, so you had to be told."

He shook his head as if her words were insects attacking him. "I don't believe that Laurel would do such a thing. She isn't a cheat. And if she needed money, she could have come to me directly."

"She's afraid of you," the woman said. "She always has been, since she was a girl in school. And remember it isn't the first time she's played this trick on the family."

"I don't believe it."

He turned to me again. His shoulders were visibly bowed now and his arms were hanging loose, as if he'd lost the principle that kept him controlled and upright.

"I know that Laurel has had her emotional problems. But she wouldn't lie to me, or cheat her own family. She simply isn't that kind of a girl." He seemed close to breaking down and crying; then his grief changed back to anger. "Damn it to hell, if she did do it, somebody put her up to it. If it was that husband of hers, I'll blow his head off. What's his name? Russo?"

"It wasn't Tom Russo." But even as I said that, I realized that I couldn't be quite sure. Tom had his problems, too; death haunted his dreams and perhaps his waking life.

The woman was watching Lennox with sharp attention. She may have realized that she had spoken too harshly. Driving her wedge into Lennox's family, she had inadvertently driven it into him. She moved toward him and put her arm around him.

"It's time you took a rest, William. You've had too much for one day."

"I can't rest. Who will look after things?" He spoke with an old man's querulousness. "Everything's going to pieces. Jack is shot and Laurel's missing and our new well blew out. And Sylvia sits up there and laughs about it. Damn Sylvia to hell. And damn Ben Somerville. Why did I have to surround myself with losers?"

The woman led him out of the room by the hand. As she passed me, she gave me a keen promising look which made me wait for her to come back.

XXIII

She was gone for some time. When she returned, she had changed her riding costume for a dress and was carrying a book in her hand.

"I gave him a tranquilizer," she said, "and got him to lie down. These grim realities are very hard on William. He lives in dreams, he always has. He came out here after the first war with the dream of founding an empire and a dynasty. All he had to start with was a few thousand dollars which he'd saved and some experience in the Pennsylvania oil fields. And he made the dream come true." Her eyes swept the room, which looked very much like a dream that had solidified around the dreamer. "Now it's breaking up around him, and he can't stand it."

"You put it to him pretty strongly about Laurel."

"I have to, or he'll go on dreaming about her. Men are so unrealistic where women are concerned. It's been

obvious for at least fifteen years that Laurel Lennox is a
schizoid personality. But her family go on treating her as
if she were perfectly normal, and being surprised and
dumfounded when she turns out not to be."

"Are you a psychiatrist?"

"No, I am not a psychiatrist." But she gave me a look
which conveyed the idea that where Laurel was concerned I was just another dreaming man. "I have studied
some psychology, and I know Laurel."

"You've known her for fifteen years?"

"Longer than that. I started teaching at River Valley
School eighteen years ago. I've known Laurel since she
was eleven or twelve. And she's always lived in a world
of her own, a not very happy world where not very nice
things happen."

"That's true of a lot of children. Ordinarily, though,
we don't blame them."

"I'm not blaming her, for heaven's sake. I'm trying to
inject a little realism into this situation. It would be a
poor bargain for all of us if Laurel picked up a little
money or a little loving at the expense of breaking her
grandfather's heart. I mean that literally. He's old
enough, and vulnerable enough, and enough involved
with her to be killed by it."

"We don't want that to happen," I said, thinking of
the powerful reasons the woman had for keeping him
alive.

Her dark gaze probed at my face. "You're not taking
me quite seriously, are you?"

"I take you very seriously, Mrs. Hapgood. I always
will," I added half seriously.

She smiled, and her whole appearance changed, the
way a young girl's will when her feelings are touched.
"Then I'll show you something that may interest you."

It was in the book in her hands, a large thin volume
with the title *River Valley Annual* printed across the
front of the green cloth binding. She opened it on a
refectory table which stood against the wall, and leafed
through the pages as I looked over her shoulder.

There were some stories and poems by the River Valley students, reports on soccer and girls' hockey and the
debating season, a message from the headmaster, and a

double-page spread of photographs of teachers. Among them I recognized Connie Hapgood herself, a girl in her twenties, with shaggy hair, wearing a bright appealing unfinished look.

She lingered over her picture for a moment, as if the girl she had been had taken her by surprise. "I forgot I was in this book."

"You haven't changed much."

"Liar. That was fifteen years ago. Fifteen long years."

With visibly nervous fingers, she turned some more pages to the photographs of the graduating seniors. The pictures were captioned with the students' names and predictions of their futures, evidently written by their classmates. Connie pointed out a rather fat-faced boy with an uneasy smile and dark angry dubious eyes. His name was Harold Sherry, and his prediction was: "World's greatest gourmet. Seriously, when Harold discovers himself, it will be a major discovery!"

Connie read it aloud in a meditative tone, and added, "I wonder if Harold ever did discover himself."

"Is this the Harold who ran off to Vegas with Laurel?"

"This is the Harold. The school expelled him, of course, in addition to what the court did, and he never did graduate. But it was too late to take his name and picture out of the yearbook."

"What did the court do?"

"Put him on probation for six years."

"That's fairly stiff."

"I agree. All he did, after all, was run off with a girl who was perfectly willing to go along. Who may have instigated the Las Vegas trip, in fact. But nothing was done to Laurel, because she was two or three years younger than Harold. And things got worse for him. He broke probation and ran away, and they brought him back and put him in jail for a while. His father turned his back on him, which did him no good with the court."

"Who is his father?"

"Roger Sherry. He was an engineer, and he lived here in El Rancho at the time. His wife still does. Mr. Sherry and his wife split up, I think over Harold. That little escapade in Las Vegas was really the end of the family."

I picked up the book and carried it to the window. Harold Sherry's unformed face seemed vaguely familiar, and it grew more familiar as I studied it. Under the thick flesh which the boy had worn like a mask, I thought I could make out the facial structure of the broad-shouldered man I had seen at Blanche's last night, and again at Sandhill Lake this afternoon. Both the boy and the man had the eyes of an angry dreamer.

The woman came up behind me, so close that I could feel the movement of her breath in the still air:

"Is Harold involved in this present mess?"

"He may be."

"You can speak frankly," she said. "I'm on Laurel's side, whatever you may think. The split in the family isn't of my making."

"I assumed you were on her side. Anybody in his right mind would want to get her back."

"Are Harold and Laurel together, Mr. Archer?"

"I don't know. They may be."

"Does that mean that the kidnapping—the alleged kidnapping—is a put-up job, as it was the other time?"

"It's possible," I said. "But events never repeat themselves exactly, especially in crime. There are too many variables, and the world has changed in the last fifteen years. It's a good deal more dangerous. Harold may be, too."

"Did he shoot Jack?"

"Someone who looked like him did."

"You're hedging, aren't you?"

"I saw the man who shot Jack from a long way off. I can't be sure of the identification on the basis of that and a fifteen-year-old picture." I closed the book and gave it back to her.

"Don't you want to know where his mother lives?"

"That was going to be my next question."

"Her house is on Lorenzo Drive." She took me to the front door and pointed across the valley. "It's a pink stucco house standing by itself on a knoll. I think the poor woman lives there alone. There are quite a few lonely women in this place. They move out here with their husbands and think they'll be taken care of forever

and ever. But then something happens and the whole illusion breaks down."

Her voice was full of feeling; she might have been
talking about herself. I couldn't tell if she was a hard
woman who had moments of softness, or a soft woman
who could be hard on occasion. It wasn't easy to tell,
about any woman.

I thanked her for her trouble and went out to the
Cadillac. William Lennox was sitting behind the wheel
out of sight of the front door, where Connie Hapgood
lingered. He had changed his dude clothes for a dark
suit and a homburg in which he looked very old and formal, like somebody getting ready for a funeral.

He regarded me truculently, but I got the impression
that a light breeze would blow him over and that any kind
of blow, physical or mental, would shatter him.

"I want you to drive me into town," he said. "Somebody has to pick up the pieces, and it looks as if I'm
elected. Jack's out of the picture, and Ben Somerville
isn't worth the powder to blow him to hell. He's a born
loser. He started out by blowing up his ship and he's
ending up by blowing up my oil business."

His speech was sibilant and a little slurred, and his
voice hurried as though he wanted to get it all out before
he forgot what he intended to say. I wondered if it was
the tranquilizer he had taken, or if there had been some
deep internal change in him.

"Let's get started," he said. "I don't have bloody all
day. I want to see my son. Is he badly hurt?"

"I don't believe so, Mr. Lennox. But he probably
won't be needing any visitors. You better stay here with
Mrs. Hapgood."

"But there are decisions to make."

"You can make them here."

His face reddened. "If you won't drive me, I'll drive
myself. This is my son's car."

"It wouldn't be a good idea for you to drive."

He took off his homburg and punched it with his
frail bony fist. "Dammit, don't tell me what to do. I
don't allow it. Get out and I'll drive myself."

His words were bold and angry, but his voice was uncertain. His white hair clung like smoke to his spotted

scalp. His eyes kept moving, like water under wind. He seemed to be caught in an old man's uncertainty, too weak to go but not content to stay.

He looked both angry and grateful when Connie approached the car and spoke to him:

"Mr. Archer isn't going into town. He has some investigative work to do out here. Anyway, you need a rest now."

"Who needs a rest?"

"You need a rest. So do I. We both do. Come on, William, or I'll get Dr. Langdale after you."

Her voice was maternal and seductive. He got out of the car and put his crumpled homburg on his head. She laughed at him and pushed it down so that his ears stuck out. He laughed, too, pleased and flattered by her horseplay. They walked back toward the house together, a pair of ill-matched comedians making the best of it.

I thought as I drove downhill across the valley that there was something real there after all. No doubt they had made a kind of bargain: that she would stay with him and look after him until he died; then his money would look after her until she died.

XXIV

The pink house on Lorenzo Drive had a slightly abandoned look. The shrubs and flowers around it were either overgrown or dying, and when I turned off the Cadillac's engine there was a waiting stillness in the air.

I went around to the back of the house and looked inside the garage. It contained an aging gray Mercedes, a woman's bicycle, and a lot of gardening equipment. No green Falcon. No bloody footprints.

I went around to the front again and knocked on the door. Mrs. Sherry was a long time answering. Eventually I heard her soft movements inside. A key turned over in the lock and the door opened on a chain.

She was a faded woman who shaded her eyes from the light as if she had spent the day immured in darkness. "What do you want?"

"A chance to talk to you for a few minutes."

"Who are you?"

"I'm a private detective." I told her my name.

"Is it about Harold?"

"I'm afraid it is. May I come in, Mrs. Sherry?"

"I don't see much point in it. He doesn't live at home any more. My son and I decided some time ago to go our separate ways." She sounded like a woman who had broken off an unhappy love affair, or barely survived an illness.

"But you jumped to the conclusion that I came here on his account."

"I did?" She sounded genuinely puzzled. "You must be mistaken. I had and have no idea why you came here."

"I'd like to discuss it with you, though. May I come in, Mrs. Sherry?"

She hesitated. The skin tightened around her mouth and eyes. She seemed to be winding up her nerve to shut the door on me.

"Harold's been wounded, I think."

Shock struck her face a glancing blow. I guess that she had been struck in that way many times before, and had learned the tricks of moral evasion. If you withdrew your spirit deep into yourself and out of sight, it couldn't be completely destroyed. But it might go blind in the internal darkness.

She unhooked the chain clumsily and opened the door. "Come in and tell me about it." She held back her crucial question until we were seated facing each other in her dim formal living room: "Is Harold going to die?"

"I don't believe so."

"Where is he?"

"I don't know that. I saw a young man who looked like him at Sandhill Lake this afternoon. He drove away in a green Falcon."

"It must have been someone else. My son doesn't have a car like that. He doesn't have any car."

"How do you know if you're not in touch with him?"

"I didn't say that. I still hear from Harold." She added with unexpected rigor, "When he wants something from me."

"Have you heard from him today?"

"Yesterday."

"What did he want?"

"To borrow my car. I refused." She looked at me with a certain desperate hopefulness, as if her refusal might make her immune to any further pain.

"Why did he want your car?"

"He didn't say. But I knew something was afoot."

"How did you know that?"

"I know my son. He sounded excited, as if he'd had another one of his grand ideas."

Another phony kidnapping? I almost said it out loud to her, but I held back. The world and I had been pressing her rather hard. I didn't want to hurt her deeply, and I didn't want to lose her. There was the further problem of identity, and the possibility that I had the wrong man and the wrong mother.

She had recovered enough of her nerve to ask, "What happened at Sandhill Lake? My husband—Harold's father used to go shooting at the lake."

"There was some more shooting there today. A double shooting."

Her hand went to her throat as if to hold back the question, but it came out: "Harold shot somebody else, too?"

"I think so. But before we go any further, I'd like to see a picture of Harold."

She brightened. "You mean you're not sure that Harold is involved?"

"Not absolutely sure. Do you have a recent picture?"

"I have one from a couple of years ago. It's in my bedroom."

She brought it to me in hopeful trepidation, carrying it as if it was a bomb that needed defusing: a small photograph of a worried-looking young man who had lost some weight and gained some years since his picture was taken for the River Valley yearbook. It was certainly the man I'd seen at Blanche's, and almost certainly the one who had ambushed Jack Lennox in the tower at Sandhill Lake.

"I'm afraid he's the one." I put the picture down on a coffee table.

"Who did he shoot?"

"Jack Lennox."

The life retreated from her face, leaving it vacant. She fell into her chair, turning sideways and covering her head with her hands.

She said:

"It's starting all over again, isn't it?"

"I don't know what you mean."

"That terrible trouble with the Lennox family. Harold was only a boy when it started. He wasn't the criminal they made him out to be. He was physically too mature for his years; that was the main trouble with him. He wanted to marry Laurel. That's why they went to Las Vegas—they thought they could get a preacher to marry them. But they ran out of money, and Laurel had the bright idea of pretending to her parents she'd been kidnapped. It was Laurel's idea, but Harold was the one who got the blame. Her father went to Las Vegas and searched them out and gave my son a terrible beating and threw him in jail. Harold was only eighteen, and he never recovered from the trauma. I've got doctors who will swear to that in court. My family and his father's family were all college graduates, but Harold never went back to school." She sat up blinking, as if she had talked her way by a subterranean route back to the present. "Where is Harold now?"

"I wish I knew."

"But you said that he'd been shot."

"He got away from the lake under his own power. Jack Lennox went in an ambulance."

"Is Mr. Lennox hurt badly?"

"I don't know. He has a head wound. It looked fairly superficial to me, but I'm not a doctor."

"Is Laurel involved in this, too?"

"I'm afraid she is, Mrs. Sherry. Laurel's been kidnapped again. Your son met her father at the lake to collect the ransom for her return. The ante has gone up since the other time in Las Vegas. This time it's a hundred thousand dollars."

"Harold is asking the Lennox family for that much money?"

"He's done more than ask for it. He's already collected it, as I said. The delivery was made to him at Sandhill Lake earlier this afternoon, by Jack Lennox. Your son and Jack Lennox evidently shot each other."

She shook her head in a flurry of rejection. "I wish I had never given birth to a son." But when she heard herself, she couldn't stand the chill of loneliness. "Laurel put him up to it. Remember it was her idea the first time."

"Maybe it was. But that was a long time ago, and people change. This time it could be real."

"You think he kidnapped Laurel?"

"He claimed he did. He took money from her father."

"Is that what you want? To get the money back?"

"I want Laurel back. I don't really care about the money. Nobody does. If you can get that message to Harold, it might help."

"I wouldn't know how to get in touch with him." But she looked at me as an agent might look, willing to barter and trade with what knowledge she had.

"You said he phoned you yesterday."

"Yes. He wanted my car."

"Where was he phoning from?"

"He didn't say."

"Was it a long-distance call?"

"I don't really know. It only lasted a minute. When I refused to lend him my car, he got angry and hung up on me." A flicker of pain crossed her face, as if the receiver had crashed in her ear again. "But I'm glad I didn't let him have it."

"You knew something was afoot, you said."

"I didn't actually *know* anything. But he sounded excited—the kind of excitement I've learned not to trust. My son is young for his years, and terribly excitable."

"Harold is at least thirty, isn't he?"

She looked at me in some surprise, as if the last ten or fifteen years had somehow passed unnoticed. Her lips moved in calculation. "He's thirty-three."

"That means he isn't a child. What does he live on?"

"I help him out. And of course he's held a number of

jobs. One thing you can say for Harold, he isn't lazy."

"What kind of jobs?"

"He's been a busboy recently, while he's looking for something better."

"Where does he live, Mrs. Sherry?"

"I don't know. Somewhere on the beach."

"It's a long beach," I said, "from San Diego to Isla Vista."

"He *was* in Isla Vista at one time. But he came back to Los Angeles. I don't know where he's living now; he hasn't told me. Except when he wants something from me, he treats me as if I were his enemy."

"Does he have girl friends?"

"He has a girl friend, yes. He mentioned her the last time we talked. But I've never seen her. I think Harold is ashamed of her."

"Why do you think that?"

"He refused to answer any personal questions about her. She may be a married woman."

"Laurel is married. Has Harold been seeing Laurel?"

She didn't answer me right away.

"Has Harold seen Laurel recently?" I said.

"Yes, he has. Apparently he met her in Los Angeles, and she invited him to her house. I warned him not to go on seeing her. She's always been a terrible influence on him."

"How do you know she invited him to her house?"

"He told me so."

"Yesterday?"

"A week or two ago."

"So you've been in fairly continuous contact with him?"

"He comes to me for money. But I haven't been able to give him much lately. What little money I have is tied up in a trust, and the income doesn't go as far as it used to."

"When he mentioned Laurel, what was his attitude?"

"He was grateful," she said with some scorn. "Grateful to her for inviting him to dinner. I told him he should have more pride, after what her family did to him. I told Harold he was demeaning himself by accepting anything from Laurel Lennox."

"What was his reaction?"

"I don't know. He didn't answer me directly. But I knew I'd given him something to think about."

She sat in silence, trying to understand her life. Her body moved as if it was wrung by pain. I got the impression that there was an almost physical connection between her and her son, stretching like an umbilical cord from where she sat to where he was laying down his bloody footprints.

"I don't know what's going to happen," she said.

"Neither do I. I'd like to think that the worst has already happened."

She took this as an optimistic remark. "Yes. I'm sure it has. And I'm sure that he hasn't—that nothing has happened to Laurel."

"I've got to find her before something does. Where do I look, Mrs. Sherry?"

"I have no idea."

"Didn't he give you an address, or a phone number?"

"Yes. But he's always kept moving on. I believe he's moved again in the last week or so."

"Since he went to Laurel's house for dinner?"

She considered the question. "Yes."

"What was his last previous address?"

"He was living someplace in Long Beach—I never actually knew where. I think he was living with a woman."

"How do you know?"

"His attitude toward me changes," she said. "He always becomes so much more independent. But then it never lasts."

"Did he ever talk about the woman?"

"No."

"Where would he go to have his wound looked after?"

"I don't really know."

"Does he have a personal doctor?"

"He did have. I directed him to send his bills to me. They were very reasonable. His name was Dr. Lawrence Brokaw." She stood up in sudden decision. "I'll see if I can find his address for you."

Mrs. Sherry came back after a while carrying a sheet

of notepaper, blue and deckle-edged, on which she had written Dr. Lawrence Brokaw's office address in Long Beach.

Her handwriting was small and elegant. She stood nervously beside me as I read it.

"You won't have to tell Dr. Brokaw about this?"

"About what?"

"The kidnapping—the supposed kidnapping. After all, I'm sure it was Laurel's idea. There's no reason why my son's name should be dragged in the dirt again."

She was trying to smile, but had become so tense she was virtually chattering. I folded her sheet of notepaper and put it in my pocket.

"A crime has been committed, perhaps a capital crime. A young woman is missing. Your son has collected ransom money for her, and he's been shot. But all you're worried about is bad publicity."

"I'm worried about a lot more than that. But I know what bad publicity can do to a boy and his family—I've seen it happen. Harold has never been the same, and neither have I."

"What happened to Harold's father?"

"He worked as an engineer for the Lennox company. Naturally he lost his job, and he had a hard time getting another. The last I heard of Roger, he was living in Texas, somewhere on the Gulf Coast. With another woman," she added bitterly.

"Are you divorced?"

"Yes, I divorced Roger. He turned against his own son." She was silent for a time. "Roger must be quite old by now. He's quite a few years older than I am. And I'm not young."

"We're all getting older. When I saw Harold in Pacific Point last night, he was with a little old man in a tweed suit. The man had lost most of his hair. It looked as if it had been burned off, and he had burn scars on his face and scalp."

She made a face. "He sounds horrible."

"He isn't, really. He was just a little old man who had seen his best days. Have you ever seen him with Harold?"

"No."

"Or have any idea who he might have been?"

"I have no idea. He wasn't Harold's father, if that's what you're thinking. Roger's a big man with a lot of hair, and no scars of any kind. Anyway, he wouldn't be caught dead in public with Harold."

Before I left, I asked her to give me Harold's picture, expecting that she would refuse. But she let me take it. I think she realized that Harold had to be found, and that I might be more likely than some others to bring him in alive.

XXV

When I passed Sandhill Lake on my way north, it was swarming with uniforms. It looked like the scene of the annual picnic of the Sheriff's Officers' Benevolent Association. I didn't stop. I would have had to tell them about Harold Sherry.

I drove directly to Seahorse Lane and found Elizabeth alone in what appeared to be an empty house. She greeted me without warmth and led me in silence into the big front room. Its front windows were now heavily smeared with oil. Through them I could see that the receding tide had left the beach dark and glistening, as if it had been covered with black oilcloth.

"Where have you been?" Her tone was faintly accusatory.

"El Rancho."

"You chose a strange time to go there."

"It paid off, though not in the way I expected. Is your mother here?"

"She's in her room. Mother is quite upset."

"About Jack?"

"It's naturally hit her very hard. And now Tony Lashman is missing. It makes me wonder if he isn't involved in what's happened to Laurel. Mother must be having the same idea."

"How did he leave?"

"Apparently he just walked away down the beach. He has no car."

"Where are the others?"

"My husband took Marian to the hospital, to be with Jack."

"How is your brother?"

"He's surviving, that's all I know." She gave me a long cold look. "I'm afraid I don't understand what you were doing when Jack was shot."

The angry feeling in her voice was more pronounced. It seemed to be directed against the world and against me as its representative. The change I sensed in her probably reflected a change in her entire family. One of them had been taken, and one wounded, and they felt under siege.

"I saw what happened at Sandhill Lake from a distance." I explained to Elizabeth how that was. "I didn't actually witness the shooting of your brother but I'm reasonably sure who did it." I got the photo of Harold out of my inside pocket. "Do you recognize him?"

She held the picture close to one of the smeared windows. "It's Harold Sherry, isn't it?"

"Yes."

"I knew he was up to something. He came out to my house in Bel-Air and did some pretty wild talking."

"When was that?"

"Just last week."

"And what did he say, exactly?"

"I prefer not to tell you."

"I would prefer not to be here at all."

I realized as I said it that I was angry with her now, furiously angry in a quiet way. We had been intimate the night before, not only in the physical sense. But the morning and the afternoon had carried us far apart, and we seemed to blame each other for the distance.

"You're perfectly free to leave," she said.

"I didn't mean that."

"But I did."

I sat down facing her. "We're both under strain. We both want to get Laurel back. That's the main thing, isn't it?"

She took a deep breath. "I suppose you're right. But where is she?"

"I'm reasonably sure that Harold knows."

"Then where is Harold?"

"That's the question. The things he said to you might bear on it."

She sat down, studying the photograph as if it was a mirror in which she could see that she had lost her looks. I said:

"Was Harold in the habit of visiting your house?"

"Far from it. I hadn't seen him in years. I didn't know who he was until he told me. He's much better-looking than he was in his teens. But I'm afraid he's still the same old Harold."

"Exactly what do you mean?"

"He pretended to have come on a friendly visit, to get my forgiveness for the past or something of the sort. He'd already been in touch with Laurel and she had forgiven him, or so he said. But I'm sure he didn't come to see me for any friendly reason." She paused, and her face turned quite bleak as she remembered the conversation. "I got the impression that he was trying to ferret out the family secrets."

"What secrets?"

"You know one of them," she said without meeting my eyes. "I shouldn't have told you what I did last night, about Ben and that young woman who came to our house with the boy. I'll ask you not to repeat it."

"I don't intend to. Was that one of the things that Harold was interested in?"

"Yes. But he had it wrong. Harold Sherry is one of those people who always get things wrong. He seemed to think that it was Jack who had been the woman's lover." She smiled very dimly. "I wish it had been."

"Are you sure it wasn't?"

"Absolutely certain. Jack was still in the East attending Navy Communications School when the woman came to Bel-Air and talked to me. And it was definitely Ben she was talking about."

"Did Harold tell you where he got the information? Or misinformation?"

"He'd been in touch with Laurel, as I said. But it's

hard to imagine Laurel talking about her father in those terms. It's possible that Harold heard the story from someone, and got it distorted in his own mind. He really hates my brother Jack, you know."

"That's obvious. I'm more interested in what he had to say about Laurel."

She sat in silence for a while. Outside the house I could hear the dull surf measuring off its long-drawn-out intervals. "He said that they were friends again. He'd had dinner at her house, and he liked her husband."

"Was he sincere, do you think?"

"It's hard to say. A man like Harold is never completely honest. He doesn't like himself enough really to like anyone else. And he's always got more than one thing going on in his head."

"What kind of things?"

"He didn't talk about them to me—at least not openly. But I can imagine the kind of things they are. Blackmail and fraud and what have you. He's a very mixed-up person."

"I know that. What I'm trying to find out is this. Did Harold kidnap Laurel this time around, as he claims? Or did the two of them take off together and make the money demand on her parents?"

"I simply can't believe that Laurel would do that."

"She did once."

"When she was a fifteen-year-old. She's changed since then. Laurel's really quite a well-intentioned person. She tries very hard. And she's always been more of a victim than a victimizer."

We were back again at the riddle of Laurel. "Perhaps," I said, "it doesn't make so much difference whether she's consciously one or the other. Harold is the one that makes the difference. He may have a kind of hex on her, going back to adolescence. I've seen it happen to other girls, especially ones that don't get along with their parents."

"I know what you mean." She added thoughtfully, "Jack can be pretty hard to take."

"Tell me this. When Harold Sherry came to your house, did he say anything about where he was staying?

Or a phone number where you could get in touch with him?"

She considered the question. "No, he didn't."

"What kind of a car was he driving?"

"An old green compact."

There was a telephone in the room, and with Elizabeth's permission I used it to make a call to Dr. Lawrence Brokaw in Long Beach. The woman who answered said that Dr. Brokaw was with a patient. If I'd leave my name and number, the Doctor would call me back.

Sylvia Lennox had come into the room as I was talking. She peered at my face as if she was afraid of what she might find there.

"What happened to my son, Mr. Archer?"

"He was wounded by a man named Harold Sherry." I was sure of it now.

"But I sent you with him to look after him."

"He needed more looking after than I could give him. He wanted to take care of the situation all by himself."

She didn't seem to hear me. Her mind was moving like a flightless bird among her troubles. "And now Tony Lashman has deserted me. What do you think has happened to Tony?"

"I don't know. When did you see him last?"

"This morning, when I put him in his place."

She moved between her daughter and me to the window. Her lean wrinked face looked softer and more shapeless, as though the blows that had fallen on her had been physical. She said, in a thin and mournful voice which was shaken by gusts of fury:

"All my life I've tried to do my duty, and this is what it's come to. My only son has been shot. My beach is covered with filth. My granddaughter is missing. And Tony left without even saying goodbye." She turned from the window, her eyes wide, full of the dark scene. "I blame the men for this."

"What men, Mother?"

"*All* the men. I've sat back all my life and watched them operate. If they want a woman, they take her. William did that. Ben put an oil well where no oil well belongs. Look at what he's done to my beach. And Jack has been shot. I want to go and see him."

Elizabeth put an arm around her mother's shoulders. "Stay here with me. You wouldn't like it at the hospital, Mother."

"I don't like it here, either." She turned to me and spoke in a more reasonable tone: "Did you say Harold Sherry shot Jack?"

"Yes."

The old woman nodded grimly. "I warned Jack to take it easy on that boy. I told him when a girl runs off with a boy, you can't always blame the boy one hundred percent. But Jack was determined to destroy him. He wouldn't let the court give him juvenile treatment, and William used his influence to see that he was put in jail. And now the boy is striking back at us." She shuddered, and wagged her head. "I want no part of it. I'm opting out. Let the men handle it. It's all their doing."

She turned and left the room, moving uncertainly. She had stumbled under the pressures of the day, and age had overtaken her.

"Mother's always felt like that, really," Elizabeth said. "She's never said it quite so explicitly, but it's been her philosophy of marriage all along. Let the men go ahead and take the responsibility and make the mistakes. And then the women can sit back and feel superior. It's not a very good kind of innocence."

"Any innocence may be better than none."

"I used to think so. But I'm beginning to wonder. You've got to use your innocence for something. You can't just keep it in a hope chest."

Her voice was low and very personal. She was talking about herself as well as her mother, and she sounded young for her age.

"What's bothering you, Beth?"

Her head came up in response to her name. "It isn't what you think it is, exactly. The fact is I've been giving my husband a very hard time generally—ever since Harold Sherry came and talked to me. I bitterly resented that young woman, whoever she was, and I took it out on Ben every way I could. And I wonder, if I'd given him some peace—a chance to think—if he might not have made the mistake that blew the well."

"You're reversing your mother's philosophy," I said, "and really reaching for a piece of guilt."

"Because it belongs to me. To the extent that Ben was responsible, then I'm responsible, too."

"How do you know he was responsible?"

"He told me. He allowed the well to be drilled without adequate casing, and even after there were signs of trouble he ordered the drilling to go ahead."

"That was his mistake in judgment. You can't make yourself responsible for it."

"I am, though, partly."

"You mean you want to be."

"I am, and I want to be."

The phone rang beside me. I picked it up:

"Archer speaking."

"This is Dr. Brokaw. Did you call me?" The voice was youngish, and a little breathy.

"Yes. It's about a patient of yours."

"What patient?"

"Harold Sherry. He's in trouble."

There was a flat silence. "I'm very sorry to hear that. Is it serious?"

"Just about as serious as it can get. He's wanted for kidnapping. He was wounded by gunfire and dropped out of sight. I thought he might go to you."

"He hasn't. Are you a policeman?"

"A private detective. Do you have an address for Harold?"

"I may have."

"Will you look it up for me?"

There was another silence, divided into equal segments by his breathing. "I'm afraid I can't give out patients' addresses over the phone."

"Not even when a young woman's been kidnapped?"

"You say you're a private detective. If a woman's been kidnapped, why haven't I heard from the police?"

"I'm the one who has your name. I got it from Harold's mother. If you want me to give it to the police—"

"No. Look. Where are you now?"

"Pacific Point."

"Can you come here to my office? I'll be finished with

my other—with my patients by half past five. Then we can talk about Harold." He hung up on me.

Elizabeth moved across the room and stood above me with her fists clenched. "Won't he help?"

"I think he will."

"If he's a local doctor, my family can bring pressure to bear on him."

"He isn't, though. He practices in Long Beach. And I'll probably get further with him by myself."

Her general anger focused on me again. "You're very self-confident, aren't you? Overconfident, perhaps, considering your failure to protect my brother."

"The only way I could have protected your brother was by putting him in irons. He didn't want me to go to Sandhill Lake with him. It looked as if he wanted to have a shoot-out. Anyway, he got one. And I'm not taking any responsibility for it. Your brother pointed a gun at me and ordered me out of the car."

"Really?"

"I'm not making this up."

"But why would he do a thing like that?"

"I don't know, but I plan to ask him. I'm going over to the hospital now."

Elizabeth didn't put up any further argument. Letting me out into the courtyard where I had left my car, she tried the knob of an outside door between the back door and the garages. The door failed to open. I said:

"What's in there?"

"It's Tony Lashman's room. I keep hoping he'll turn up. I'm worried about him."

"Are you sure he isn't in his room?"

"I'm not sure about anything."

The lock on the door was of the Yale type, easy to open with a plastic credit card. The room on the other side of it was large but rather makeshift, incompletely walled with knotty pine. The single bed was unoccupied and unmade. There was no one under the bed and no one in the closet. The floor of the closet was piled with dirty clothes intermingled with sections of a black rubber wet suit.

A windup alarm clock sat on the table beside the bed. It wasn't ticking. It had stopped a few minutes short of midnight, or of noon.

XXVI

I drove across town to the hospital and learned, after some palaver at the front desk, that Jack Lennox was in a private room on the top floor. In the hallway outside his door, I found Sergeant Shantz sitting on a metal folding chair which his flesh overlapped.

"Where have *you* been?" he said.

"I returned Jack Lennox's car, and got involved with the family. How is he doing?"

"Okay. His wife is in there with him." Shantz rose heavily, pushing his chair back against the wall. "If you're going to be here for the next few minutes, I should make a phone call. The Sheriff asked me to let him know when Lennox was able to talk."

The Sergeant moved down the hall toward the elevators, and I went into the room. It was dim, with the curtains partly closed over the windows.

Marian Lennox was standing in a protective attitude by the head of the bed. She looked rather resentful of my intrusion, as if she valued this time alone with her husband. His face was sallow and pinched under a turban of bandage.

"Archer?"

He tried to sit up. His wife pushed him gently back against the pillows. "Please, Jack. You're not supposed to get up."

"Stop making like a nurse, for God's sake." He moved rebelliously under her hands. "You're not good at it."

"But the doctor says you need complete rest and quiet. After all, you've been shot."

"Who shot me?"

"Don't you remember?" I said.

"No. The last thing I remember is opening the door

of the tower—the lookout tower at Sandhill Lake." He groaned.

"Why did you go there?"

"It's where I was supposed to leave the money." His voice was losing its force.

"Who asked you to leave it there?"

"Nobody I knew." He looked at his wife. "Do you know who it was?"

She shook her head. "I only talked to him once, when he made the first call. I didn't recognize his voice."

"It hardly matters, anyway," I said. "It was probably the same man who shot you. And I know who that was."

They waited in silence for me to tell them. When I gave them Harold Sherry's name, Jack Lennox seemed blankly puzzled by it, as if the shot that had wounded him had driven all memory of Harold from his brain. But Marian's face changed. She looked as if she could feel the recurrence in her body of an old illness.

"Don't you remember Harold?" I said to him. "You shot him in the leg."

"*I* shot him? You've got to be kidding." He sat up, balancing his head like a heavy weight. "Does that mean you've captured him?"

"Not yet."

"What about the money? The hundred thousand?"

"He got away with it, at least for the present. I'm going to have to tell the police about the money."

Lennox seemed uninterested. He didn't ask me about his daughter Laurel. I wondered if he had perhaps forgotten her, too. He let out a long sigh and collapsed against his pillows.

Marian interposed herself between us. "I'm afraid Jack is exhausted. Couldn't we talk outside?"

"Of course."

She pulled up her husband's covers, pressed his shoulder, and followed me out. She seemed to be under better control than she had been earlier. Her face was strained but focused. It occurred to me that she was one of that disappearing species of women who live in their husbands' shadow and can only step out of it when the husbands are out of action. She said, when the door had closed behind her:

"You haven't said anything about Laurel, Mr. Archer."

"There hasn't been any word on Laurel."

"You don't know where she is, then?"

"No. The way to her is through Harold Sherry."

"He got his money. What more does he want?"

"I don't know. He may want some assurance of personal safety. The money's no good to him if he doesn't live to spend it."

Her gaze moved past me, pale and desolate, looking down the long arctic slope of the future. "Jack shouldn't have shot him."

"No. It upset the bargain. But Harold may have fired at your husband first."

A puzzled cleft appeared between her eyes. "Why would he do that?"

"I'll have to ask him."

"Do you have any hope of finding Harold Sherry?"

"Some. I know the name of a doctor he's gone to in the past. With his leg wound, he'll be wanting to get to a doctor."

"Would I know the doctor's name?"

"I doubt it. He practices in Long Beach."

"We know quite a few people in Long Beach."

"But I don't think I better mention his name to anyone, even you. He's my only decent lead so far. The chances of getting Laurel back aren't quite as good as they were this morning. I guess you know that, Mrs. Lennox."

She shook her head. "I don't know. Everything is so confused. It was a sorry day for Laurel—for all of us—when she met Harold Sherry. This isn't the first time he's abducted her, did you know that? He ran away with her when she was just fifteen."

"I've heard about it. But I don't understand his motive."

"He was always envious of our family."

"Was he attracted to Laurel?"

"Perhaps he was, in a sick way. I remember once he came to the house—this was before he took her to Las

Vegas. He couldn't keep his hands off her. She had to ask her father to intervene."

"Laurel asked your husband to intervene?"

"That's correct. Jack threw him out of the house." Her voice was cold and featureless, like a medium reciting words whose meaning was not clear to her. "My husband has always had a violent temper."

"I've seen a few indications of that. Tell me, Mrs. Lennox, has his temper ever been turned against Laurel?"

"Of course it has. Many times."

"Recently?"

"Yes. They haven't been getting along at all well lately. Jack hasn't been too happy about her marriage. In fact he's done his best to break it up." She overheard herself and gave me a worried look. "What do you suspect Laurel of doing?"

"There is a possibility that she threw in with Harold of her own free will."

"When they went to Vegas?"

"Then," I said, "and now. Do you think Laurel was genuinely kidnapped last night?"

"I don't know what to think." She looked at me suspiciously. "What are you getting at, exactly?"

"The possibility of collusion. There's some evidence that Laurel and Harold have been seeing each other."

"Where did you get that story?"

"I'm sorry, I can't name my source." There was enough bad blood between Harold's mother and the Lennox family.

"Anyway, I don't believe it," she said.

She turned away to go back into her husband's room, and paused with her hand on the door. I could see how thin and vulnerable she was. Her graying hair, cut in a long shag, curled like wispy feathers at the nape of her neck. Her shoulder blades stuck out under her dress like unfledged wings.

She had lost her daughter, and her husband had been shot. It was the kind of experience that used people up in a hurry. A week from now, if the attrition continued, she could be old and defeated like Sylvia.

"I'm sorry, Mrs. Lennox. I thought you should know some of the possibilities."

She turned quickly and almost lost her balance. "Yes, of course. You're right. I want you to keep me informed."

"I'll try to do that."

"If Laurel is involved with Harold Sherry—I don't believe it, you understand, but *if* she is—I want to know about it before anyone else. Particularly before you tell the police."

"I understand you." But I made no promises.

XXVII

It was a long day. When Marian Lennox left me, I sat down in Shantz's folding chair, leaned back against the wall, and let my mind go loose. Black waves washed over it, carrying me in to a black shore. I sat up with a start.

Shantz stepped out of the elevator. He came toward me quickly, his belly swinging over his heavy gun belt. Drops of sweat stood out on his forehead.

"Sorry I kept you waiting. There's been another death at the beach."

"Whose death?"

"We don't know yet. A young fellow with black hair. We've got him downstairs in the pathology department. If you want to take a look at him, it's on the first floor, to your right as you leave the elevator. Captain Dolan is there with the Sheriff."

The elevator Shantz had left was still waiting. I touched the first-floor button and leaned on the wall of the descending cubicle. I felt as if I was going down to the bottom of things.

A Chicano girl in a nurse's-aide uniform leaned in through the door as it opened. "Is something the matter?" Her soft black eyes were solicitous.

"No. There's nothing the matter."

"I'm going up. Do you want to go up?"

"No."

"Are you a patient?"

"No."

Her question jolted me into movement. I stepped out into the first-floor corridor and walked toward the "Pathology" sign unwillingly. There had been too much violence for one day.

I hunched my mind around a little until my scar tissue was back in place. Then I knocked on the door and went in.

A grimly maternal woman behind a fixed desk dispatched me down a further corridor, through what seemed like zones of deepening cold, to the room where the dead man lay. He was still strapped to the aluminum stretcher on which the Sheriff and Captain Dolan had brought him in. His body was enclosed in a transparent plastic bag which had been opened at the top to reveal his head.

It was Tony Lashman, with oil in his eyes, oil in his open mouth. "This is Lew Archer," Dolan said. "Sheriff Sam Whittemore, Lew."

We shook hands across the body. Whittemore had a jolting blue glance which came at you unexpectedly out of a lined and worried face. He used his handshake to guide me to the other side of the room.

I told him that the dead man was Sylvia Lennox's secretary, and that I had seen him alive at noon. "Where did you find him?"

"Just down the beach from Sylvia Lennox's house. You can't see it in that position, but the back of his head was bashed in, apparently by a rock."

"Did you find the rock?"

The Sheriff's bright blue eyes came up to meet mine. "We didn't find the rock. There're a million rocks, all of them covered with oil, around where he was lying." He leaned toward me. "You know the Lennox family, do you?"

"I've met most of them in the last twenty-four hours."

"Just off the top of your head, now, do you have any idea who's doing these killings?"

"I'm afraid I don't."

"Or why?"

"I'm working on it, Sheriff. But at this point I can't see much light."

"Neither can we." He added quickly, "Don't quote me."

Captain Dolan took his turn. "Is this the fellow you saw at Sandhill Lake when Lennox got shot?"

"No. It isn't."

"Are you sure?"

"I'm quite certain. This is Sylvia Lennox's secretary."

"Why would somebody knock him in the head? Was he involved in that deal at the lake?"

"I don't know."

The Sheriff said, "What was the nature of that deal? I never did get it straight."

"Jack Lennox was supposed to pay over some money."

"Pay the other man some money?"

"That's correct."

"What happened to the money?"

"The other man took it away with him."

Dolan said. "Why didn't you tell me that before?"

"I had to check with the Lennox family."

"Is that where the money came from? The Lennox family?"

"Yes"

"And who were the Lennox family paying off?"

I sat in silence for a while, trying to think of a way to leave Laurel out, and a way to preserve my sense of not being an auxiliary policeman. But Laurel was far beyond the reach of my protection, and there seemed to be no point in protecting Harold Sherry.

I gave them Harold's name, and told them where he came from and what he had been doing. The only thing I held back was Dr. Lawrence Brokaw's name and address in Long Beach. I wanted to be the first to talk to Brokaw.

"So it's a snatch." Whittemore spoke with some disgust.

"Why didn't you tell us that before?" Dolan said. "I'm still not sure."

"What else could it be?"

"A run-out on her part, with Harold Sherry cashing in on it. Or he may have her stashed somewhere."

"Dead or alive?"

"She could be either. She could be alive but in danger. That's why I'm anxious to find her."

The Sheriff spoke: "Or the two of them could be on a plane, with fifty thousand apiece for their day's work."

"That's a possibility, but I doubt it."

"Do you know something more that you haven't told us?"

"No, I've given you the essential facts. But of course you can get a lot more from Laurel's family."

"What *about* the Lennox family?" the Sheriff said. "Could this be a case of malice, do you think? Is somebody trying to make them look real bad?"

"Harold Sherry has reason. I told you that."

"What about other suspects? There's been a lot of feeling against the Lennox people since the oil spill. There was a near riot at the wharf today, did you know that?"

"I was there."

"Then you know what I mean. Do you think a gang of eco-freaks are trying to blacken the Lennoxes' reputation?"

"By killing people and putting them in the oil?"

"If you want to put it that way."

"No. I think the oil spill and the other crimes are probably unconnected."

Then I remembered what Elizabeth had told me, about the effect of Harold's earlier visit on her husband and her marriage. Perhaps there was a psychological connection, after all.

"Are you having second thoughts?" Whittemore said.

"Yes, but they're a little off the subject. Harold Sherry has a grudge against the Lennoxes, but it goes back fifteen years."

As I told them about it, I became aware that time was slipping away. I was going to have to hurry to catch Dr. Brokaw. Resisting further questions, I moved toward the door.

"Are you in a hurry?" the Sheriff said.

"Yes. I have an appointment."

"That's okay. As long as it isn't with Harold Sherry."

He laughed. I went out laughing.

Dolan followed me into the corridor. "You might want to stick around for a little while. We've got a witness on his way over here now."

"A witness to what?"

"That isn't too clear. When I spoke to him on the phone a little while ago, he talked as if he could identify the man you pulled out of the water this morning. He's got a wild idea that the decedent is somebody he knows. Or somebody he knew over twenty-five years ago when he was an officer in the Navy."

"What makes the idea so wild?"

"The naval vessel he was on burned off Okinawa. And this guy seems to think that the body floated all the way in from there—that it's been in the water for the last twenty-five years." Dolan tapped the side of his skull with his fingers.

"Your witness wouldn't be Captain Somerville?"

"No, but he works in public relations for Somerville. His name is Ellis. He came around early this morning when we brought the body in here, wanting to keep the whole thing as quiet as possible. He didn't say a word about knowing the guy. I noticed he did have a bad reaction when we showed him the body. But I figured he was just one of those sensitive types."

"I think he is. I also think something's bothering him."

"You know Ellis?"

"I met him today around noon. He seemed very jittery."

"Was he drunk?"

"No. But he'd been drinking."

"He's drunk now," Dolan said, "and maybe a little crazy in the bargain."

"Is he a suspect, in your opinion?"

"I don't know. He sounded like a guilty man on the phone. I'm not sure what he's guilty of, but I took the precaution of sending a car for him."

The Sheriff left, and a few minutes later Ellis arrived, accompanied by a uniformed deputy. Ellis had deteriorated since I'd seen him at noon. He walked loose-kneed, and he didn't appear to recognize me. But he saluted Dolan, raising his hand to his damp forehead in a gesture that seemed intended to ward off evil.

I followed them into a room where we could see our breath. Dolan pulled a drawer out from the wall and uncovered the little old man. Ellis bent over the drawer and almost fell. Tears fell from his face onto the dead man's face.

"It's Nelson," he said in awe. "It's Nelson, all right." He turned to Dolan. "But how did he get so old? He was just a young man when he went into the water off Okinawa."

"He was alive yesterday."

"No, you're mistaken. He was lost off the *Canaan Sound* over twenty-five years ago. And it was my fault." The awe was still in his voice. He turned to the dead man and touched his scarred face and said, "I'm sorry, Nelson." He got down on his knees, holding onto the edge of the drawer with his fingers. "Forgive me."

Half carrying him, we got him out of the cold room and sat him down in a chair. Dolan wet a towel and wiped his face. But he wouldn't look at us. He sat with his head hanging down in shame and sorrow, water dripping from his nose and chin.

Dolan drew me to the far side of the room and spoke in a low voice. "Do you think he's off his rocker?"

"He could be. He's drunk and hysterical, anyway. But there may be something in what he says. Captain Somerville told me himself that Ellis was with him at Okinawa. And I know the ship caught fire."

We moved back to Ellis, who seemed to be getting himself under better control. "Why do you think it was all your fault?" I said.

"Because it was." His mournful eyes came up to mine. "I was the avgas officer on the *Canaan Sound,* and I was responsible."

"You were the what?" Dolan said.

"The avgas—the aviation-gasoline officer. We were taking on gas at sea and I must have made a mistake, because one of our tanks ruptured. The ship was running with gasoline. Before we could get it cleaned up, something sparked and the whole thing blazed up. Some of the crew went overboard. Most of them were picked up by the oiler, but some were lost. Five or six were lost. And *he* was one of them." Ellis pointed uncertainly toward the cold room.

"You called the dead man Nelson," I said. "Is that a first name or a last name?"

"I don't know. We all just called him Nelson. He was a Communications messenger on the *Canaan Sound*."

A worried-looking woman came down the corridor. She walked like a soldier advancing, angry and fearful, on the enemy. Ellis looked around for a place to hide. But there was only the door of the cold room.

"What are you doing here?" the woman said to him. "You promised me you'd stay at home until you sobered up."

He sat with his head down, mumbling in reply. "I had to take another look at the man."

"What man?"

"The man they pulled out of the water. We called him Nelson. He was on the *Canaan Sound*. Poor Nelson. He'd still be alive if it wasn't for me."

"That's nonsense," the woman said. "He only drowned last night."

"You're mistaken. There were five or six of them drowned, and I was responsible."

"That isn't true. None of it is true. It was an accident, pure and simple, which means it wasn't your fault. We've been over it and over it."

"I was responsible," Ellis said. "I was the one overseeing the work when the tank ruptured."

"Shut up." She turned her back on him and spoke to us. "My husband can't be trusted on this subject. He's a very sensitive man, and he was involved in a terrible accident. His ship was nearly lost in a gasoline spill, and because he was the gasoline officer he assumed responsibility. But it wasn't really his fault."

"Whose fault was it?" I said.

"It was Captain Somerville's fault, if it was anybody's. I've gone into the subject with my husband's shipmates. Some of them think the Captain must have called for more pressure than the tank would stand. He was the only one with the authority."

Ellis raised his head. His drunken blowzy grief had been dried and canceled by another emotion.

"Shut up, please shut up. Do you want me to lose my position?"

"You'd be better off without it. I've always said so. You're nothing more than a hired flack, and you're not good at it. I've always thought we should go away and start over."

"I'm going to have to," Ellis said.

His moment of truth had passed, along with his illusion that the dead man had floated home across the Pacific. Ellis was just a middle-aging man afraid of losing his job.

XXVIII

Late afternoon traffic crawled on the boulevards. My route took me through a working-class tract where I had lived when the earthquake had hit Long Beach, back near the drop-off edge of memory. The streets looked old and run-down, except for one where yellow acacias were blossoming like an exposed vein of gold.

It was past five-thirty when I parked my car in front of Dr. Brokaw's office. He had a corner office on the second floor of an old building which had survived the earthquake. The waiting room was sparsely equipped with some faded chintz-covered furniture, a desk, and an old metal filing cabinet. Nobody was waiting there, but vanished patients had left behind faint matching odors of fear and poverty.

A harried-looking chemical redhead in an off-white uniform came out of the inner office. "Are you Mr. Archer?"

"Yes."

"I'm sorry, the Doctor couldn't wait for you. He had an emergency call, just a few minutes ago."

"Will he be coming back here?"

"I doubt it. He asked me to tell you he was sorry."

"I'm sorry, too. Where can I reach him later?"

"I'm not authorized to give out his address. But if you call the office number, you'll get the answering service. They may be able to help you."

"Maybe *you* can," I said. "I'm trying to locate a man named Harold Sherry."

"That's funny, he's the—" She stopped abruptly in mid-sentence.

"He's the what?"

"I was going to say, he's one of the Doctor's patients."

"Is he the emergency Dr. Brokaw went on?"

"I don't know. I really don't."

"Where does Harold Sherry live?"

She glanced at the filing cabinet, then back at me. "I'm sorry, we don't give out that information. If you'll excuse me now, my husband is picking me up and I've still got work to do."

She went into the inner room. I opened the door to the hallway and closed it without going out. I moved quietly across the room to the filing cabinet and opened the Q-R-S drawer. Several addresses were given for Harold Sherry; all but the bottom one had been crossed out. The remaining address was c/o Cup of Tea, which was a public eating place hardly more than a block from where I was standing.

I left my car where it was, and walked to the Cup of Tea through gathering dusk. It was a big old cafeteria where people of all ages and classes met. There were long-haired girls and bearded young men, family groups with children, old people hunched protectively over their meager suppers. A pair of Chicano busboys were cleaning off empty tables and gathering up the dishes with noise and élan.

I went up to the serving counter to ask for the manager. But I was overcome by the sight of food. I couldn't remember when I had eaten last. The serving girls moving around in the steam looked like buxom angels.

I ordered fried liver and onions, mashed potatoes, pumpkin pie, and coffee; and said I wanted to speak to the manager. He came up to my table as I was drinking my coffee—a balding man wearing a light washable jacket.

"Is something the matter, sir?"

"I hope not. The food was okay."

"We try to make it that way."

"I'm looking for Harold Sherry. He gave this address."

"Oh. Harold. He doesn't work here any more."

"Where can I find him?"

The manager made an open-handed gesture which looked at if it was borrowed from one of his busboys. "Harold didn't tell me that he was going to leave. He just didn't turn up for work last week."

"Why?"

"Too much imagination for the kind of work he was doing. That's the nice way to put it. Are you a relative of Harold's?"

"Just a friend. He didn't leave any kind of forwarding address?"

"Maybe he did. I'll check with the cashier. He spent a lot of time hanging around her."

Her name was Charlene. She had level blue eyes and clean brown hair, and she sat behind the cash register as if she was piloting a plane. When the manager asked her about Harold, she blushed and became upset and shook her head. He retreated, making his borrowed Spanish gesture.

I waited for her to calm down, and paid her for my meal. "If you can put me in touch with Harold, you'll be doing me a big favor."

"You wouldn't be his father?"

"No. I saw his mother this afternoon."

"I didn't know he had a mother. He's always talking about his father. He said his father is a big oil man in Texas. Is that the truth?"

"I guess he's moderately big."

She breathed deeply, and her bosom rose. "So Harold had his reasons for starting here at the bottom."

"What reasons?"

"You know, he wanted to learn the food business. His father promised to buy him a pizza franchise. But first of all he had to learn the food business."

Her level eyes were on my face. I realized that she

wasn't so much telling me about Harold as asking me. She wanted to know if Harold was a liar.

I answered the question with another question: "Can you tell me where he is, Charlene?"

"That depends on what you want him for."

"I can't go into details. But Harold has come into some money."

"Big money?"

"You might call it that."

She didn't believe me. In spite, or because, of that, she told me what I wanted to know: "The last time I saw him was in the liquor store. He was supposed to be in Texas visiting his father. But he was right here in Long Beach, with a big fat woman. He said her name was Ramona." Her eyes were chilly. "He was buying her beer."

"Do you know where I can find her?"

"You can ask them at the liquor store, I guess. They talked to her like she was a regular customer. It's Tom and Jerry's, down that way." She gestured toward the waterfront.

I walked down that way. To the left were the space-age buildings of the Convention Center, high-rise apartments pierced with lights, parking lots where the beaches used to be. Off to the right was an indeterminate area, a kind of skid row for people with money in their pockets. Beyond it, harbor water glinted.

Sailors prowled the semidarkness. A drunk in a well-cut dark suit was sitting on the curb outside of Tom and Jerry's reciting poetry which sounded as if he was making it up as he went along. The smiling hard-faced little man behind the counter in the liquor store looked ready to shoot me or serve me, depending on what I said to him.

"Do you know a girl called Ramona?"

"I know a Ramona. I wouldn't call her a girl. I suppose you want to know how much of her income goes for liquor."

"I'm not a welfare investigator," I said. "I'm looking for a friend of hers, is all."

"Harold?"

"That's right."

"I haven't seen Harold lately."

"Where does Ramona live?"

"Next street up on your right." He pointed inland. "It's the first three-story building past the corner. She's on the second floor, in Apartment D. If you want a friendly welcome, bring her a six-pack."

I took his advice. In the lobby of the building, a boy in naval uniform was leaning with a woman against the wall. I climbed the stairs, sliding my hand up the alligatored banister, and knocked on the door of Apartment D.

A woman opened the door, looked me over swiftly, and said, "Hello, there."

She had a broad handsome face, jet-black eyes, tar-black hair. Her body looked swollen in its tight black dress but, like her face, it had a heavy beauty.

"Hello, Ramona."

"Who are you?"

"I'm just a friend of a friend," I said.

"Who's your friend?"

"Harold Sherry."

"He didn't mention you."

"Does Harold live here?"

"Not any more he doesn't."

"Did he leave a forwarding address?"

"He did not." She leaned toward me in the doorway. Her shoulders were massive and magnificent. "Is there a beef out on Harold?"

"No," I lied. "He owes me some money."

"Me, too. We should get together. Come in, why don't you?"

She moved out of the doorway, making room for me to enter. The room was cramped and ancient as a cave. An open day bed took up about a third of its space. A pair of worn armchairs faced each other across a table on which a quart bottle of beer stood empty.

"I was just having a beer," she said.

"I brought some more."

"That's nice. Harold must have said I liked beer, eh?"

I wondered what her background was. She spoke without an accent but with a touch of angry mimicry, as if to suggest that the language wasn't exactly hers by choice. She flipped off the top of a can of beer, handed me the can, and opened one for herself.

"Sit down. Here's *to* you. And here's to Harold and his new girl."

"He has one, has he?"

She nodded. "He has one. She came with him when he stopped to pick up his things the other day."

"Did you see her?"

"Not really. I looked out the window, but she stayed in the car. You know her?"

"I might. What kind of a car was she driving?"

"A little green car, not new."

"A Falcon?"

"I guess that's what it was. A little green sporty model. You do know her, eh?"

"I'm not sure."

"I wanted to go down and meet her. Harold wouldn't let me. He didn't want me to see her. All I saw was the top of her head. She's a brunette, like me."

"Why didn't he want you to meet her?"

"Because I'm half Indian. For a boy who's been over the jumps like Harold, he's got some very old-fashioned prejudices. Also, he thinks I'm too fat." She nodded her head in agreement. "I *am* too fat. Do you want to guess how old I am?"

"Thirty-five."

I thought I was flattering her, but she shook her head. "Twenty-nine. If you were me, how would you get rid of some of this weight?"

"Give up beer."

"Besides that, I mean. I've got to have something in my life besides sitting and waiting."

"What are you waiting for?"

"Something good to happen. Like winning the daily double." Her voice was shallow, mocking her own emptiness or the emptiness of the place where she was living.

"Don't you want something better than that?"

"You mean marriage and children, or a job? I've tried those things. I've held good jobs. And I've got a husband and three children. Only he kicked me out. And I'm not allowed to see my children." She looked down at her lap. "They live in Rolling Hills. Sometimes

I go down and look across the water and pretend I can see them." She lifted her head. Her face was like a moon rising over the hill of her body. "Are you married?"

"I have been. I'm divorced."

"Just like me, eh? What happened to your wife?"

"I don't know. I haven't seen her recently."

"Then worry about your wife. Don't worry about me." She drank up the rest of her can of beer. "Incidentally, my name isn't Ramona. People just call me that; it started as a joke."

"What is your name?"

"I don't tell strangers." She rapped her can down on the table. "You haven't told me *your* name."

"Archer."

"Where's your bow and arrow, Archer?"

"Out in the back of the Pontiac."

She laughed suddenly. "You're kidding me. Does Harold really owe you money?"

"A little money."

"You can kiss it goodbye."

She opened another can and offered it to me. When I refused, she drank from it herself. The lonely, irregular rhythm of her life was beginning to get to me. Under it I could sense her leashed anger.

"Try his mother," she said. "I'm betting he'll go back to his mother. He's the type that always does—in the end they always settle for clean sheets. Clean sheets and dirty minds," she added in a meditative growl. "What kind of a girl has he got now?"

"I don't really know."

"I thought you said you knew her."

"I was wrong. I was thinking about another girl."

"But you knew about the green car."

"I saw Harold driving it today."

"It figures," she said. "I think he went with her because he needed a car. He wanted me to buy him one, but I don't have that kind of money—not any more."

"What did he want a car for?"

"He had a plan, if you can call it that. He didn't spell it out to me, but he said it would make a fortune and at the same time get back at the people that wrecked his life." Her gaze moved on my face like a dark ray. "Is Harold in trouble?"

"He could be. Who were the people he wanted to get back at?"

"His father was one of them. Harold got into some really bad trouble at one time. His father walked out on him and let him take the rap. He never forgave his father for letting him go to jail. Or the other people."

"Who were they?"

"I don't remember the name of the family, but they're in the oil business. When Harold got high, he used to talk about blowing up their oil tanks and stuff like that."

"Would he know how to go about it?"

"He might. His father was an oil engineer—he started here in Long Beach—and Harold told me his father trained him to follow in his footsteps. That was before the big break in the family."

"Did he ever tell you what caused the break?"

"He never did. But he blamed it all on his father. He was getting pretty paranoid on the subject—you know what I mean? It's one reason I wasn't too sorry to see him go."

"Where did he go?"

"He wouldn't tell me. Of course he had something worked out with that girl. He probably moved into her apartment."

She looked around the narrow horizons of her own apartment. As the conversation and the evening wore on, she seemed to grow older and more melancholy. The gleam of beauty I had noticed on her at first had been absorbed by her body, like something swallowed by a grieving monster.

She lived in twilight, I thought, just as Harold's mother did. I wondered if Harold's new girl was another twilight woman.

"Can you tell me the girl's name?"

"I don't think so."

"It wasn't Laurel?"

She thought about the question. "He knew a Laurel, I think. The name came up, anyway. But I don't believe this was the one."

"What was this one's name?"

She shrugged her heavy shoulders and put out her hands like a woman expecting rain.

Down in the dark street, sailors were standing around in disconnected attitudes, like dim purgatorial souls waiting for orders.

XXIX

I walked uphill to my car. The area was almost deserted, as if when the sun had dropped into the sea it had sucked the people along with it.

There was a single light in Dr. Brokaw's building, on the second floor at the corner. I went up in the laboring elevator and tried the outer door of his office. It was locked.

A man's voice on the other side of the door said, "Who is that?"

"Lew Archer. I talked to you on the phone, about Harold Sherry."

"I see."

He was still and silent for a moment. Then his keys clinked, and one of them turned harshly in the lock. The door opened inward, slowly, as if against pressure. Silhouetted by the light from the waiting room, Dr. Brokaw was a man of medium height with an enormous head.

I saw when he stepped back to let me enter that his macrocephalic head was mostly hair and beard. Between them, his eyes looked out like a forest animal's, dark and sensitive and vaguely alarmed.

"I'm sorry I couldn't meet you earlier. I really didn't expect you to wait. But now that you're here, come in."

I followed him across the waiting room into his private office. He shut the door and leaned on it, looking at me with something like repugnance. His beard was shot through with gray, but his eyes were young. They seemed to soften as they looked at me.

"You're very tired, aren't you?"

It sounded more like an expression of sympathy than

a medical opinion. But it made me aware of my tiredness, which seemed to rise in waves up through my body to my head.

"I've covered a lot of territory in the last twenty-four hours. And been getting nowhere."

"This *is* nowhere, isn't it?" His teeth flashed in his beard. "Sit down, Mr. Archer. Rest your feet."

I waited until he had closed the door and moved to the other side of the desk. His black medical bag was on the desk beside a photograph of a woman whose eyes resembled Brokaw's. He reached out and turned the picture face down, as if he didn't want our conversation to be witnessed. I said:

"The emergency patient you went to see just now— was it Harold Sherry?"

"I prefer not to discuss it."

"That means it was Harold."

"You're jumping to an unwarranted conclusion."

"Then tell me who it was."

He leaned forward across his desk, and spoke with surprising force. "My patients are my own responsibility. You have no right to cross-question me about them."

"If you think this is cross-questioning—"

He raised his voice. "Don't threaten me, Mr. Archer. Attempts have been made to threaten me before now, and I can assure you they were counter-productive."

"I wasn't threatening you, or even trying to. I think you're involved in a situation you don't understand."

His mood, or what he chose to show me of it, went through a quicksilver change. "That would be nothing new. It's the story of my life."

"I don't pretend to understand it, either. I do know there's been a major crime, possibly several. A young married woman named Laurel Russo disappeared last night. This afternoon, Harold Sherry collected a hundred thousand dollars' ransom money. At the same time, he shot Laurel's father, who shot back. Both men were wounded, and the woman is still missing."

As I told him what had happened, his face changed as if it was being exposed to the events themselves. Brokaw seemed to be a very sensitive man, almost too sensitive to be a doctor. I wondered if he wore his beard as a mask.

"Did you see Harold this evening, Doctor? You can understand why the question is important."

"I can understand why it's important to you. You call yourself a private detective, but you're still what my patients call fuzz. You're the willing representative of a punitive society, and all you really want to do is arrest people and put them behind bars."

"Is that all I really want to do?"

"I suspect it is."

The quiet accusation stung. I tried to move like a neutral in the no man's land between the lawless and the law. But when the shooting started I generally knew which side I belonged on. Polarized by Brokaw, as perhaps Brokaw was polarized by me, I felt very little different from the man in harness I had been twenty years before when I resigned from the Long Beach police force.

"What do you want to do with criminals, Doctor?"

"Treat them. But your word 'criminals' begs the question. I want to treat them before they become criminals. It's one reason I came back here and opened this office."

"Are you a Long Beach boy?"

"For my sins, I am."

"Me, too." I was glad to find some common ground with him. "It was a good place to grow up in." My words sounded rather hollow in my ears.

"It isn't so good any more. Half the diseases I treat are drug-related. A large percentage are venereal. Another large percentage are emotional."

"Have you been treating Harold for emotional trouble?"

He gave me a quick darting look. "How did you guess that?"

"I know something about his background. I talked to his mother this afternoon."

"I haven't had that privilege. In fact I've had very little time with Harold himself. I've only seen him four or five times. Five times."

"Including this evening?"

"You're very persistent. But I'm standing on my right to remain silent."

"I don't know where you get that right."

"Harold Sherry is my patient."

"I can understand your concern for him," I said. "What I don't understand is your lack of concern for the young woman he kidnapped."

"The young woman was not kidnapped. I saw her."

"Tonight?"

He waved his left hand loosely. "Yes, tonight."

"Where did you see her?"

"In a motel."

"With Harold?"

He nodded his shaggy head. "She was obviously there of her own free will."

"Describe her, Doctor."

"She's a nice-looking brunette, rather tall, about five foot six, age about thirty."

"Did you talk to her?"

"Not really. She stayed very much in the background."

"Then how do you know she was there of her own free will?"

"By the way she acted—the relationship between them. It was a warm relationship. She wasn't concerned about herself; she was very much concerned about Harold."

"Is Harold badly wounded?"

His head sank like a buffalo's between his shoulders. "You're putting me in an untenable position, Mr. Archer. You won't be satisfied until I tell you all about Harold and lead you to where he is. But that I refuse to do. My primary duty is to my patients."

"If Harold is badly hurt, you're doing him no favor."

His eyes grew smaller and darker. "I'm a professional man. You have no right to talk to me in this way."

"Then you do the talking, Doctor."

"I have nothing to say to you."

We sat in stalemated silence. I looked at the framed diplomas on the wall behind him. He had been trained in good schools and hospitals, not so very many years ago. Judging by the dates on the diplomas, Brokaw wasn't out of his thirties.

He pushed back his chair. "If you'll excuse me, I haven't had anything to eat all day."

"Go ahead and eat," I said without moving. "Don't let the dead man spoil your dinner."

"What dead man? There is no dead man. Harold's wound is not serious."

But Brokaw was upset. What I could see of his face had lost its color and turned sallow. I said:

"You have to report treatment of gunshot wounds to the police."

"But not to you."

"You think the police will give Harold a better break than I will? He could be shot on sight, and you know it."

He shook his head. "That would be a tragedy, a real tragedy. I don't believe he's responsible for what happened."

"Psychologically not responsible, or morally not responsible?"

"Either or both. I'd be willing to bet a good deal that Harold committed no serious crime."

"You already are betting a good deal, Doctor. Whether or not the girl went with him willingly, there's no question that he shot her father, and no question that he took the ransom money."

"How do you know that?"

"I was there. I virtually saw it happen. You picked the wrong patient to bet your professional life on."

"I don't pick my patients; they pick me."

His voice was defensive. He was losing his fine free self-assurance, and I was a little ashamed of what I was doing to him. But I had to get to Harold.

"You mentioned a dead man," Brokaw said. "The girl's father didn't die, did he?"

"No, and he's not expected to. But I pulled a body out of the sea this morning." I told him about the man in the tweed suit.

Brokaw's face went through another change. He looked badly shaken. "Are you telling me that the little man is dead?"

"You know him, Doctor?"

"Harold brought him here to my office yesterday. He wanted me to treat him."

"What for?"

"The man was in pretty poor shape, both physically and mentally. He had burn scars on his body and face, and he looked as though he'd been through a major disaster at some time in his life. Emotionally, too, he showed indications of severe trauma. He was a dilapidated man, almost too frightened to talk. He seemed very dependent on Harold. He had the dependency and the lack of affect of a man who has spent much of his life in institutions."

"What kind of institutions?"

Brokaw considered his answer. "Hospitals, possibly mental hospitals. I asked Harold if the man had been a patient, but Harold claimed not to know. He said that he had picked him up on the waterfront and brought him to me because he was in poor shape. But their relationship, when I think of it, wasn't a casual thing. I got the idea that Harold had a use for the man, and he wanted me to give him something to hold him together. I did give him some tranquilizers. But when I suggested that he should be hospitalized, the two of them walked out on me." He spread his hands on the desk in front of him and looked at them with distaste. "I'm afraid I didn't handle it too well."

"The little man died of drowning. You couldn't have warded that off."

"He belonged in a hospital. I should have insisted on getting him into one then and there."

Brokaw shook his head from side to side, and a loose lock of hair fell in his eyes. He was close to crying. It seemed to me that he allowed himself to feel too much, and that it interfered with his power to act. He spoke haltingly:

"Harold lied to me. He told me that he'd put the man in a hospital."

"When did Harold tell you that, Doctor?"

He gave me a startled look which melted into guilty sorrow. "When I saw him tonight. He claimed that he had taken him back to the government hospital."

"Which government hospital?"

"He didn't say. He was lying, in any case, if what you tell me is true."

"I'm not lying. I saw the two of them together last night. They had dinner on the Pacific Point wharf, near where the man was drowned. Early this morning, I pulled his body out of the water. Don't you think Harold should be questioned about this?"

A further change occurred in the face behind the beard, a painful grimacing followed by a hardening. "Yes. I do."

"Where did you see him tonight?"

He answered reluctantly. He had made a heavy emotional investment in Harold—the kind a man sometimes makes just before the market breaks—and it couldn't be easily withdrawn. "He's staying in a motel with the young woman."

"I know that. Where is the motel?"

"Redondo Beach."

"And what's the name of it, Doctor?"

"The Myrtle Motel."

"Will you come there with me?"

"What good could that possibly do?"

"The last man who walked in on Harold got shot in the head. I don't want it to happen to me. But Harold would never shoot you."

"What could I say to him? Tell him that I'd betrayed him?" His voice broke.

"You're fond of Harold, aren't you?"

He bowed his head in acknowledgment. "Yes. I thought he had promise, in spite of everything. I was hoping to straighten him out, open a better life to him. But I didn't have the skill or the time."

"You can do something for him now. Help me take him peacefully."

He was silent for a while, struggling with his feelings, then resolved the conflict in anger. "I will not. I'm a doctor, not a detective."

I got up to leave. He followed me to the door of the waiting room.

"I'm sorry, Mr. Archer, I simply can't face Harold

under these circumstances. If there's anything else I can do . . ." His voice trailed off.

"There is something. Will you see if you can trace the other man to one of the veterans' hospitals? I believe his name is Nelson."

He thought about it. "Yes, I will. I'll be glad to."

XXX

The Myrtle Motel was on old U.S. 101. Hillside apartment buildings clung to the slopes above it. The area below was garish with the lights of liquor stores and restaurants and gas stations.

The buildings of the motel were made of indestructible concrete block, as if in preparation for an obscure war. The green Falcon wasn't among the cars in the parking spaces.

I parked under the neon "Vacancy" sign and went inside. A man who had been defeated in an obscure war of his own came out of the back and gave me a questioning look across the desk. His hair was thin, but massive sideburns hung like stirrups on either side of his face.

"Can I help you?"

"We may be able to help each other," I said. "You wouldn't have any way of knowing this, but you've got a wanted man in one of your rooms."

He shied away in what seemed a practiced movement. His eyes never left my face. "I certainly didn't know it. Are you a policeman?"

"A private detective." I gave him my name and showed him my photostat. "His name is Harold Sherry."

After a moment's thought, he said, "We've got nobody of that name registered."

"He's probably using another name. He's a man in his early thirties, dark-haired, dark-eyed, height about six feet, heavily built with very broad shoulders, probably walks with a limp."

The key man shook his head. "I've never seen him, and I've been on the desk since noon. We've only got three or four people *in* the place. Business will probably pick up later," he added hopefully.

The thought that Brokaw had lied to me rose like a touch of nausea behind my throat. I swallowed it down, and tried again:

"The woman may have registered. She's a good-looking woman, aged about thirty, dark hair, dark eyes, height about five feet six, very good figure."

A dim light appeared behind his eyes. "It may be the woman in Number 8. Mrs. Sebastian? She did say her husband was under the weather."

"What kind of a car are they driving?"

"A little old green Falcon about five or six years old. I noticed it because she forgot to put down the license number. So I went out and filled it in on the card myself."

"May I see it?"

He fumbled in a drawer and came up with the card for Number 8:

Mr. and Mrs. Frank Sebastian
408 Vistosa Street
Los Angeles, California

The address given was Tom Russo's, but the handwriting didn't look like Laurel's to me. It was rather childish, round and large.

"The woman filled in this card?" I said to the key man.

"All except the license number."

I made a note of the license number. "Describe the woman, will you?"

"Your description was pretty close, except that I wouldn't call her very good-looking. And she's just a little plumpish for my taste." His hands shaped a lopsided hourglass in the air.

"Show me her room, will you?"

We went out together. There was no car in front of Number 8. But there was light in the room, leaking out around the edges of the closed blinds. I went back to the office, out of sight of the window, and the key man followed me.

"It looks to me as if they might of left," he said.

"Do you want to check?"

"Not if there's going to be any shooting."

"Tell them you have to inspect the heater or something."

He shook his head. "I'm not being paid for this."

But he left me and moved reluctantly in the direction of Number 8. A minute later he came back.

"I don't think there's anybody in there."

"Did you look?"

"No, but the key is on the outside of the door."

We let ourselves into the room and found it empty. The double bed was unmade. There was some blood on the sheets, neither fresh nor old. Smoke still hung in the air. The place had the quality of a discarded life from which Harold and the woman had barely escaped.

I made a search of the room, with its closet and bathroom, and found nothing significant except for more blood on the bathroom tiles. I went back to the office with the key man and used the pay phone there to make a series of calls.

The first was to Captain Dolan in Pacific Point. I told him where I had found and lost Harold Sherry, and gave him the license number of the green car and a description of the young woman with Sherry.

"Who is she, Archer? Laurel Lennox—Laurel Russo?"

"No. It's a different woman."

"Then where is Laurel?"

"I don't know."

"Who is this other woman, anyway?"

"I don't know, Captain," I said, though I thought I did know.

I called Tom's house in Westwood, hoping that Cousin Gloria would answer. But it was a man who came to the phone. He said that Tom wasn't there, and hung up abruptly.

I called the drugstore. A male voice I didn't recognize told me that Tom was taking the evening off, for a change. No, he had no idea where Tom was now, but he had seen him earlier. Tom had come by the drugstore to pick up some bandages.

"Bandages?" I said.

"That's right. Tom said a friend of his needed them."

"Did he mention the friend's name?"

"I don't think he did, no."

I called Dr. Brokaw's number, expecting to have to talk my way past his answering service. But he answered the phone himself, on the first ring. I told him what had happened.

"So they got clean away." He didn't try to conceal the relief in his voice.

"They got away, but not cleanly. We have the license number of their car now. They'll be picked up."

"The woman went with him, did she?"

"Evidently."

"Then it's pretty clear she isn't his prisoner."

"This isn't the same woman," I said. "I don't know what he did with Laurel Russo."

"Who is the woman with him?"

"I think her name is Gloria. You wouldn't be likely to know her. Have you had any luck with the hospitals, Doctor?"

"As a matter of fact, I have. I'm not sure that luck is the word, though. The big hospital in West Los Angeles reports a patient missing—a Navy veteran named Nelson Bagley. He was taken out for dinner the night before last, and never came back."

"Who took him out for dinner?"

"That isn't clear. Do you want to follow up on this?"

"I intend to. It would help a good deal to have a doctor along, especially at night. These government hospitals can be pretty stuffy about giving out information."

Brokaw didn't answer immediately. "All right, I'll meet you there."

XXXI

I parked in front of the hospital and went in rather reluctantly. I had been there before, and knew how dim and depressing the lobby was—a warning of what could happen to any man. Some men to whom it had happened were sitting around the big room. A few of them had friends or relatives with them.

Dr. Brokaw was at the desk talking to a woman who looked rather like a veteran herself, but more like an old sergeant than a private. She had that glazed look of limited command. "This is Miss Shell," Brokaw said. "Miss Shell remembers checking out Nelson Bagley the night before last."

"Indeed I do." She chopped at the air with her profile. "He was supposed to be back by ten that same night. I didn't want to let him go in the first place, but Dr. Lampson said it would be all right."

"Was Dr. Lampson his doctor?"

"Yes. I have a call in for him. The Doctor is the one who should be talking to you. All I did was check Bagley out. Dr. Lampson was the one who authorized it." The woman was very tense.

"Nobody's blaming you," Brokaw said in a soothing voice. "There was no way you could foresee what was going to happen."

"What did happen?" she said.

"We don't really know. Nelson Bagley was found in the ocean off Pacific Point this morning. Mr. Archer here was the one who brought him in."

The woman turned back to me. "Was he a suicide?"

"I doubt it very much. I think he was murdered."

Her lips tightened and her eyes dilated. "I had my suspicions of that young man. If I had had the final say, I wouldn't have trusted him out of my sight with any of the patients."

"Why wouldn't you trust him, Miss Shell?"

"I didn't like his demeanor. He wouldn't look me in the eye."

"What reason did he give for taking Bagley out of here?"

"He was going to treat him to a home-cooked dinner. That was his story, anyway."

A man in a white coat came striding across the lobby. Miss Shell gave him a single flashing accusatory look, then assumed the official mask that nurses wear in the presence of their superiors.

"Here's Dr. Lampson now."

He was a tall dark man with a face that had known pain. His black hair was short, almost military in cut, and his body was spare. He nodded soberly to Brokaw, who introduced himself and then me. Lampson led us to a deserted corner of the room where the three of us sat down on plastic chairs.

"What happened to Nelson?" he said.

I told him in some detail. Lampson listened carefully. Like the building in which he practiced, his eyes were full of shadows.

"I don't understand it," he said when I had finished. "You saw Nelson last night—Wednesday night—at a seafood restaurant in Pacific Point. But he left here Tuesday night, about five-thirty, supposedly to have dinner with some friends. What happened in the meantime?"

"I can tell you one thing that happened," Dr. Brokaw said. "Harold Sherry brought him to me in Long Beach yesterday."

"You know Harold Sherry?"

"He's my patient."

"What sort of a man is he?"

Brokaw shot a questioning glance at me, which I returned. He lowered his head in embarrassed thought, cupping his bearded chin in his hand.

"I can't really answer that question."

"How long has he been your patient, Doctor?" Lampson said.

"A couple of months. I didn't get to know him well. I realized that Harold had certain problems."

"What sort of problems?"

I said, "Harold shot a man this afternoon, and got shot himself. The police are looking for him now, and so am I. He's wanted on suspicion of kidnapping."

Lampson's eyes winced, but otherwise he gave no sign of shock or surprise. "Harold does seem to have his problems. What were you treating him for, Dr. Brokaw?"

"He came to me with what he thought was V.D. It turned out to be a minor infection which was easily cleared up. I went on seeing him because he obviously needed someone to talk to. He was quite bitter about his father and certain other people, and I suppose I sensed that he was bent on trouble. Which I wasn't successful in heading off, I'm afraid." Brokaw hung his shaggy head and blew his nose.

Lampson turned to me, a little impatiently. "Do you know Harold Sherry?"

"I'm getting to know him, at a distance. I've never talked to him. I'd like very much to know what his interest was in your patient Nelson Bagley."

"So would I. I don't understand it at all."

"How did he contact Bagley, do you know?"

"A young woman brought him here sometime in the last week or so. She'd visited Bagley before. I believe she had some kind of family connection."

"With Bagley or with Harold?"

"With Bagley. Her connection with Harold was obvious enough. She was crazy about him."

"Can you describe her, Doctor?"

Lampson raised his eyes to a corner of the ceiling. "A rather large girl, quite nice-looking, brunette—age, I'd say, close to thirty."

"Is her name Gloria?"

"Yes, it is. I never did get her last name."

The dim air of the place oppressed me. I felt as if I was lost in the catacombs under a city where no one could be trusted or believed.

"Flaherty. I know the woman," I said. "She's on the run with Harold now."

"I'm surprised to hear that, frankly. She seemed to be quite a decent girl."

Brokaw raised his head. "She is. I saw her—"

He stopped, his mouth open like a red wound in his beard. His eyes shifted from Lampson's face to mine. Then he hung his head again, hiding his face under the thatch of his hair.

Lampson looked at me and raised his eyebrows questioningly. I shook my head in answer. As if he had heard the inaudible interchange, Brokaw got up and walked away. He looked back once before he reached the door, but made no gesture of farewell.

"What's the matter with him?" Lampson asked me.

"I'm not sure. I think he bought a large piece of Harold Sherry, and now he's embarrassed by it."

"He acts as if he's guiltily involved."

"No. I'm pretty sure he isn't."

"What was he going to say about seeing the girl? Do you know?"

"No."

I was surprised to find myself fronting for Brokaw. Perhaps I owed him that. He had been painfully honest with me. But his departure left questions hanging in the room.

"Did you say you knew Gloria, Mr. Archer?"

"I've talked to her a couple of times. I got the same impression of her as you did—that she was well-intentioned and reasonably honest. She may be, at that. She wouldn't be the first nice girl that's taken up with a sociopath."

"Is that what Harold is?"

"He has some of the earmarks."

"What's this about a kidnapping?"

I told him, omitting Laurel's name. Lampson screwed his face up as I spoke, and smoothed it out with his hand. He repeated the gesture several times.

"It hurts me to think that I let my patient leave the hospital with Sherry."

"Why did you?"

"I didn't see how any harm could come to him with Gloria involved. And Harold Sherry seemed genuinely interested in him. It was the first invitation of the kind that Nelson had had in the time I've been working with him. When I became his doctor, he was very nearly catatonic, completely uncommunicative, oblivious to the world. I'd been trying to bring him out of that, and succeeding. At the same time, his physical health had improved. I thought he was ready to do a little socializing. Anyway, I could see no harm in trying it." He showed his teeth in an unsmiling grin. "How wrong can a man be? When I signed him out of here, I signed his death warrant."

There was grief in his voice. Though Lampson kept his feelings under firm control, I was reminded of Ellis's wild outburst in the morgue. Neither the doctor nor the avgas man had killed Nelson Bagley, but both of them felt guilty in his death. I said:

"You're not the only one who feels responsible for what happened to Nelson Bagley. This afternoon in the Pacific Point morgue, I talked to a man named Ellis who believed that he had killed him. He had been an avgas officer on the *Canaan Sound,* Nelson's ship, and he told me he made the mistake that burned the ship. Ellis was pretty distraught, close to hallucination. He thought, or said he thought, that Nelson's body had been in the ocean for over twenty-five years—that he had floated in all the way from Okinawa."

"He might as well have," Lampson said. "He didn't have much life in those years. Did this officer—Ellis?"

"Ellis."

"Did this Ellis explain what he did that caused the fire on the *Canaan Sound?*"

"He said he made a mistake in pressure which ruptured one of the gas tanks."

"Really?"

"I'm not lying. I don't think Ellis was either."

"No. He wasn't lying."

"Have you talked to Ellis, Doctor?"

"I talked to Nelson." His mouth was twisted in a complex smile. "It doesn't matter now—now that he's dead—but his memory was gradually returning. Just last week, he told me about the ruptured gasoline tank on his carrier. It was the last thing he remembered about the *Canaan Sound*—the last thing he remembered for many years."

"What brought his memory back, Doctor?"

"I'd like to attribute it to my art." He pinched his nose as if to punish his pride, and looked at me over his fingers with black intent eyes. "But the truth is, I'm not that good. I'm not even a trained psychiatrist. I have to admit that Nelson got more of a charge from Gloria's visits than he ever got from mine. You can understand why I encouraged her to take an interest in him. I felt that between the two of us we were bringing him back to life. I could sense forgotten material coming up to the surface, or near the surface, of his mind. Even his poor body seemed to be responding. But all I succeeded in doing was to set him up for death."

His voice was harsh, full of the general anger which young men often turn against themselves. He closed his eyes, and his face became vulnerable

"Nelson Bagley was quite important to you, Doctor."

"He was my Lazarus." He spoke with irony and regret. "I thought that I could raise him from the dead. But I should have let him lie."

"Why do you say that?"

He leaned toward me, the plastic chair complaining under his weight. "I'm wondering—at least it's possible that Nelson was killed because his memory was coming back. Some pretty explosive material came up the last time I talked to him."

"What kind of material?"

"Some of it had to do with the death of a woman. He talked about her as if she was his wife. But I checked his records, and there was no indication that Nelson had ever been married."

"What happened to the woman?"

"Apparently she was murdered a long time ago. It may have been in the same year that the gas tank ruptured and sent him into the sea. The dead woman and the ruptured gas tank came up together in the same interview."

"Just last week?"

"That's right."

"How was the woman killed?"

"She was shot. Nelson may have shot her himself, though he didn't say so."

"You think Nelson was murdered because he remembered the murder of the woman?"

As if he had made himself more vulnerable, Lampson raised his fist to his mouth and spoke behind it. "I'm not offering it as a theory, exactly. But the possibility did occur to me. There aren't too many conceivable motives for killing a poor little man like Nelson Bagley. He had no money and no connections that I know of." He dropped his fist.

"You said he might have shot her himself. There's a

possible motive in that for killing him. Have you made any attempt to find out who the woman was?"

"No. I intended to, but I've been too busy."

"What was her name?"

"Nelson called her Allie, I believe."

"What makes you think he shot her?"

"He blamed himself."

"Exactly what did he say?"

Lampson brooded over the question. "I don't recall his exact words, and exact words are important. As a matter of fact, I wasn't sure if he was talking about killing a woman or making love to her, or possibly both." He looked up at me with a certain resentment. "I didn't mean to tell you this."

"I'm glad you did."

"What good can it possibly do? The woman is dead, and so is Nelson."

"You want to know who killed him," I said, "and why. Unless we do find out, his death is meaningless, and maybe his life is, too."

Lampson nodded quickly, once. "You're right. It's what it's all about, isn't it?—to find some meaning. That's what Nelson was trying to do. He lived like a vegetable for over twenty-five years. But towards the end he was coming back to life, struggling for meaning. And I was trying to help him."

Lampson was opening up. I liked what I saw in him, and I asked him:

"What got you interested in Nelson?"

"He seemed so utterly hopeless, physically and mentally. I gave him quite a lot of my time—more than I should have, perhaps. I'm afraid I stole some time from my other patients."

"Why?"

"I don't know why. Yes, I do. Nelson reminded me a little of my father." Lampson's eyes focused as if he were looking down a dark mine. "My father was killed on Guadalcanal when I was quite young."

"And that's why you're here?"

"In this hospital, you mean? I'm sure it's one reason. But you're not here to investigate me. Or are you?" He was getting nervous again, and closing up.

"I need your help, Doctor. I'm trying to find a woman who was abducted last night. This afternoon, Harold Sherry collected a hundred thousand dollars ransom for her and shot her father. The way to the missing woman seems to lead through here."

Lampson peered out across the lobby as if he might catch a glimpse of the woman, or see some trace she had left. The room was almost empty now. Many of the visitors had gone, and the patients were drifting back into the interior of the hospital like ghosts at cockcrow.

"What is the woman's name?"

"Laurel Russo."

Lampson reached out and took hold of my wrist. "Russo?"

"That's correct."

His grip on my wrist tightened. "That was the name of the dead woman."

"The one that Nelson was talking about?"

"Yes. Her name was Allie Russo."

We sat facing each other like linked mirror images. I rotated my wrist to remind him that he was holding on to it. He dropped it as if it was hot.

"Did you keep any record of your conversation with Nelson?"

"I made a few notes."

"May I see them, Doctor?"

"I'm afraid they're private."

"So am I. I don't intend to take them away with me. I simply want to have a look at them."

He hesitated. I said:

"There's a woman missing, remember. Apparently she's in the hands of a dangerous man. That should override a dead patient's right to privacy."

Lampson gave me his quick nod of assent. "Come into my office."

I followed him down a corridor, the hospital atmosphere thickening around me. The scarred metal desk in Lampson's office was piled with papers, which he shuffled through. He handed me a sheet of yellow foolscap on which he had written in pencil:

Name was Allie Russo I wanted to marry her

*but she turned against me I used to follow her around
saw the life she led. One night I watched through the
Venetian blinds they were doing it and I blew my top
and I did a terrible thing to her. I asked the Lord to
forgive me but he didn't. He busted the gas tank and
set us on fire and I been living in hell here ever since
then.*

Lampson and I sat in silence for a minute. The small
office seemed crowded with past life.

"What do you think he did to her?" I said.

"He seemed to feel responsible for her death. But he
may not have done what he thought he did. Sometimes a
man like Nelson feels terribly guilty simply because he's
been punished so terribly."

XXXII

There was a light in Tom Russo's house. I knocked
on the front door, and after a while I heard slow footsteps behind it. The door opened slightly.

I thought at the first uncertain glance that the face
that appeared in the opening belonged to Tom, and that
it had been deeply marked by grief. Then I saw that it
was the face of an older man who resembled him. I
said:

"Is Tom at home?"

"What do you want with him?"

"We have some business."

"What kind of business?"

In a younger man, his abrupt questions would have
been rude or even hostile. But I sensed the anxiety behind them, the old man's vulnerability.

"I'm a private detective, and I've been helping Tom
to look for his wife. Do you happen to know where he
is?"

"He had to give his cousin a lift someplace."

"Redondo Beach?"

"I think he mentioned Redondo. He asked me to stay

here in case anything came up. But he should have been back long ago."

"Are you his father?"

"That's right." His dark eyes showed some pleasure. "There always was a resemblance between he and I. A lot of people made a comment about it. Do you want to come in? Tom should be home any time."

"I'll wait. I have some information for Tom."

He took me into the front room and we sat facing each other. He was a fairly good-looking man of seventy or so, with a lot of wavy iron-grey hair. He wore a dark suit which had recently been pressed.

"Information about his wife?" he asked me after a long polite pause.

"About his wife," I said, "and about his mother."

He flinched and looked down at his hands, which were slightly misshapen and lined with ineradicable grime. "I was married to Tom's mother."

"What happened to her, Mr. Russo?"

"She was shot to death in this house when Tom was a little boy." He looked up anxiously. "Has Tom been asking questions about his mother?"

"He was dreaming about her this morning."

Russo leaned forward stiffly from the waist. "What did he say?"

I avoided answering his question. "Nothing that made much sense. Does he know what happened to her, Mr. Russo?"

The old man shook his head. "He knew at the time, all right, but then he forgot about it. I let him forget. Maybe I made a mistake. I was thinking tonight that maybe I made a mistake. When he picked me up at the home today, I hardly knew my boy. He wasn't the happy, cheerful boy I raised. But if I made a mistake I had my reasons. He was so young when it happened—no more than five—I didn't think it would leave any mark on him. I thought we could move back here, him and I, and start together with a clean slate." His voice and eyes were profoundly disappointed.

"Move back here from where, Mr. Russo?"

"Bremerton, in the state of Washington. It all started during the war, when I went to Bremerton to work in the shipyards. I rented this house to some people and took Allie and little Tom along with me. But they didn't stay. Allie made up her mind to leave me. She brought little Tom back here and they lived in this house for a year while I stayed on in Bremerton by myself."

"When did you come back?"

"Not until after Allie was dead. They brought me down here when they found her body. Somebody shot her. I guess I told you that."

"Where did they find her body, Mr. Russo?"

"On the floor in the back bedroom." He flung out a heavy careless arm toward the room where Tom had been dreaming that morning, dreaming as if he had fallen asleep as a child and had never fully awakened.

"And where was Tom?"

"He was here in the house with her. He must have been here alone with her for a while. The police said she was dead for several days already when they found her." Sudden tears brightened his eyes. "Tom went to the neighbors when he finally ran out of anything to eat. Don't ask me why he didn't go before. I think he was scared to. You know how little kids are. They think they'll get blamed for everything that happens."

"Did you talk to him about it?"

"Not very much. I let the sleeping dogs lie." He dashed his tears away with his fingers, first from one eye, then the other. "Maybe you think I made a mistake when I stayed on in this house with Tom. But it was my house, and I had a right to live here. It was the only house I ever owned. I got a real good buy on it when I married Tom's mother in 1937. Tom has his reasons to be grateful for this house. I borrowed on it to send him to pharmacy school. He makes good money as a pharmacist, and now he's buying the place from me. With Social Security, it's what I'm living on at the home. I don't know where I'd be without this house."

"Nobody's criticizing you, Mr. Russo."

"That's what you think. His mother's people criticized me plenty for living here with Tom. I thought me and him could live it all down, you know?" But he glanced around the room as if the past had surrounded him and closed ranks. "What did Tom say to you this morning?

Did he remember his mother and what happened to her?"

"I think he was trying to."

"Did he name any names?"

"Not to me," I said. "Did he name any names to you?"

The old man shook his head. I studied his face, which was lined and segmented like a puzzle.

"Do you have any idea who killed her?"

He gave me an evasive look. "The way the police talked at first, they thought I killed her myself. But I could prove I was in Bremerton. I hadn't even seen Allie for a year. More than a year."

"Why did they suspect you?"

He made an explanatory movement with his open hands. "You know how they are. The husband is always the first one that they look for. And by the time they finished with me, the man that done it—the man that did it was halfway around the world."

"Halfway around the world?"

"That's what I said."

"Do you have somebody definite in mind?"

"Yes, sir, I do." He leaned toward me. His large-knuckled fingers closed on my knee. "I'm pretty sure who killed Allie. It all hangs together, see? She met him in Bremerton—he was in the skeleton crew of one of the escort carriers I helped to build. The *Canaan Sound*. He was the reason she left me in the first place. We had a fight about him and she walked out. She only stayed in Bremerton as long as the *Canaan Sound* was there, with Bagley aboard her—his name was Nelson Bagley. And when Bagley's ship moved out of there, Allie moved out, too, and took my boy along with her."

"How do you know Bagley killed her?"

"It all hangs together. When I came down from Bremerton to look after little Tom, he told me Bagley'd been here at the house."

"Did he name him?"

"He described him to me. But when I tried to get Tom to talk to the police he clammed up. They said they had no evidence on Bagley—I could see it was me they wanted to hang it on. So I made my own investigation, and I got a reporter interested. He wrote a story about Bagley with everything in it except Bagley's name —description and everything. I'm still as certain as I live that Nelson Bagley was the man."

"What made you so certain?"

"The clincher," he said, "was when I found out the *Canaan Sound* was anchored in Long Beach Harbor the night Allie was killed. That was Nelson Bagley's ship, and Bagley had shore leave that night. He came into town here and killed her and went back aboard his ship. The very next morning—that was May 3, 1945—she sailed for Okinawa. By the time they found Allie's body, Nelson Bagley was halfway around the world."

I made a note of the date he had given me. "Why did he kill her, Mr. Russo?"

"I think she took up with another man. It was crazy jealousy on Bagley's part."

"Do you know who the man was?"

"It could of been one of his shipmates, I don't know. They were a wild-living crew in Bremerton. And they came to a bad end. I found out later what happened to that ship. She burned off Okinawa. Do you know what happened to Bagley? He was fried in oil, and that was heaven's judgment on him. The final clincher."

"There's been another judgment on him," I said. "Bagley was drowned last night. But I don't think heaven had much to do with it."

The old man rose and stood over me, swaying slightly. "How could he be drowned? He was a patient in the vets' hospital."

"He was. But Cousin Gloria and her boy friend took him out of there."

His brow knitted. "How could they? The hospital people told me he was nothing more than a living corpse. They wouldn't even let me see him."

"When was that, Mr. Russo?"

"A long time ago, just after the war."

"He improved a lot since then, apparently. But it didn't do him much good in the long run."

Russo walked to the far end of the room and came back very slowly. "You don't think Gloria killed him, do you?"

"I don't know. How does Gloria feel about the death of her aunt?"

"I never discussed it with her," Russo said. "After Allie got herself killed, I never saw much of her side of the family. Gloria's mother—that's Allie's sister Martie —is an unforgiving woman. Even after I proved to the authorities that I was in Bremerton when Allie was killed, her sister Martie never forgave me. She always believed that Allie left me in Bremerton because I treated her bad. But that was a lie. I treated Allie the best way I knew how." He looked at me with eyes like the charred ends of memory. "Sometimes I wish I never bought this house. Never took up with Allie. Never had the boy. The whole thing went sour on me."

"Why, Mr. Russo?"

He sat with his face quiet and open to the past. "This is a bad house for marriages. Look at what happened to my son's marriage. I made a mistake to ever buy this house."

XXXIII

There was the sound of a car in the street. It stopped in front of the house, and Russo lifted his head.

"That's Tom's car now. I know cars. I had my own filling station until gasoline rationing set in back in the forties." He spoke as if it had happened yesterday.

Tom came in and greeted his father with anxious solicitude. "How are you doing, Dad?"

"I'm all right. Why shouldn't I be all right?"

"I didn't mean to keep you waiting so long."

"It's okay. Mr. Archer and me had things to talk about."

Tom turned to me. His eyes were wide, still full of the night outside. "Did you want to see me?"

"I have a few questions to ask you. Where have you been, by the way?"

"I dropped Gloria off. Then I did some driving around. I went to Pacific Point to find out if Laurel's parents had heard anything. But there was nobody in the house."

"Laurel's father was shot this afternoon. He's in the Pacific Point hospital, and his wife is with him."

"Who shot him?"

"Harold Sherry." I told Tom what had happened at the hunting club.

He sat on a hassock, leaning forward with his arms on his knees, his hands dangling limply, his eyes puzzled and hurt. I asked him if he had seen Harold. He shook his head.

"Do you know where he is, Tom?"

"Gloria asked me not to say."

"Did Gloria know he was wanted by the police?"

The question jolted him. "No. I mean, if she did know she didn't tell me."

"What did she tell you?"

"He phoned her here. He said that he was injured. He didn't say anything about a shooting. I thought it was an accident, and that was why he needed bandages."

"Did you see him, Tom?"

"No. He didn't want me to come into the motel."

"Was it the Myrtle Motel, in Redondo Beach?"

He shook his head. "I'm not supposed to say."

"You're not on Harold's side, Tom. And he's not on yours. He grabbed your wife last night, and apparently he's holding her for ransom. I told you about it this morning. Don't you remember?"

"No. I didn't talk to you this morning, did I?"

"You were in bed, just waking up."

"Oh, yes, I remember." But I could see that he didn't.

His father leaned toward him and prodded his shoulder. "Talk to the man. He's on your side. He wants to get your wife back."

Tom grimaced in pain, as if his father had poked him with an electric rod. "Okay, okay. It was the Myrtle in Redondo Beach."

"They're not there any more," I said. "Where would they go from there?"

"I don't know. I don't understand what's going on. Is Gloria mixed up in this?"

"One way or another, she has to be. How did she meet Harold, do you know?"

He answered after a while: "It happened right here in this house. Laurel met him in town someplace, and they were old school friends and she brought him home for dinner. Then Gloria dropped in, and Gloria and Harold hit it off. I guess they saw quite a bit of each other after that."

"Where did they see each other?"

"Partly here, and partly at her place, I guess. Mostly at her place. I didn't like the idea of him hanging around here too much, especially when I was working nights. Laurel and me—Laurel and I had one or two discussions about it. As a matter of fact, I think that's one reason she moved out on me. He had a very funny effect on Laurel."

"How close were they?"

The question bothered him, perhaps because his father was there to listen to the answer. Tom got up from his hassock and moved away from both of us, very tentatively, like a blind man exploring a strange room. He turned and spoke softly across it:

"They weren't sleeping together, if that's what you mean. I mean, Gloria was the one he was interested in in that way. But he had a very peculiar effect on Laurel. He could make her get excited by saying things. I don't mean in a sexual way, exactly—it was more like somebody taking amphetamines and drinking. I don't mean she was doing that, but that was the way she acted. She'd get funny and loud and silly. I didn't like it. So the last time he came here, a week or so ago, I told him not to come back."

"And Laurel moved out on you?"

"That's right."

"Do you think she's been seeing Harold since?"

"You told me he kidnapped her. That's seeing him," he said miserably.

I repeated the question I had asked him that morning. "Could it be a fake kidnapping, Tom? Something they cooked up together to raise money from Laurel's relatives?"

Tom had been avoiding his father's eyes. Now he

turned and looked at him. The old man's face had darkened and changed shape, as if it had been squeezed into a rectangular box.

"It's getting late, Dad. I better take you back to the home."

"So I won't hear what's been going on in this house?"

"Nothing's been going on in this house."

"Don't try to kid me, and don't try to kid yourself. You've been sitting around and letting it happen, making my mistakes all over again. I thought you'd learn from what happened to your mother."

"What *did* happen to my mother?" Tom's voice was thin and desperate, as if he dreaded the answer to his question.

"She was murdered here in this house, in the back bedroom." Russo spoke with the half-conscious cruelty of an old man who had failed to learn from his suffering. "You ought to remember, you were here in the house when he did it to her. You remembered at the time."

Tom's face lost blood as if a plug had been pulled. He clenched his fists and raised them beside his head and ran at his father. Old Russo half rose to meet him, but was flung back into his chair by Tom's assault.

I caught Tom around the waist and dragged him clear. The old man was bleeding at the side of the mouth. I maneuvered Tom into a chair against the opposite wall and stood over him. He began to sob.

"Ask him who shot his mother," the old man said behind me. "He was here in the house when it happened. Go ahead and ask him."

Russo was angry and excited. The harsh memory of the past had been too much for him, and he seemed to be taking revenge on his son for the loss of his wife. I wondered if he had been doing that ever since he came back from Bremerton to look after the boy.

Tom's dry sobs were like hiccups which convulsed his entire body. The old man took him by the shoulders. "Was it Nelson Bagley?"

"I don't know. I don't know." His voice was high and level.

"Was he wearing a sailor suit?"

"Yes. But he took it off and they made jingle bells."

Violence repeats itself like a tic, and the room was full of potential violence. Old Russo began to shake Tom.

"Why didn't you tell the police that at the time? It's too late now."

"That's right, Mr. Russo. It's too late. Why don't you lay off him now?"

"He's my son."

"Treat him like one. He's scared and upset and he's lost his wife——"

"I lost my wife, too," the older man said.

"I'm aware of that. All the more reason why you should go easy on your son."

Like a fighter after a hard round, Russo moved to the far side of the room. He sat down and looked at the floor. I could hear his breathing gradually slowing down.

He rose and approached his son and touched him on the face. Tom returned the gesture.

"It's okay, Dad," he said.

Then Tom walked a little unsteadily out of the room. I followed him down the hall toward his bedroom. I had an impulse to stop him, keep him out of the dangerous lair of the past. But when he turned the light on it looked no worse than any other room with an unmade bed.

I stood in the doorway. "When did you start remembering your mother again?"

"I never forgot my mother."

"I mean about her death—how she was killed."

"It just started today, I think. Anyway, since Laurel went away. It keeps running through my head like a film clip—her on the bed, and the man on top of her."

"Was there more than one man?"

"No. I don't know."

His voice was rising again. He sat abruptly on the edge of the bed and, like a bivalve closing, covered his face with his hands.

"I won't make you talk about it now. But think about it, will you?"

"I don't want to think about it," he said behind his hands.

"Give it a try anyway. Make some notes, if you can. Anything you remember may be important."

"Why? It won't bring her back."

"No, but it may help with Laurel. Did you see Laurel today, Tom?"

"No. Of course not."

"Where do you think she is?"

He dropped his hands. "How should I know? Laurel doesn't tell me where she goes."

I sat on the bed beside him. "Do you think she's been kidnapped?"

"No." Then he reconsidered. "I don't know. I didn't think Harold was that rough."

"He's rough."

Tom screwed up his face. "I must have been crazy to let him into the house. I thought he was her old school friend. And then he got interested in Gloria. Since she divorced Flaherty, she hasn't had too many fellows interested in her."

"Harold was interested in her car, wasn't he?"

"That's right. Her car was one of the main attractions."

"Did he give any indication of what he wanted it for?"

"He wanted to take somebody for a ride. I don't mean that the way it sounds, exactly. They were just going to take somebody to her mother's place for dinner. I heard Gloria talking to him about it on the phone."

"When?"

"A couple of days ago. What day is this?"

"Thursday."

"Then it was Tuesday."

"Who were they going to take for dinner?"

"Somebody from the hospital. I didn't catch the name."

"Where does her mother live?"

"Aunt Martie runs a motor court on the Coast Highway. It isn't much of a place. She's had some reverses since her husband left her."

"Topanga Court?"

"That's right. Do you know the place?"

"I was there this morning." And Aunt Martie had lied to me about the tweed suit.

XXXIV

There were several cars in the yard under the cliff, but none of them was the green Falcon that belonged to Gloria. I parked in front of the office and went inside.

The bell jingled over the door. Behind the archway, the television set was talking in brash young voices that sounded like descendants of the voices I'd heard that morning. Mrs. Mungan appeared, wearing her red wig lower on her forehead.

"How are you, Mrs. Mungan?"

"Surviving," she said. "Do I know you?"

Her eyes seemed to peer at me through a glaze of time or distance, as if my morning visit had occurred a long time ago. Then she remembered me.

"What do you want now?"

"A little help. You weren't much help this morning. You said you gave Joe Sperling's tweed suit to a little old man who took off down the beach. You didn't mention his name or his background, but I'm pretty sure you knew both. You didn't mention that he came here in the company of your daughter and her boy friend, and probably took off with them as well."

She didn't deny any of it. She leaned across the counter, supporting her weight on her arms. If I had lit a match, I could have set fire to her breath.

"What have you got against us, anyway?"

"Nothing."

"Then why don't you go away and leave us alone? My daughter is a good girl. All she ever did was try to do the right thing. Which is more than you can say for most of us."

"What about Harold?"

She considered the question. "I didn't say I'd vouch for him."

"Are they here?"

"No. They're not."

"Have you seen them tonight?"

She shook her head. "I didn't see Gloria last night, either. She lent her car to Harold, and spent the night at her cousin's."

"Where is Gloria spending tonight?"

She looked through the open door toward the highway. Her eyes seemed to reflect the light-streaked darkness.

"I wish I knew. I've been expecting to hear from her."

"I know where she was a couple of hours ago," I said. "In a motel in Redondo Beach looking after Harold."

"Is there something the matter with Harold."

"He was shot. He kidnapped Tom Russo's wife, and her father shot him when he picked up the ransom money."

"You've got to be kidding."

But she knew I wasn't. She put her face down on her arms and rested it there for a moment. When she lifted it and showed it to me again, it hadn't changed very much, except for the glint of terror in the eyes.

She licked her dry lips. "I was afraid she'd get into trouble if she took up with Harold." She paused, and sucked her breath in. "Did you say he kidnapped Laurel?"

"That's right. Could we sit down in the back and have a talk, Mrs. Mungan?"

She glanced behind her through the archway as if she had to ask permission of someone or something there, perhaps the television voices. "I don't know."

"It could be important, to you and Gloria. She's in trouble, probably through no fault of her own."

"That was the story of her marriage. Bob Flaherty ran up a pile of debts and left her holding the bag. The same thing happened with me and her father—"

I cut in: "This is worse. If Gloria goes along with Harold and helps him get away, she'll be treated the same as he will. And Harold has a good chance of being shot on sight."

Her fingers went to her mouth, pressing it back into shape. "What can I do?"

"You can talk to me. I think this present trouble goes back a long way, at least as far as the murder of your sister Allie."

"You know about that?"

"Not as much as you do, Mrs. Mungan. May I come in?"

She opened the gate at the side of the desk and let me into the back room, where she turned off the television set. I could hear the background noises of the highway. Before I sat down in the armchair she offered me, I glanced at the pictures on the walls. One of them was a photograph of a young woman who looked as Mrs. Mungan might have looked when she was young.

Her breast nudged my arm. "That was my sister Allie. I guess you've seen her picture?"

"No, I haven't. She was very pretty."

"Yes, she was the pretty one in the family." She opened a drawer and handed me a smaller and younger photograph. "This was her graduation picture when she graduated from Fresno High in 1935. She was a real stunner, as you can see."

I nodded in agreement, though the fine eyes which confronted me in the picture had long since been closed.

"She was nice, too," the woman said. "It isn't fair, what happens to some people. It would have made more sense if I'd been shot instead of Allie."

She slumped in a chair. I was afraid she might dissolve in tears, and be lost as a witness. But perhaps her tears had all run out long ago. The only effect of the shocks she'd been experiencing seemed to be that she was sobering up.

"Who shot Allie?" I said.

"That's the question I've been asking myself for more than twenty-five years. I lie awake in the middle of the night thinking about it."

"And what do you think, Mrs. Mungan?"

"I used to think it was her husband, Russo. Allie married beneath her, and he was an older man, insanely jealous." It sounded like a line she had repeated many times, until it had become a piece of family folklore. "But the police said he couldn't have done it. He didn't miss a day of work in the shipyards, and it would have taken him a couple of days anyway to make the trip back and forth between here and Bremerton."

"What made Russo jealous?"

"That's just the way he was."

"Were there other men in your sister's life?"

"I didn't say that."

"I'm asking you, Mrs. Mungan."

"I'm not answering. Let her rest in peace, why can't you?"

"Other people are being killed. Tom Russo's wife has been kidnapped, and your daughter Gloria is involved with the kidnapping."

"You told me that before. I don't believe it."

"After everything that's happened in your family, you don't believe it?"

Her mouth opened and stretched wide. The flesh around her eyes crinkled. She looked as if she had seen a ghost and was getting ready to scream. But she was silent, looking inward as if the ghost was in her mind.

"Was Nelson Bagley your sister's lover?"

"No. He wanted to be. He used to follow her around like a dog. But Allie wasn't really interested in him."

"How do you know that?"

"She wrote me about him from Bremerton. Russo was jealous of him, but he was a joke to Alison."

"Sometimes a joke like that turns out to be not so funny."

"What do you mean?"

"Russo thinks Bagley killed her."

"I know that. He tried to nail Bagley after he got back from the war. But by that time Bagley was a helpless cripple. His ship burned and he went overboard and it knocked all the sense out of his head. The police said even if it was true they had no way or proving it at that late date. And they couldn't drag a man like Bagley into a courtroom."

"But you dragged him here Tuesday night."

"I didn't drag him. I had him here for dinner. Anyway, it was Harold's idea. He was interested in what caused the fire on the ship, and he thought maybe Nelson Bagley could tell him something."

"What did Nelson tell him?"

"I don't know. I got pretty upset myself, and I drank too much before dinner. When I saw Nelson Bagley and tried to talk to him, the whole thing fell on me like a ton of bricks and I started drinking. I didn't sober up until the next morning, and by that time they were long gone."

"Harold and Gloria and Nelson Bagley were gone?"

"That's right. I naturally thought they took him back to the hospital. When you came in this morning—and told me Bagley was dead, I panicked. I told you the first thing that came into my head."

"Did you say you talked to Bagley Tuesday night?"

She hesitated. "We exchanged some words, yes."

"What did he say?"

"He said that he was sorry about Allie."

"Is that all?"

"Let me think." She frowned as if she was listening to an imperfect playback. "He didn't say much, and even then I wasn't able to catch everything he said. He couldn't talk very well, and I was upset just having him here. He was like a ghost from the past, you know? A poor little roughed-up hammered-down ghost."

"Did you ask him any questions?"

"I tried to, but we didn't get very far. I asked him who killed my sister. He said he didn't know. I finally got him to admit that he knew Allie in Bremerton before she left her husband. He claimed he didn't know her intimately, that she was interested in another man. I asked him some questions about the man. He said he didn't remember. It may have been true—he had a memory like a sieve. And the truth is, I got tired of pressing him. Talking to that poor little incinerated man made me realize that Allie had been dead for over twenty-five years and no amount of questions or answers would bring her back.

"Anyway, Harold came in and broke it up. He said it was time to watch some television. I needed a drink real badly by that time—to put down the past, you know? I try not to drink in front of Gloria—it sets a bad example—so I took the bottle into my room and locked the door and I guess I must have passed out." She closed her eyes, miming the passage of the night. "When I woke up, it was morning and they were gone and all the dirty dishes were in the sink."

"Have you seen Gloria since Tuesday night?"

"I don't think so. No, I haven't. She phoned me last night, from Tom Russo's house. She said she couldn't get home because Harold had her car. It's the only car in the family, and I'm dependent on Gloria for transportation since I lost my license—"

I interrupted her. "If Gloria calls again, will you tell her I want to talk to her? Tell her it's a matter of life and death."

"Whose life and death? Hers?"

"It could be. Did she tell you what Harold was doing with her car?"

"No. I didn't ask her. I thought it was sort of funny, though, since they just started going together."

"How long ago did they start?"

"A week or two, maybe. But things happen fast these days. The men are so impatient, and the girls have to go along."

"Did Gloria mention Nelson Bagley on the phone last night?"

Mrs. Mungan hesitated. She looked at me sidewise and licked her upper lip with the tip of her tongue.

"Did she mention Nelson Bagley?" I repeated.

"I guess she did, at that."

"What did she say about him?"

"That Harold was taking him for a little vacation. And if anybody asked about him, I wasn't to tell them anything. That was why I lied to you this morning. God knows I didn't know he was dead."

"How did he happen to be wearing that tweed suit?"

"I gave it to him. The clothes he had on weren't warm enough for him when he got here. It struck me that he was about Mungan's height—when Mungan was younger, I mean. I got out the old tweed suit and it was big, but he could wear it. I had to help him on with it, though, he was so shaky on his pins. When I saw that shriveled little throwaway of a man without his clothes, it really brought it home to me."

"Brought what home, Mrs. Mungan?"

"That we're all human. And we're all due to waste

away and die. I felt as though he climbed out of the same grave where my poor sister was buried. Now he's dead, too."

She fell into silence, peering from under the low red fringe of her wig at the blind eye of the television set. Gradually her face composed itself, as if everything she had told me had happened on an external screen which could be switched off.

I said, "What did Harold want to watch on television?"

My question startled her. "When do you mean?"

"You said he interrupted your talk with Bagley because he wanted to watch some television."

"That's right. He said that Bagley's old Captain was scheduled to come on at the start of the ten o'clock news."

"Captain Somerville?"

"I guess so. I didn't pay much attention. It was supposed to be something about oil. Did somebody spill some oil someplace?"

"Captain Somerville did."

"That's too bad," she said without comprehension.

"What was Bagley's reaction?"

"He came and sat where I'm sitting now."

"Did he see Somerville on the screen?"

"I don't know. That was when I went to get a drink." She gestured toward the closed door, and moved impatiently in her chair. "Would you object if I had a small one now? I didn't realize this was going to last so long."

"Neither did I. Go ahead and have a drink."

She got up and crossed the room, turning at the kitchen door. "I'd offer you one, but I've barely got enough for myself. You know how it is."

I knew how it was with drunks. They ran out of generosity, even for themselves. I was glad to be left alone in the room, relieved of the woman's worried presence.

Sitting among the sibilant echoes of her voice, I remembered something I had been told the night before by another woman. According to Elizabeth Somerville, a woman with a little boy had visited the Somervilles' house in Bel-Air when Elizabeth first came to live there. By now, the little boy would be thirty or so, Tom's age. The woman would be fifty or so, or dead.

I put my business card on the table beside Allie's graduation picture. Then I picked up the picture and took it with me into the wilds of Bel-Air.

XXXV

The Somerville house was blazing with lights as if there were a party going on inside. But there were no sounds of any kind except for the remote whir of traffic on the boulevards.

I pressed the doorbell and heard it ring inside. Quick footsteps approached the door. It was opened on its chain.

"Is that you, Ben?" Elizabeth Somerville said.

"Archer."

She hesitated. Then she unhooked the chain and opened the door. "Come in. I'm all alone. Smith drove down to Pacific Point to pick up my husband and sister-in-law."

"How is your sister-in-law?"

"Marian is taking this very hard. I didn't think she should spend the night by herself. So we're keeping her here for the duration." Her blue eyes gave me a swift appraisal in the lighted hall. "You don't look as if you're bringing us good news."

"I haven't found Laurel. But I have been making some progress. This is turning out to be a complex case. It isn't a simple kidnapping for ransom."

"Is that good, or bad?"

"Both. I have more to work with. But it's taking too much time. Harold Sherry may get impatient. He collected his hundred thousand, but unfortunately he and your brother exchanged shots. Sherry's wounded, and I don't know how that will affect the bargain."

"You think he might kill Laurel?"

"I wouldn't put it past him."

Her face became grave. "What do you want me to do?"

"Take a look at this picture and tell me if it means anything to you."

I got out Allie Russo's picture and showed it to Elizabeth. Her eyes became very intent.

"Do you recognize the woman?"

"I'm afraid I don't." She handed me the picture without looking up, and remained standing with her head bowed as if a heavy weight had fallen on her shoulders. "Ought I to?"

"It was just an off chance."

"Who is she, anyway?"

"Tom Russo's mother. Her name was Alison. They called her Allie."

"I didn't even know Tom had a mother."

"Most people do," I said. "Tom's mother was murdered here in Los Angeles in the spring of 1945. And I've got a feeling in my bones that her death was the beginning of all this present trouble."

She took the picture from between my fingers and studied it under the light. This time, when she handed it back, she stared directly into my face and denied very firmly that she knew the woman. But the look of her eyes was inward, as if a whole hidden world had opened behind them.

"You told me last night," I reminded her, "about a young woman with a little boy who came here to the house shortly after you were married. I believe your husband was overseas at the time."

"Yes." It was a question as well as an answer.

"I thought this might possibly be the woman."

I offered her the picture once again. She made no move to take it. "It isn't. It wasn't." But then she said, "Even if it was—supposing that it had been—what could it possibly have to do with Laurel?"

"We may know that when we find out who killed Allie Russo."

"Surely you don't suspect my husband of killing her."

"Do you suspect him?"

"Of course not. I didn't even know she was dead."

But the woman's death was very much with her now. Her eyes were heavy with it. She took me into her husband's study and slopped some whisky into a couple of glasses. She drank hers down, while I saved mine.

Her spirits rose superficially. Her color improved. But

the hidden world behind her eyes seemed to be changing and darkening. She couldn't keep herself from talking about it.

"What has Allie Russo's death got to do with us?"

"Her son married your niece Laurel, for one thing."

"Is that a crime?" she said in a brittle voice.

"No. I don't think it was a coincidence, either."

"Please explain that."

"I wish I could. So far, it's only a suspicion."

"And my husband's connection with all this is just another suspicion?"

"It's a little more than that."

She was silent for a minute, studying both my face and the situation. "I had no idea that Ben might conceivably be involved in all this. I still don't. But what did you mean when you said that it's more than a suspicion?"

"If I told you that, you'd have me shunted off the case."

"How could I do that?"

"I think you could do it. At any rate, you could make things very hard for me."

"I wouldn't, though, I swear I wouldn't."

I didn't quite believe her. She was having a reaction from the night before, when she had expressed her anger with her husband in every way she knew. Tonight she had pulled back into the shell of marriage, beyond my reach. She said:

"Do you *know* that Ben was involved with Allie Russo?"

"No, I don't. But I think he was one of several men in her life. Another was Nelson Bagley."

"I never heard of him."

"He was a messenger on your husband's ship. He went overboard when the ship burned at Okinawa. And by what appears to be a weird coincidence, he floated onto your mother's beach this morning."

"The little man with the tar on him?"

"That was Nelson Bagley."

"And what was his connection with Allie Russo?"

"He may have killed her. He may have seen her killed."

"But now he's dead himself."

"Yes. That's the point."

"Was he really a crew member of the *Canaan Sound?*"

"I'm sure he was."

Her eyes looked through me into the complex inner world that was growing like a city in her mind. "If Bagley was accused of killing the woman, does it mean that the *Canaan Sound* was here on the West Coast when she was killed?"

"Yes. The ship was at Long Beach. According to my information, Allie Russo was murdered the night of May 2nd, 1945. The *Canaan Sound* went to sea the following morning."

I could read the thought that followed in her mind, because it had followed in mine. Since the *Canaan Sound* was in port that night, its Captain was another possible suspect.

"How was she killed?"

I told Elizabeth. I told her further that the child Tom had been alone in the house with his mother's body for several days. I wanted her to understand what murder and its consequences could be like.

She shook her head as if to lose the knowledge. "My husband may be no great paragon. But he couldn't have done a thing like that. In fact, I know he didn't. He spent that whole last day and evening with me."

"Are you sure that's what you remember?"

"It certainly is. What's more, I believe I can prove it. I kept a diary that first year of my marriage. I think I still have it."

She excused herself and left the study. I sipped my drink, feeling some compunction about drinking the Captain's liquor under the circumstances. Elizabeth came back with a small locked book bound in padded white leather, with "1945 Diary" printed in gold on the cover. She unlocked it with a key, and opened it on her husband's desk to the entry for May 2nd.

I read it over her shoulder:

It's midnight and I'm very tired, diary, and very happy. Ben's station wagon just took him back to the ship. We had a lovely, lazy day in El Rancho and for the first time in months I felt really married. We let Jack and Marian and Laurel have the Bel-Air house to themselves—it was Jack's last day, too—and Ben and I spent the day with Father. Ben and Father really hit it off, which bodes well for the future. I showed Ben over River Valley School—someday we'll send our own children there!—and Ben told me something about his Navy experiences. I felt like Desdemona listening to Othello. And I forgave him (silently, dear diary—we didn't discuss the matter)—I forgave him for that woman who came to the house in March with her little boy. I feel as if I've finally become a woman myself. But now that he's gone, and I'm alone again, I'm just a little scared, diary. There's a terrible battle going on at Okinawa, and I think the Canaan Sound *is headed for there. Come home safely, husband.*

She raised her head. "I was only twenty-two, and still quite romantic. However, I had to show you this. It proves that Ben wasn't involved in that woman's death. He couldn't have been. He was involved with me, all day and all evening, and he went directly from Father's house in El Rancho back to his ship."

"How did he travel?"

"He had a Navy station wagon."

"Who drove it?"

She answered after a pause: "Some Navy man—I don't remember who."

"Smith?"

"It might have been Smith. I think it was. But please don't question him about it, will you?"

"Why not, if your husband is innocent?"

"He *is* innocent."

"Then you shouldn't object to my questioning Smith or anyone else."

Her eyes went dark with anger, sudden and stormy. "Don't tell me what I should or shouldn't do. This is my house you're in, and my life you're meddling with—"

"The point is that you have a life. Allie Russo lost hers."

I picked up Elizabeth's diary from the desk and riffled

through the pages. She made a move to stop me, but drew back. Her look of anger had changed to something more definite and personal. I got the impression that she was willing now to see the whole truth come out.

"Did you say the woman with the little boy came to your house in March?"

"Yes. It was early in March of 1945."

The entry was easy to find, under March 5th: "A strange thing happened today. A young woman and a small boy, aged about four or five, came to the house. She told me something so terrible that I'm not going to write it down, diary. But I'll never forget this day. It's made me a doubting Thomas. (The little boy's name was Thomas, the woman said.)"

I read it out loud to Elizabeth. She bowed her head: "I didn't remember what his name was. Or that I'd written it down."

But I wondered if she hadn't remembered the entry unconsciously, perhaps brought the diary out so that I would find it. I said:

"Do you want to take another look at Allie Russo's picture?"

Her eyes met mine. "It isn't necessary. I recognized her the first time you showed me the picture. She was the woman who came here with the boy."

"How often did she come here?"

"Just the one time. I went and lived with Father after that, and eventually Jack and Marian took over this house until Ben came home." She held out her hand. "May I have my diary back, please?"

I handed it to her. Holding it tight against her body, she left the room.

I bade a silent farewell to her narrow-waisted back. The night before had been a one-time thing, not without passion but without consequences. Except that I would never forget Elizabeth.

XXXVI

Captain Somerville got home a few minutes later. I heard him and his wife talking quietly in the front of the house, too quietly for me to understand what they were saying. Then Somerville came into the study and closed the door behind him. He looked old and tired.

"My wife says you want to speak to me."

"If you have a minute."

"Can't it wait till morning? It's very late."

He yawned at his own suggestion. Tears of exhaustion and exasperation ran down his face. His beard had grown out in the course of the day; it caught the light and glinted.

"It's a matter of priorities," I said. "You're trying to stop an oil spill—"

"And succeeding," he insisted. "The whole thing will be over in another day or two."

"I hope so. I'm trying to stop another kind of spill—a series of murders and other crimes."

"A *series* of murders?"

"There have been three that I know of. The first one occurred on the night of May 2nd, 1945, when Allie Russo was shot in her bedroom." Somerville flinched, but I went on. "Last night or early this morning, a hospital inmate named Nelson Bagley was drowned off a Montevista beach. Sylvia Lennox's secretary was beaten to death on the same beach."

Somerville's face lost its remaining color. His eyes closed for a moment, and he swayed. He reached out and took hold of my arm, his fingers hooking painfully into the flesh above my elbow.

"Who told you about Allie Russo?"

I shook his hand off. "Her death is public knowledge. And her son happens to be my client."

"Laurel's husband?"

"Yes. Laurel still hasn't been heard from, and she's in danger. We don't want her to be the fourth victim."

There was a sound in the hallway, a small sound such

as a dog makes when he's left outside. The door was opened, and Marian Lennox came into the room. She moved with awkward diffidence in her dark clothes.

"You were talking about Laurel, weren't you?"

"Her name came up," I said.

She moved toward me with one hand outstretched, like a blind woman, but her eyes were bright and fearful. "Did you say Laurel was the fourth victim?"

"I said she's in danger of becoming that. It's what we're trying to head off."

"And you're not helping much," Somerville said to her. "Mr. Archer and I are having a very serious private discussion. Or we were hoping to have one."

"I'm sorry. When I heard Laurel's name, I thought you might have some new information." She looked into her brother-in-law's face, and then into mine. "Where is she, Mr. Archer?"

"Harold Sherry has the answer. I don't, at least not yet."

"Where is Harold Sherry?"

"Somewhere out in the boondocks, dragging a wounded leg."

"And Laurel is with him?"

"She may be. At any rate, he probably knows where she is."

"What can we do to get her back?"

Somerville had been pacing the room, and now he stepped between us. "That's what Archer and I are trying to talk about, Marian. Or were, when you interrupted." He moved toward her, clasping her shoulders in his hands, and speaking in a softer voice: "I'm well aware of what you've been through today, and I don't mean to be unfeeling. But I suggest you go to bed now. Did you get any sleep at all last night?"

"I don't remember. No. I don't think I did."

She half closed her eyes and hung her head as if she took comfort from the support of his hands. He rocked her gently:

"You're half asleep, old girl. Now get off to bed. Do you want me to pour you a drink to take along?"

"No, thanks. You're very kind, Ben, but it would just excite me. Elizabeth promised me a sleeping pill."

"Get her to give you a couple of chloral hydrates. It's what I use when I can't rest."

He turned her, slid one arm around her shoulders, and walked her out into the hallway. Then he bent down and kissed the side of her face. The gesture seemed unforced, and it gave me a new impression of Somerville. In spite of his long trouble with his wife, he liked women and, in an old-fashioned patriarchal way, was good at handling them.

The contact with Marian seemed to have calmed him. "I'm sorry about the interruption. I'm afraid my sister-in-law is close to breakdown. Her whole life has been just about wiped out in the last thirty hours."

"How is her husband, Jack?"

"I saw him this evening, he's doing all right physically. But he doesn't handle trouble too well, and Marian handles it very badly. She's at loose ends without him. And you can imagine what these uncertainties about Laurel have done to her." He rapped his knuckles together. "We've got to get Laurel back."

"I think I've been making some progress. You can help me, Captain."

"Just tell me how."

"By answering some questions."

"All right. I'll do my best."

Somerville looked out into the hallway, then shut the door. We sat almost knee to knee in the chairs that his wife and I had occupied. I said:

"Did you know Allie Russo?"

His face became completely grave and still. "I won't deny it. But I want it understood that anything I tell you about her is in confidence."

"It has to be further understood that if you have important evidence it goes to the police."

"Who decides its importance?"

"Both of us, or either."

Somerville moved uneasily. "I can't accept that."

I said without much emphasis, "Would you rather talk directly to the Los Angeles police? Allie Russo's death occurred in their jurisdiction, and they never close the books on unsolved murders."

His hand wrenched and scoured at the lower part of

his face as if he was trying to reshape it. "I had nothing to do with her death."

"Who did?"

"There were several suspects, including her husband. She had a rather disordered life after she left Russo."

"How do you know that?"

"I saw her from time to time."

"Did you see her on the night she was killed?"

"I did not. I was with my wife at her father's house that evening. I went from there directly back to the ship, and we sailed for Okinawa the following morning."

"Did you know she was dead when you sailed?"

"I certainly did not. Ask my wife, and she'll confirm what I just told you."

"She already has."

"Then what is this all about?"

"You said you wanted to help."

"I do. That should be obvious. But I can't solve your problems for you by confessing something that I didn't do."

"What about something you did do? Were you Allie Russo's lover?"

"Not in any real sense. I may have slept with her a few times."

"You may have."

"I did. It was no great matter. I wasn't married at the time, and she had already left her husband when I met her. We were good friends, that's all."

"How did you meet her?"

"One of my crew members asked me to help her out. She was living with her little boy in a cheap hotel in Seattle, and he got the flu. I arranged for some medical treatment."

"What was the crew member's name?"

"Nelson Bagley." His voice was flat. "Bagley was crazy about her, but I don't think he ever got to first base. Which is probably why he killed her."

"You know that he killed her, do you?"

"Yes. I think I do."

"Were you there when it happened?"

Somerville took a deep breath and let it out, making an angry noise. "Certainly not."

"Did you know about her death on the night she was killed?"

He thrust out an impatient hand which pushed the idea away. "I didn't say that. I wasn't aware that Allie was dead until nearly three weeks after it happened. We were at sea off Okinawa. The battle for the island was still going on, and the *Canaan Sound* was providing fighter support for our troops—"

"What about Allie's death?"

"I was getting to that. We withdrew from the battle area to refuel—that was the night of May 22nd—and the oiler put some mail aboard before we started the fueling operation. My personal mail included an envelope containing a newspaper account of Allie's murder. Some kind soul had clipped it out and sent it to me." His voice was dry and harsh.

"Do you know who the kind soul was?"

"There was nothing in the envelope to identify him or her. Of course, I've thought of various possibilities, including her husband and my wife." Somerville gave me a rapid questioning look.

"I don't think it could have been your wife. The clipping may have been sent by Allie's murderer."

He shook his head. "Allie's murderer was aboard the *Canaan Sound* with me."

"Do you mean Bagley?"

"Yes. The newspaper clipping gave a fairly accurate description of Bagley as he was then. One of Allie's neighbors saw him sneaking around her house on the night she was killed. Apparently he was spying on her through the back windows. As soon as I read the description, I sent for Bagley, but he failed to show up. Then something happened that put the whole thing out of my mind."

"Was that when the ship caught fire?"

"No, it didn't happen immediately. That came later, and Nelson Bagley was responsible for it."

I studied Somerville's face. His look was grim and driven. I wondered for a moment if Bagley had become his monomania, the imagined source of all the trouble in his life, killer of his mistress, wrecker of his ship.

"I've heard it suggested that you were responsible for the fire on the *Canaan Sound*."

The Captain showed neither anger nor surprise. "I may have been partly responsible."

"You're very candid."

"I'm trying to be honest with you," he said. "The captain of the oiler reported later that I called for too much pressure when we were filling the avgas tanks, and that was why one of them ruptured."

"Did you?"

He lifted his hand like a statue coming alive, then dropped it as if coming alive was too much effort. "I don't remember the details of that night too clearly. I've spent a lot of other sleepless nights trying to. But I honestly don't remember making the request for higher pressure. Possibly I did. Certainly something went wrong." His eyes were puzzled. "I'd just received the news of Allie's death. It stunned me, and it's left me with a very foggy recollection."

It was an extraordinary admission. It seemed to me that for the first time I was hearing the truth about the loss of the Captain's ship and the Captain's mistress.

"Wasn't your avgas officer blamed for the rupture of the tank?"

Somerville's eyes moved with difficulty, like stone eyes, to my face. "Have you been investigating the *Canaan Sound* disaster?"

"Not exactly. But it keeps coming up."

"Has Ellis been talking?"

"Some. He took it very hard when he was shown Bagley's body. He seems to blame himself for the whole thing."

Somerville looked down at the floor between us.

"Did you encourage him to take the blame, Captain?"

"That was hardly necessary. Ellis was a willing volunteer. Anyway, it didn't really matter to him."

"It didn't matter? You should have seen him today."

Somerville shook his head abruptly. "I mean in the sense that he wasn't a career officer. It was just a job, and when he left the Navy I saw to it that he got a better job. But I lost my command. I lost the possibility of any future command. I sat out the rest of the war."

The Captain was still and quiet for a time. He seemed to be mourning obscurely, for his lost honor, or his lost pride. I had the queer impression that he had been sitting out those last few months of the war ever since, while some unreal alter ego carried on the business of peacetime life.

"You said that Bagley set fire to the ship. Were you serious, Captain?"

He roused himself from his gray dream. "I can assure you I wasn't joking. Bagley took a gun out of the communications shack and tried to kill himself. He gave himself a superficial wound in the head, but the damage he did was incalculable. This was some time after the avgas tank ruptured. Parts of the ship were awash with gasoline and fumes, and of course the smoking lamp was out. The flash of Bagley's gun started a fire in the passageway and set fire to him as well. He ran up to the flight deck and jumped overboard. We lost him—it was still dark, and we had to mobilize all hands to fight the fire. But the oiler found him in the sea and picked him up, along with some other men who had gone overboard. My steward Smith was one of them. Several other men were lost, either burned or drowned."

Somerville was breathing hard. It had cost him an effort to tell me about the fire that had ruined his ship and his career. He closed his eyes as if to shut out the memory.

"I don't understand why Bagley tried to shoot himself, Captain."

He opened his eyes reluctantly. "Whoever sent that clipping to me apparently sent one to Bagley as well. Bagley realized the game was up, stole a gun from the comm office, and went down into an empty passageway and shot himself, or tried to."

"How did he get hold of the clipping? Had the mail been distributed to the crew?"

"No. But remember that Bagley was a messenger in the comm office, where the mail was handled. It gave him special access."

"Do you *know* he saw a copy of the clipping?"

"I didn't see it in his hands," Somerville said. "But a copy of it was later found in a drawer in the comm office. It's all in the official record of the inquiry into the cause of the fire. You can refer to that if you don't believe me."

I neither believed the Captain nor disbelieved him. I had been in the Army, though, and traveled on naval vessels. I knew something about the power of their captains to create their own reality aboard ship—a power that sometimes could extend long past the event, and shape the record of official inquiries. I said:

"I still don't entirely understand why you didn't have Bagley brought in and questioned."

Somerville looked at me in some confusion. "When do you mean?"

"When you sent for him and he didn't show up."

"I had more pressing things on my mind. I was sitting on top of an oil spill, man."

"An oil spill?"

"A gasoline spill." The Captain turned red, as if the fire in his memory was showing through. "I mean to say a gasoline spill. I'm very tired, I'm afraid."

"So nothing was said to Bagley?"

"Not that night. Certainly not by me. I didn't see him at all until several months later. He was in a Stateside hospital, and he was hardly more than a living corpse. There was some idea of prosecuting him, for the sake of the record, but I helped to get it quashed."

"Prosecuting him for Allie Russo's murder?"

"Yes. There's no doubt he was guilty. But the authorities, both naval and civilian, saw no point in pressing the matter further, and neither did I. It appeared very unlikely at the time that Bagley would ever get out of bed again, or regain his powers of speech. It's a miracle that he did."

"Maybe that's why he was killed," I said. "He was learning to talk again."

Somerville glanced up sharply. "He was learning to talk again?"

"Yes. I spent some time with his doctor earlier this evening. Bagley had been doing considerable talking."

"About Allie—about Mrs. Russo's death?"

"The subject came up," I said.

"Did Bagley confess?"

"Some of the things he said could be taken as a confession. I'm not sure that's what they were, though. He may simply have been a witness to the murder. Or he may have done something to her after she was dead."

I watched Somerville as I named the possibilities. His face seemed to undergo a process of aging. "Exactly what did he say?"

"That he did something terrible."

Somerville inclined his head abruptly, his chin chopping down like an axe. "He killed her. His own death last night only confirms it."

"How does it do that?"

"I think he was killed in revenge by one of the Russos, Allie's husband or her son. You may not know those hot-blooded types as well as I do—if they have a stain on the family honor, they wash it away with blood."

The guilt of one of the Russos was a possibility I had considered. But I wasn't prepared to discuss it with Somerville. I tried to change the subject, unsuccessfully, since the possible guilt of the Captain himself was involved in what I said.

"Nelson Bagley saw your face on television Tuesday night. Did you know that, Captain?"

"I certainly did not. You mean to say that Bagley was watching television?"

"Somebody put him up to it."

"Somebody?"

"I think it was arranged by Harold Sherry."

"What was the point?"

"To get something on you and possibly other members of your family. Apparently Harold Sherry took Bagley out of the hospital for that purpose."

The Captain's face went through still another aging process which ended in a bitter smile. "Are you suggesting that I'm a suspect in Bagley's death?"

"The suggestion is yours."

"The hell it is. Where would I find the time, man? I've been working a twenty-hour day. And if there's anyone more in the public eye than I've been this week —" He opened his hands loosely and let them fall.

What he said was true. But he seemed to be an unreal

man even when he was saying true things. We sat and looked at each other, the unreality expanding between us until it lay like a pollution over the endless city and across the endless sea, all the way to Okinawa and the war.

XXXVII

Somerville escorted me to the front door, apologized for being very tired, and said good night. His wife didn't appear.

I sat in my car for a minute, looking out over the city which stretched like a luminous map to the horizon. It was hard to pick up its ever-changing meaning. Its whorls and dots and rectangles of light had to be interpreted, like an abstract painting, in terms of everything that a man remembered. The thought of Laurel, still lost somewhere in that maze, went through me like a pang.

A door opened at the back of the garage, spilling out light. Smith emerged and came toward me, trampling on the heels of his long shadow. I got out and went to meet him.

"I wanted to ask you," he said, "has Miss Laurel turned up yet?"

"Not yet. I've been looking for her."

"You're Mr. Archer, isn't that correct?"

I said I was.

The black man reached into his trousers pocket and brought out a plastic tube or vial between three and four inches long. "Is this yours?"

I took it into the lighted toolroom at the back of the garage. The label on the vial was that of a Pacific Palisades drugstore which I patronized, and had my name clearly typewritten on it.

"Lew Archer," it said. "Take one at bedtime as needed for sleep—Dr. Larry Drummond. (Nembutal Gr. 3/4 #100)."

After a blank moment, I realized that it was the vial

which Laurel had taken from my medicine cabinet. It was empty. Hope and fear collided in my chest.

I turned to the man behind me. "Where did you get this?"

"Right here. It was in the wastebasket in the tool-room bathroom."

"And it was empty?"

"It sure was. I didn't take anything out or put anything in. Was there some medicine in it?"

"Sleeping pills," I said. "The same ones that Laurel took from my bathroom."

"Are they dangerous?"

"I'm afraid they are. Will you show me where you found this empty tube?"

He opened a painted green door at the end of the toolroom and pulled the chain of a light over his head. The small room contained a toilet and a washbasin with a mirror on the wall above it and a white plastic wastebasket on the floor underneath.

The wastebasket was empty. There was no sign of Laurel anywhere in the room. I found myself peering intensely into the mirror as if her vagrant image might somehow have left its traces on the glass. I caught a glimpse of Smith's face looming dark and opaque over my shoulder.

"When did you find the vial?"

"Just now, since I got back from the Point. I didn't think it meant anything, and then I saw your name on it. With what you told me, it means that she's been here, doesn't it?"

"I think so. I hope so. Who uses this room?"

"Just me, and sometimes the man who helps with the gardening."

"Does he live in?"

"No, sir. He's Mexican. He comes over here from the barrio."

"When did you last come in here—I mean before you found the vial?"

He thought about the question, chewing at his lips with gold-glinting teeth. "Sometime this morning, early."

"Did you happen to look in the wastebasket then?"

"No, sir. I can't say I did. But I might have noticed if that tube had been in it."

"And you don't think it was?"

"I couldn't swear to it one way or the other."

"When was the last time you can swear the wastebasket was empty?"

"I emptied it yesterday," he said. "The garbage was collected yesterday."

"So Laurel could have been here any time since?"

"I wouldn't say any time. I've been around here part of today, between the two trips I made to the Point, this morning and this evening." He gave me an anxious sidewise look. "I hope you don't think I did anything wrong."

"There's no suggestion of that."

"I'm glad to hear it." But he sounded incredulous, and far from glad.

Trailed by Smith, I went back to the front door of the house. He unlocked it for me and let me in. The interior was dark and silent, and it made me feel like a burglar.

Elizabeth appeared at the end of the hall. She was still fully dressed and wide awake.

"Archer? I thought you'd gone long ago."

"I was on my way, but Smith found something interesting." I showed her the empty vial and explained its importance. "I don't want to raise your hopes too much, but this probably means that Laurel's been here in the last twenty-four hours, possibly even tonight."

"But it's empty. What does that mean?"

"I don't know. It worries me."

Elizabeth's eyes turned blue-black. "You think she swallowed the capsules?"

"It's possible."

"She could be on the property now somewhere. She may be dying."

I got the flashlight out of the trunk of my car. Smith turned on all the outside lights. The three of us made a search behind the trees, under the wet hedges, and through Laurel's old hiding places.

The bloody rat was still on the floor of the pool house. The Captain's picture looked down through cracked glass from the storage-shed wall. It seemed strangely like the memento of a dead man, a man who had died long ago on the far side of the ocean.

Smith came into the shed and found me standing in front of the picture. He stood beside me, and said with some feeling:

"He was the best captain I ever had in the Navy. I don't know what happened to his career."

"What caused the gasoline spill on the *Canaan Sound?* You were there, weren't you?"

He glanced down at his withered hand. "I was there. But don't ask me what caused it. Things go wrong for some men. First the gas tank went bad on him, and now it's happening again with this underwater oil. The Captain does everything by the book, but gas tanks and underwater oil wells don't know about the book. You have to be lucky dealing with them, and the Captain doesn't have that kind of luck. He'd be better off doing what he always wanted to do—teaching at Annapolis."

As we moved back toward the house, empty-handed and anxious, Marian came out of the open front door. Her gray-streaked hair was rumpled and her dress was twisted on her hips, as if she had dressed in the dark and in a hurry. She looked around rather wildly under the lights.

"What's going on out here?"

"Apparently Laurel paid us a visit today," Elizabeth said. "But she didn't stay."

I told Laurel's mother what Smith had found, and what I thought it meant. She grasped me by the shoulders. She was surprisingly strong, like a hurt cat, and she shook me:

"You've got to find her."

"It's all I'm trying to do, Mrs. Lennox."

"Where do you think she is now?"

"I have no way of knowing. It's possible she went home."

"Which home?"

"You'd know better than I would. You're her mother."

She rushed into the house. I followed her and found her telephoning in the Captain's study.

"You've got to help us look for her, Mr. Russo," she

was saying. She sounded close to hysteria. I lifted the receiver from her hand and spoke to Tom:

"Have you seen her or heard from her?"

"No, sir, I haven't. You think I should go out looking?"

"It's a big city, Tom. You might as well stay home. She may try to contact you."

"Okay, I'll stay home."

"Have you seen Gloria, by the way?"

"Not since I dropped her off in Redondo Beach. That makes two of them missing."

"At least there's some hope that Laurel is alive." I hung up.

Marian was at my elbow. "You told him he should stay home, that she might try to contact him. She might try to do the same to me. After all, I'm her mother."

"That's true."

"But our house is standing empty. What if she goes home and there's nobody there? I've got to go home."

"You're tired, dear," Elizabeth said.

"Not really. I couldn't possibly sleep, anyway. I seem to have given up sleeping. Will you lend me a car?"

"You shouldn't drive yourself," Elizabeth said.

I would have liked to volunteer, but I was so tired I didn't trust my driving. Smith said he would take her back to Pacific Point.

She promised to let me know if she heard from Laurel.

Turning down the hill toward home, I noticed that the view of the city had changed. It seemed larger, more luminous, and less abstract. It stretched between the mountains and the sea like a living substance with the power to be hurt and to hurt.

I switched off the thinking and feeling part, and drove home on automatic pilot.

XXXVIII

My apartment looked as if years had passed in the thirty hours since I had been there with Laurel. There was a drabness in the light, a sourness in the air. It gave me a shock to realize that the change was not in the apartment but in me.

I sat down on the chesterfield and closed my eyes, trying to separate myself from what had happened to the room and the light. Waves of darkness started to come in level with my eyes.

They carried with them a message which was repeated over and over: Laurel was long gone, and very likely dead; the empty vial in Somerville's garage had probably been left there to mislead us. I tried to explain to myself how this could happen, but I was too tired to think straight. I lay down with a cushion under my head and sank into sleep.

The telephone dredged me up from the black depths. I made my way across the room and picked up the receiver. It was my answering service.

"Mr. Archer? There's a woman trying to get in touch with you. I told her it was too early, but she insisted—"

"What woman?"

"She wouldn't leave her name."

"Did she leave any message at all?"

"She said something about her daughter coming home —the one you wanted to talk to."

"Did she say her daughter had come home?"

"I think that was the message. It didn't come through too clear. She talked as if she was slightly looped."

I thanked the operator, shaved myself and changed my shirt, and went out into the gray early morning. The traffic on Wilshire was sparse. I turned off onto Pico and followed it down toward the sea, then turned north on the highway.

A yellow miasma of smog left over from the day before floated above the coast and out over the water. The morning light that filtered through it was unkind to Topanga Court. With the broken cliff and the earth slide rising behind it, it looked like an abandoned mining settlement, a ghost town dominated by a pile of slag.

Remembering that Harold had a gun and the will to use it, I parked my car a couple of hundred feet up the highway. On the way back, I passed a carful of children parked on the shoulder. They were sitting in an old

Cadillac with a Texas license and fenders like crumpled wings. A sticker on the rear bumper of the Cadillac read, "Honk if you love Jesus." The children's dark eyes looked out at me in solemn question. Was this the promised land?

Gloria's green Falcon was standing under a carport at the rear of Topanga Court. Its license plate, caked with what looked like carefully hand-molded mud, was illegible. I moved around the building to the front. There was a light inside and, stitched among the sounds of highway traffic, I could hear the murmur of voices.

I tried the front door. It was locked. Then there were footsteps, and Mrs. Mungan looked out at me through the glass pane. If the place resembled a ghost town, she looked like a buried miner who had struggled up for one last glimpse of daylight.

She unlocked the door and stepped outside. The bell jangled harshly over her head. I could smell whisky on her, but her eyes were cold sober.

"You got my message, did you?"

"Yes." I thanked her.

"You took long enough to get here. I've had a hard time holding Gloria. She's scared."

"She has some reason to be. She's been involved in a kidnapping."

"She says not. She claims she hasn't set eyes on Laurel."

"May I talk to her directly, Mrs. Mungan?"

"Yes. I want you to. Why do you think I called you?" She peered up at the yellow sky. "I realize we're in trouble."

Gloria was waiting in the room behind the archway. She stood up when I came in, raising her clenched hands to the level of her breast, as though I might attack her physically.

"Good morning, Gloria."

"Good morning," her dubious mouth said.

She had lost her cheerfulness and her looks together. She was one of those girls who were almost pretty when they were feeling good, and almost ugly when they were depressed. She turned to her mother, scowling with apprehension:

"Martie? Could I please talk to him in private?"

"But you've already told me everything." The older woman looked at her suspiciously. "Or haven't you?"

"Certainly I have, but that's not the point. I'm embarrassed."

Mrs. Mungan retreated, closing a door behind her. Gloria turned to me:

"My mother means well, but she's got so many problems of her own, particularly since my father walked out on us. I've really been mothering Martie since I was about twelve. Her problems always loomed so large that I never had time to wonder if I had problems, let alone do anything about them."

This came out in an emotional rush, but the emotion dissipated as she spoke, and the words slowed. I didn't interrupt her. Every witness has his own way of creeping up on the truth. She said:

"It isn't easy to grow up with an alcoholic mother. Martie's been drinking for as long as I can remember—ever since Aunt Allie died. Do you know about Aunt Allie?"

"I know she was murdered. You told me about her yesterday morning, remember?"

"Was that just yesterday morning? It seems like about a year ago. Anyway, I know more about it now. Aunt Allie was shot by one of the men in her life—a man that she rejected."

"How did you find that out?"

"Harold told me last night, in the motel."

"In Redondo Beach?"

"No. We went to another motel after that. Harold didn't trust the doctor not to turn him in."

"Is Harold still in the other motel?"

"Not any more," she said.

"Where is he?"

She looked at me in distress. She had given her feelings to Harold and, damaged and disappointed as they were, they were hard for her to withdraw.

"Tell me where he is, Gloria. He's the key to this whole business."

"That isn't true," she said defensively. "Harold never

kidnapped anybody. And he never shot anybody, either."

"Who told you that?"

"He·did, and I know he was telling the truth. He was just trying to bring Aunt Allie's murderer to justice."

"Do you mean Nelson Bagley?"

She nodded. "He was the one who did the actual shooting. But there were other people involved—people who covered it up."

"Who were they, Gloria?"

"Harold made me promise not to tell. He said that he could take care of it himself."

"Are we talking about Captain Somerville?" I said.

"I didn't say that."

"But wasn't that the point of bringing Bagley here, to catch Somerville on television?"

She turned and looked at the television set as if it might be able to answer for her. But it was dark and silent.

"If you know so much," Gloria said, "why ask me about it?"

"All right, I'll tell you. Somerville was your aunt's lover. Bagley either had been or wanted to be. She rejected Bagley, and I think she took another lover. Bagley shot her. Somerville used his influence to keep the whole thing quiet, probably because he was afraid of being connected with it. But Harold Sherry's been digging it up again. Is that the general picture?"

"You know more about it than I do."

"But you spent considerable time with Harold last night. Didn't he tell you anything? Didn't he even explain how he got shot?"

"Laurel's father tried to kill him, he said."

"Why?"

"He said that Laurel's family always hated him."

"Did he tell you the reason?"

"No."

"Or mention that he tried to kill Laurel's father?"

"No." But her eyes were wide and thoughtful, scanning the night she had just gone through with Harold and watching all its meanings change their shape.

"How did Harold explain the box of money?"

"He said he cashed in his securities. His father left him all those securities, stocks and bonds. He was planning to leave the country and take me along."

I was getting tired of Harold's lies and her reluctance to let go of them. "Look, Gloria. You called me and I came here on the supposition that you wanted to talk. There's not much use in your holding back now."

"I didn't call you. My mother called you."

"Anyway, here we are. And you're not talking."

"What do you want me to say?"

"Tell me where Harold is."

"I don't know where he is, and I don't care."

"Where did you leave him?"

"I didn't leave him. He left me."

"How could he do that? Did somebody come and pick him up?"

"That's one thing I'm not going to tell you."

But something in her voice told me, and something in the angle at which she held her head, as if she had been struck by a human hand, or was about to be.

"Was it another woman, Gloria?"

After a long silence, she said, "Yes. It was an older woman. Harold made me promise not to look, but I peeked out the motel window and saw her."

"How old?"

"At least Martie's age. She was driving a big Mercedes. Harold crawled into the trunk and rode that way."

"With the money?"

"Yeah, he took the money with him."

"And the gun?"

She nodded dismally. "What's the matter with me?" she said. "Why do I always have to get the wrong ones?" She sat hunched over like a woman trying to give birth to a new life. "My cousin Tom was the one I really wanted. But the one *he* wanted was Laurel—ever since he was a little boy."

After a moment's delay, I was struck by the implications of what she said. "Since he was a little boy?"

"That's right."

I sat up straight. "Has Tom known Laurel that long?"

"Almost all his life," Gloria said. "They used to play together when he was four or so, and she was three. After his mother died, he lost track of Laurel, and he didn't see her again until a couple of years ago. Then she walked into the drugstore in Westwood one day and asked him to fill a prescription for her. Her name was on the prescription. It was a name that he had never forgotten and he sort of recognized her, too, from her baby days. But she was out of the store before he believed that she could actually be the same Laurel Lennox. Then he ran after her into the parking lot and told her who he was, and she remembered. It wasn't more than two months before they were married."

I had heard the end of the story before. "Who told you this, Gloria?"

"Tom did. Many times," she added with a hint of bitterness. But the bitterness was mixed with more positive feelings, including a touch of bridesmaid's sentimentality. The coming together of Laurel and her cousin was probably the main romantic event in her family's history.

But I was interested in its unromantic aspects. "I wonder how Tom and Laurel happened to be playmates when they were children?"

"I don't really know. I never thought about it. Maybe Martie will know."

Gloria opened a door into the back passageway and called her mother, who came out walking in a mist of alcohol. Her long day's drinking had already begun. But the eyes with which she searched her daughter's face were as sharp as a fortune-teller's.

"Is he taking you in?" She turned to me. "Do you have to take her in?"

"I don't think so. But it would be a good idea if Gloria went to the police on her own and gave them a full account. Do you have any friends in the Sheriff's department?"

The two women exchanged glances. "There's Deputy Stillson," the older one said. "He always liked you."

"Will you go and talk to Deputy Stillson, Gloria?" I said.

She clenched her fists and shook them, sending a tremor through her entire body. "I don't know what to say to him."

"Just tell the truth—what you told me—and ask him to pass the word to Captain Dolan in Pacific Point. Dolan is in the Sheriff's office there."

Tears sprang into her eyes, as if her head had been subjected to sudden pressure. "I don't want to tell on Harold."

"You have to, Gloria. And you better do it before I bring him in."

"You're going to bring him in?"

"Yes."

"Do you know where he is?"

"I think so."

"Where?" She stepped toward me eagerly.

"I can't tell you." I turned away from her and spoke to her mother: "Gloria's just been saying that your nephew Tom used to play with Laurel Lennox when they were children. Do you know anything about that, Mrs. Mungan?"

"I have a vague memory of it. Why?"

"Do you know how the connection came about?"

"I can't say I do." She spoke brusquely to Gloria, "If you're going to go and talk to a deputy sheriff, you better wash your face and change your clothes."

Gloria gave her mother a defiant look, but turned submissively and left the room.

"I didn't want her to hear this," Mrs. Mungan said. "I don't recall if I told you last night about my sister and Captain Benjamin Somerville."

"No, I don't think you did. What about Somerville, Mrs. Mungan?"

"He was the one that Allie fell for when she was in Bremerton. She thought for a while he was going to help her get a divorce and marry her. But then he turned around and married a girl half his age—a girl with high connections in the oil business. That girl was Elizabeth Lennox, Laurel's aunt."

She gave me a look of satisfaction, like a mathematician who had solved an equation. Then her face darkened, as if the product of the equation had saddened or frightened her.

"It all comes back to me now," she said. "Allie was hard up for money after she left her husband in Bremerton and came back here with Tom. Mungan and I helped her out as much as we could. But she was having a hard time holding on to the house and living from day to day. So I suggested she should go to Somerville and get something from him. After all, he was the one who broke up her marriage. And, being in real estate, we knew that he'd just paid fifty thou for a big new house in Bel-Air. That was a lot of money in those days, back in the spring of 1945.

"Allie told me she went to his house, but he wasn't there. He was at sea. His new little wife was at home, though, and Allie got some money from her, enough to carry her for a few weeks. Then she ran out again.

"Mungan and I couldn't help her. In those late war years, we were just about losing our real-estate business, which we eventually did. So she went back to Somerville's place again. This time his new wife wasn't there, but her brother was—the same man we saw with Captain Somerville on TV Tuesday night. The brother and his wife hired her to do some babysitting for them, which Allie did right up to the day she died. That was how Tom and their little girl got together."

She stood in silence, swaying a little, listening to the flat echoes of her story. But her eyes remained uncomprehending. She wasn't a mathematician after all: more like an idiot savant who remembered all the details of her own and her sister's life but couldn't detect any over-all meaning in them.

XXXIX

I took the freeway south to Pacific Point, then switched to the old highway. Where it veered close to the ocean, I could see oil lying thin and rainbowed on the water, thick and black on the beaches.

Sandhill Lake was once again deserted. I could see no official cars and no Sheriff's men around the hunting club. But I remembered something I had forgotten. There was an armed guard and a barrier at the entrance to El Rancho; and I couldn't ask Harold's mother to pass me in.

I asked the guard to call William Lennox's house. A servant brought Connie Hapgood to the phone:

"Mr. Archer? I've been thinking about getting in touch with you. William appears to be missing."

"For how long?"

"At least an hour. His bed was empty when I went to wake him with his Postum. All of the cars are here, which means that someone took him, doesn't it?" Her voice rose high and cracked on the question.

"What do you mean took him?"

"I don't know exactly what I mean. But I'm frightened, and I don't frighten easily. Somehow this place seems terribly empty and dead."

"He could have left under his own power. He almost did yesterday."

"That worries me, too," she said. "We have a very large acreage here. Some of it is rough country. His heart isn't in very good shape, and he tends to overdo, and if he wandered off by himself—" She left the sentence unfinished.

I'll get there soon as I can. That won't be immediately, though."

"Where are you going first?" Her voice was sharp with a kind of jealousy.

"I'm on the track of Laurel."

I hung up before she could question me further. The guard lifted the barrier and waved me through.

I parked on Lorenzo Drive below Mrs. Sherry's hedge and walked up her driveway. It wasn't very steep, but it felt that way to the muscles of my legs and to my will. Harold had a gun and was probably in good enough shape to fire it.

I studied the windows for any gleam of metal or movement. But the only movements around the house were those of a pair of hummingbirds making aerobatic love.

I walked around to the back, as I had done the day before, and inspected the contents of the open garage. Very little seemed to have changed. The aging gray Mercedes was there, but this time the lid of the trunk was up and when I looked inside I found dried blood on the floor.

The back door of the house creaked. Mrs. Sherry appeared, moving rather stealthily toward the garage. She started when she saw me. But she had enough presence of mind to come up close to me before she spoke, and then to speak in a whisper.

"What are you doing here?"

"I want to talk to Harold."

"Harold isn't here. I told you that yesterday."

"Then why are we whispering?"

She touched her mouth with her hand as if it had given her away. But she couldn't bring herself to raise her voice.

"I've always had a very low voice," she whispered.

She moved past me in an elaborately casual way and shut the lid of the trunk as noiselessly as possible. Her movements were tense and awkward, and interrupted by glances in my direction. Her eyes had grown deeper and brighter in the course of the night.

"Where is he, Mrs. Sherry?"

"I don't know. We went into that subject yesterday, I believe. I gave you all the information I had—all there was." She spread her hands to show me how clean they were, and how empty.

"But this isn't yesterday. Harold is here with you, isn't he?"

Her deep bright eyes made the rest of her look even more faded and forlorn. She didn't answer my question directly:

"Some German philosopher—I think it was Nietzsche —said that history just goes on repeating itself—the same old story, like a worn-out record endlessly repeating itself. When I first heard that in college, it didn't make sense to me. But now I think he was right. It's the story of my own life."

"Can you tell me what the story is?"

She shook her head. "I don't know what it is. That's the strangest part of it. It seems to be repeating itself, and yet it always takes me by surprise."

"It's true of all of us, Mrs. Sherry. But not all of us have sons."

"I wish I didn't." But then she rebuked her mouth with her stern fingers. "No, that isn't true. I don't wish Harold dead, or unborn. I know if I didn't have him, I'd be even less of a person than I am."

"How is he, Mrs. Sherry?"

"He seems feverish. I've been making up my mind to call a doctor. Do you think Dr. Brokaw would come out here from Long Beach?"

"You could ask him. But I think you'd do just as well to call a local doctor."

Her face crumpled. "I can't. The whole thing would be common knowledge in no time."

"It's going to become common knowledge anyway. It already is, except for the names and the places. The one positive thing you can do for Harold is to get him to talk before he's forced to. If he'll tell us where Laurel Russo is, it should count for something with the law."

Mrs. Sherry's face lengthened as if of its own weight, like dough. "He doesn't know where she is. I've asked him."

"He doesn't know?"

"That's correct. He says he hasn't seen her for several days."

"Then he's lying."

"He may be." The admission came hard to her. "I don't always know when Harold is lying."

"Where is he?" I repeated.

"In the house. In his own room."

"Is he armed?"

"He was," she said. "But I took it away from him. He got quite excited in the course of the night—I think it was the fever. He was calling me names and cursing and waving the gun at me. So I took it away from him." She sounded ashamed, as if in some way she had defrauded Harold of his manhood.

"What did you do with the gun?"

"I unloaded it and put it away in my closet. I put the shells in another place, in the laundry hamper in my bathroom."

"You acted wisely. Now will you let me talk to him?"

The shadow of imminent loss fell across her face, dulling her eyes. "Harold will never forgive me."

"Worse things could happen. There's no future in the present situation, Mrs. Sherry. I'm surprised the county police aren't here now. And when they do get here you're going to be in trouble yourself, for harboring a fugitive."

"But I'm his mother."

"Then let me talk to him. And while I'm doing that you better call your doctor. Don't you have one in the neighborhood?"

"There's Dr. Langdale. He lives in El Rancho."

She took me to the back door and let me into the kitchen. A pan of burned bacon was smoking on the electric stove. She lifted it and burned her hand and dropped it. It was a day when nothing was going right for Mrs. Sherry.

While she was running cold water on her hand, her son called from somewhere in the house:

"What's going on out there? Mother?" He sounded angry and frightened.

"I'm coming," she said in a voice that was probably too low to be heard by him.

She led me quietly through the house to the door of his room, made a sign for me to wait, and went in.

"What is this?" I heard him say. "I thought you were making breakfast."

"I was. I burned my hand."

"Is that what it was? I thought I heard you talking to somebody."

There was a silence in the room. I could hear one of them breathing.

"There is someone here," she said at last. "A man in the hall wants to talk to you."

"What are you trying to do to me?"

He hopped on one foot to the door, swung it wide, and saw me. There was a bloody bandage on his leg, with the pajama leg cut off above it. His hair hung down in his hot eyes.

"Who are you? I don't know you."

"My name is Archer. I'm a private detective."

"What do you want?"

"I want Laurel."

He turned on his mother once again, as if she was the

source of his whole troubled life. "Was this your idea, you rotten old fool?"

She bowed her head as if she was accustomed to such epithets. "You mustn't talk to me like that, Harold. I'm your mother."

"Then why don't you act like it?"

I put my hand on his chest—his heart was beating wildly—and I pushed him backward into the room. He sat down suddenly on the edge of the bed.

"Harold and I have things to discuss," I said to Mrs. Sherry. "It'll be easier for you if you don't listen in. Easier for all of us."

She gave Harold her look of unbearable loss and moved past me toward the door.

"One thing before you go," I said to her. "Where's the box of money?"

"I put it in my closet." She added in a flustered voice, "I wasn't intending to keep it, you understand. Do you want me to get it?"

"Leave it where it is for now. It might give you a little something to bargain with."

She looked at me without comprehension. There had been too many demands on her understanding. Harold was watching us like a spectator at a ping-pong match on which he had bet heavily and was losing.

"That's my money you're talking about," he said. "I got that money the hard way."

"You seem to do everything the hard way, Harold. If I had your percentages, I'd start looking for a little advice."

"And how much is that going to cost me?"

"Nothing. I already have a client. His name is Tom Russo. But what you've done to Russo's wife may cost you the rest of your life."

He looked up at me in fear. "I didn't do anything to her. I haven't even seen her this week."

"That's the truth," his mother said. "He said the same thing to me."

"I heard you, Mrs. Sherry. Now could I possibly have a few minutes alone with Harold? The police will be turning up here any time now. The first thing they'll want to know is where Laurel is. If he can tell them, they may be prepared to forget some things."

"I don't know where Laurel is. Isn't that true, Mother?"

"Yes." She moved protectively between us. "Harold would never do anything to Laurel. He's always adored her."

"That's right, I've always adored her."

I sensed what was happening. Mother and son were picking up on a dialogue which had probably been going on for fifteen years and become as unreal and powerful as a dream. And I was cast in the third role in this dream play—the punitive father who had gone to live with another woman but returned to haunt them.

XL

I felt like walking out on both of them. Instead I spoke to Mrs. Sherry in a firm unfriendly voice:

"Get out of this room for a few minutes, will you, please? And call Dr. Langdale."

She was shocked into compliance. I slammed the door behind her. Harold said:

"You don't have to get violent. Mother isn't used to that sort of thing."

I laughed in his face. I would have liked to hit him. But there had to be a difference between the things that he might do and the things that were possible for me. I said:

"Where is she, Harold?"

He gave me a look of crafty innocence. "Who are we talking about?"

"Laurel Russo."

"Ask her father. He can tell you."

"Don't try to con me. Jack Lennox is in the Pacific Point hospital with a hole in the head. Which you put there."

"He shot me first. I shot him in self-defense."

"Extortioners have no rights of self-defense. If Jack

Lennox dies, you'll be in the worst hole a man can be in. You already are, with this kidnapping on your hands. If you were as smart as you think you are, you'd make some move to start climbing out of the hole."

His gaze moved around the room, restless and fearful. The room looked as if it had been kept for him just as it was when he was a boy in his teens. There were college pennants on the walls, faded like whatever dreams he had had. A bookcase full of young people's classics stood hopefully in one corner.

He tried to speak, licked his dry lips, and tried again. "I didn't kidnap Laurel, any more than I did the other time."

"You mean that she's in on this with you?"

He shook his unkempt head. "I haven't even *seen* Laurel."

"Then why did her father pay you a hundred thousand dollars?"

"That's between him and me."

"Not any more, Harold."

He was silent for some time. "All *right*. It was hush money."

"What does that mean?"

"He gave it to me to keep quiet. If *you* keep quiet, we can split the money."

His eyes were full of sudden hopefulness. He leaned toward me and almost fell out of bed. I steadied him with my hand against his shoulder.

"What have you got on Jack Lennox?" I said.

"Plenty. If it wasn't for all the loot his family has, the Navy would have put him in Portsmouth Penitentiary."

"For something he did during the war?"

"That's right. He shot a man in the head and set fire to his ship. But when you've got the kind of clout the Lennoxes have, you can even hush up a crime like that."

"How do you know this, Harold?"

"The man he shot lived to tell me about it."

"Do you mean Nelson Bagley?"

He looked at me in blank surprise. Like other half-smart alienated men, he seemed to find it hard to believe that there was knowledge in the world besides his own. The realization made him angry and insecure.

He said, "If you already know all this, I don't want to bore you."

"You're not. Far from it. Apparently you've been doing some detective work."

"That's right. You're not the only one."

"How did you get on the track of Nelson Bagley?"

"I've been doing some research on the Lennox family. I found out from a girl I know about a murder that was done in the spring of 1945. It was her aunt who was murdered. What made it interesting, the aunt had been the girl friend of bigshot Captain Somerville, who married Elizabeth Lennox. I looked the murder up in the old newspaper files, and I found out that Nelson Bagley was the main suspect. He was never brought to trial, supposedly because he was a mental case. But there were other reasons."

"What were they?"

"People like the Lennoxes own the courts, along with everything else. And they look after their own."

I didn't believe it, and I said so. Harold struck the air with his fist:

"I tell you I'm not lying. There's nothing old man Lennox wouldn't do for his son Jack. And nothing he hasn't done, either. He hushed up that Navy fire by bringing Captain Somerville into the family business."

"How do you know that?"

"I figured it out for myself—I've been making a study of these people. And Jack Lennox didn't deny it when I called him on it the other night. He didn't deny that he murdered the woman, either."

"Are you talking about Allie Russo?"

He nodded rapidly several times. "Jack Lennox was with her the night she was killed. I got that from an eyewitness."

"Nelson Bagley again?"

"That's right. Nelson was spying on Allie the night she was killed. He saw Jack Lennox in her bedroom with her."

"I thought Captain Somerville was her lover."

"He was. But Somerville went to sea. And Jack Lennox came back from the East where he had been going to Navy school, and sort of inherited her. He hired her to do some baby-sitting with Laurel, but she spent more time with Jack."

"That doesn't prove Jack killed the woman."

"No, but it all fits in. Nelson Bagley wasn't lying to me, and he practically saw it happen."

"Bagley never was a very good witness," I said, "and now he's unavailable."

"Naturally he is. I'm surprised that Bagley lived as long as he did, knowing what he knew about Jack Lennox. He knew that Lennox shot him and set fire to the ship. He knew that Lennox murdered Allie Russo."

"Are you sure he knew these things, or did he imagine them?"

"I'm sure, man, I made sure. Last Tuesday night, I set up a controlled experiment. I found out that Lennox and Somerville were going to make a television appearance, so I got Bagley out of the hospital and took him to my friend's place. Bagley recognized both of them when they came on the tube. He said Lennox was the one he saw in Allie's bedroom, and Lennox was the one who shot him."

I wasn't as sure as Harold was, or as he pretended to be. The facts of Allie's death and Bagley's shooting were reaching me filtered by time and probably distorted by the minds of two damaged men, one of whom was now dead himself.

"What happened to Bagley, Harold?"

"I took him to Lennox's house on the cliff in Pacific Point. I wanted to make absolutely certain of the identification. But I had to stay out of sight because Lennox knew me."

"He knew Bagley, too."

"Yeah. He knew him, all right. He took him for a walk out the back of his house and shoved him over the cliff into the surf."

"Did you actually see this happen?"

"I didn't have to. Lennox offered me money to keep quiet. He said that he could raise it overnight if we made the whole business look like a kidnapping. I can see now that he was baiting a trap with that money, planning to double-cross me from the begining. He thought he could shoot me dead and still be a hero. But I beat him to the draw."

Harold licked his fever-cracked lips. His accusations against Jack Lennox sounded like a sick man's delusions. But they were beginning to join together in a kind of weird reality. It corresponded at several points with the weird reality I had been living through, and provided an explanation for the double shooting at Sandhill Lake.

But one death hadn't been explained—the death of Tony Lashman. I said to Harold:

"The night before last, when you visited Jack Lennox's house on the cliff, did you go there directly from the wharf?"

"No. When I asked for Lennox, the woman at the restaurant gave me the wrong address. She gave me the address of old Mrs. Lennox on Seahorse Lane. But her secretary told me where Jack Lennox lived."

"The secretary sent you to Jack Lennox?"

"That's right."

"Did you know the secretary has been killed?"

Harold appeared to be shaken by the information. But all he said was, "It figures. Lennox would knock anybody off to cover up his tracks."

It seemed to me that he was repeating himself, ringing changes on a single paranoid theme. I had a sudden strong desire to get away from him and I went out into the hallway.

Mrs. Sherry came toward me with a solemn face. My own face must have changed, because she looked at me with alarm:

"Has something else happened?"

"No. We've just been talking. But your son isn't in very good shape. Did you call the Doctor?"

"I tried to. Mrs. Langdale said he was at the William Lennox house, and she could reach him there. Apparently something has happened to old Mr. Lennox."

"Did she say what had happened?"

"He had a heart attack and fell off a tractor. I don't know what a man his age was doing on a tractor."

"That's all the Lennox family needs," I said.

Mrs. Sherry's eyes failed to soften. She had no sympathy for the Lennox family.

I asked her for the money and the gun. Without argument, she brought them out of her bedroom into the hallway. I checked to make sure that the carton of money was full and the gun empty.

"May I use your phone, Mrs. Sherry?"

"You're going to phone the police?"

I said, on the spur of the moment, "It would be better if you did."

"Better for Harold?"

"Yes. Call the Sheriff's office in Pacific Point. Ask for Captain Dolan."

She nodded once and didn't raise her head. I followed her into the room where we had talked the day before. The drapes were closed against the morning sun, and shadows lay behind the furniture like vestiges of the night.

She dialed the Sheriff's number and asked for Dolan. "This is Mrs. Sherry—Harold Sherry's mother. Mr. Archer suggested I call you. Harold has been shot, and he isn't armed. He wants to give himself up and turn over the money to you."

She began to answer questions, and was still on the phone when the front doorbell rang. I let in a heavy white-haired man who said he was Dr. Langdale. I told him that Harold was in his room.

"How is William Lennox doing, Doctor?"

"Mr. Lennox is dead." His strained blue eyes came up to my face. "He was dead before I got to him. He was driving a bulldozer down the beach, and he had a heart attack."

"What was he doing on a bulldozer?"

"Trying to get rid of the oil, apparently. Mr. Lennox always hated any kind of pollution on his beach."

XLI

I passed Dolan's official car on the highway a few miles beyond the entrance to El Rancho. I kept going toward Pacific Point.

It was still fairly early in the morning when I stepped off the elevator on the top floor of the hospital. There was no deputy on duty outside Jack Lennox's door.

Lennox was sitting up in bed with a breakfast tray in front of him. His face was stippled with beard. His eyes looked jaded under the helmet of bandage. But there was nothing edible left on his tray.

"I'm sorry to disturb you, Mr. Lennox."

"What's up now?"

"We've taken Harold Sherry and recovered your hundred thousand. He made a rather full statement."

The air in the room seemed to freeze into solid silence. Outside, the sounds of life went on, the clink of dishes and the other morning noises of the hospital, the intermittent sounds of traffic sixty feet down in the street.

Lennox looked at the window as if he might decide to jump out through it. I moved around to that side of his bed. He averted his face and looked at the blank television set which hung like a scanning device high on the gray wall.

He gathered his strength and his wits together, and faced me. "What did Sherry say?"

"He made some serious allegations against you."

"He would. Sherry is a psychopathic liar, and he hates me. He hates my entire family. He mistreated Laurel when she was just a child, and I clobbered him for it. Ever since then, he's been trying to pay me back. What lies has he been telling now?"

"He said that in the spring of 1945 you shot two people. One of them, Allie Russo, died. The other one, Nelson Bagley, was wounded in the head and burned in the ensuing gasoline fire on the *Canaan Sound*."

Lennox swung his arm in a wide gesture of dismissal. "That's a lot of garbage."

"I wonder. Nelson Bagley identified you himself."

"How could he? Bagley is dead."

"He saw you on television Tuesday night. Wednesday night he went to your house with Harold Sherry. According to Sherry's story, you pushed Bagley over the cliff. Then you set up a meeting with Sherry intending to kill him. Unfortunately for you, he survived."

"And you buy this nonsense?"

"I wanted to check with you first. But you're not very responsive."

"What do you expect? You accuse me of a couple of murders that I had nothing to do with. You expect me to fall over backwards and confess?"

"Three murders," I said. "I omitted one. Your mother's secretary, Tony Lashman, was killed because he knew that Harold Sherry and Bagley went to your house Wednesday night."

Lennox looked really dismayed for the first time. "I didn't even know Lashman was dead."

"His body is in the cold room on the ground floor of this hospital. So is Bagley's. As soon as you're strong enough, I'll be glad to take you down and show them to you."

"You're helpful, aren't you? Now why don't you get out of here?"

"We haven't finished. I want to hear you tell me how Bagley died, and why. I have a kind of personal interest in him. I was the one who pulled him out of the water."

"I didn't put him there."

"Sherry says you did."

"That doesn't make it so. Sherry probably drowned him himself."

"What was his motive?"

"A psycho like Sherry doesn't need a motive. But if you have to have one, Sherry probably did it so he could pin it on me."

"That isn't very credible."

"You don't know Sherry, or how he feels about me."

"I think I know. I also know he didn't kill Bagley."

"But I did?"

"Either that," I said, "or you're covering for someone."

His eyes came back to my face, exerting an almost tangible pressure there, as if he was trying to read what was in my mind.

A nurse's aide knocked lightly and came in for his tray. "Did you enjoy your breakfast, Mr. Lennox?"

He was so deep in thought that he didn't hear her. She gave him a reproachful look and me a questioning one, then rattled out. When the automatic door had closed itself completely, I said to Lennox:

"Who are you covering for?"

There was a second interruption which postponed his having to answer me. The phone beside his bed rang. He picked it up:

"Jack Lennox here. . . . He's dead? . . . Why in God's name was he driving a tractor? . . . I see. . . . Really? Where is she? . . . I see. Well, take it easy. And don't let anyone in."

He hung up and leaned back against his pillows, drawing a series of deep breaths which didn't appear to be manifestations of grief. Excitement had colored his cheekbones and lit his eyes.

After a while, he sat up tall in bed. "That was my wife. My father was killed this morning. I happen to be his main heir, which means I've taken all the crap I'm ever going to take from anybody."

"Good for you."

"Don't mock me, little man." His gaze roved around the walls, as if the room had become too small to contain him, and came back to my face. "What would you do for a hundred grand?"

I was silent.

"Would you keep quiet about the subject of our conversation this morning?"

"Are you offering me a hundred grand?"

He nodded, watching me the way a cat watches a bird.

"The same hundred grand you offered Harold Sherry?" I said.

"Maybe that could be managed."

"And do I get a bullet to go with it, the way Harold did?"

He wrinkled up his face and made a dry spitting noise. "To hell with you. You're not serious."

"It's too late to make a deal," I said. "Harold is talking to the Sheriff's men now. They'll be coming to you shortly." I waited, giving him a chance to absorb this information. "What are you going to tell them?"

He lay back against his pillows and looked at the ceiling. The surge of excitement and power that he had felt when he learned of his father's death had passed through him and left him quite inert. He spoke in a different voice, a questioning tone that didn't come naturally or easily from him.

"You know my daughter Laurel, don't you?"

"Yes, I know her slightly."

"And you like her, don't you?"

"I like her very much."

"Would you be willing to do Laurel a service? I'm not asking you to do it for me, but for her."

"I've been trying to, as you know. I've been looking for her since Wednesday night."

"You can stop looking. My wife just told me that Laurel came home last night. I found out in the same minute that my daughter was alive and my father was dead." He spoke with a kind of egocentric sentimentality, as if he saw himself as a figure in a drama.

My heart was beating hard. "Where has she been?"

"Wandering around, I gather. Trying to get up the nerve to turn herself in."

"What kind of shape is she in?"

"Not too good. Marian had to put her under sedation. Laurel's still not over the idea of hurting herself."

There was a silence between us. Lennox lay very still with his arms stretched out at his sides, as if he was trying to share and understand his daughter's predicament.

"Did Laurel hurt anyone else?" I said.

"Yes. I'm afraid she did."

"Did she push Nelson Bagley over the cliff?"

He nodded almost imperceptibly. "We have a cliffside patio with a low wall, and Laurel was sitting there trying to clean the oil off some kind of bird. Bagley must have seen her from the road and wandered down there. He took her by surprise, and she pushed him over."

"Did Harold Sherry see this happen?"

"I don't think so. He was up the road in his car. Laurel's mother was the only witness, fortunately. But Sherry figured out what had happened—I couldn't keep Laurel quiet, and she was yelling and sobbing—and he asked for a hundred thousand to forget it. I had to go along with it. There were other matters involved, going back a good many years."

"Do you want to tell me about those other matters?"

"No, I don't. I was willing to pay a hundred thousand to keep the whole thing quiet, and I still am."

"Who suggested the kidnapping ploy?"

"I did. It fitted in with what the family knew about Sherry. And I couldn't think of any other way to raise the money."

"It had another advantage," I said. "If you had managed to kill Sherry yesterday, nobody would have blamed you."

He gave me a sharply interested look, but kept his mouth shut. I said:

"I still don't understand why Laurel pushed Bagley over the cliff."

"Neither do I, really. My wife thinks Laurel may have remembered him from the time that she was a little girl. Maybe she even saw him shoot Allie Russo."

"Was Laurel in the Russo house when the shooting occurred?"

"It's possible that she was. Allie Russo used to baby-sit for Laurel."

"Did Allie baby-sit for Laurel the night she was killed?"

"I don't remember."

"It was the night before you went to sea on the *Canaan Sound*. You should be able to remember what happened your last night ashore."

"Maybe I should, but I don't. I was drinking all day. They practically had to pour me on board the ship."

"If your daughter was at the Russo house that night, somebody must have taken her there. Did you?"

"I said I don't remember."

"Wasn't Allie Russo your girl at the time?"

"No. She was not."

"If Allie wasn't your girl, why did you shoot Nelson Bagley?"

Lennox sat up abruptly. "Has Somerville been talking?"

"It doesn't matter who's been talking. The question is why you shot Bagley."

He grimaced and peered from side to side like a man entrapped in the maze of his own nature. "So it was Somerville. Too bad for Somerville. All right. Allie was my girl for a short time while I was waiting for sea duty. When I went aboard the ship in Long Beach that night, I didn't know she'd been killed. And I didn't find out for several weeks, when our first mail came aboard in Asiatic waters. They'd made me the mail officer, so I got to it fast. Somebody sent me a newspaper clipping about Allie's murder, and it gave a full description of the main suspect."

"Which fitted Bagley."

"That's right. Whoever sent the clipping to me sent one to Somerville, too. It made him so jittery that he accidentally ruptured one of the gas tanks. And I can tell you it did nothing for me. I called Bagley up to the communications shack and got a forty-five out of the safe and held it on him while I asked him some questions. He admitted he was there at her house that night. When I showed him the newspaper clipping, he broke and ran. I followed him, and without really intending to, I squeezed off a shot. It hit him, and the flash set fire to the ship. But the fire was really Somerville's fault—he was the one that ruptured the gas tank. If Somerville wants to make an issue of it at this late date, he's the one who has a lot to lose. I'm the head of the company as of this morning."

But Lennox looked around like a dauphin who had waited too long and was already weary at his coronation. I wondered how long he would exercise the power his father had had, and I thought not long. I said:

"Who sent those clippings to you and Somerville?"

"I don't know."

"Were there any messages with them?"

"Not in mine."

"Any writing on the envelope?"

"No. The address was typed."

"Fleet Post Office address?"

"That's right."

"Why were those clippings sent to you, do you think?"

"To make us suffer," he said.

"Then whoever sent them must have known that you and Somerville had been close to Allie Russo, isn't that right?"

"I suppose so."

"How many people knew you were her lover?"

"Nobody knew."

"What about the children? Laurel and Tom?"

Lennox leaned toward me, his eyes wide, as if he had been hit by a long shot fired from below the curve of time. "You think that little boy sent the clippings? Or Laurel? She was only three, and the boy wasn't too much older."

"They were both old enough to talk."

Lennox lay back and absorbed the idea. His face became pale and anxious. He gnawed his lips.

"Have you thought of someone they might have talked to?" I said.

"No. There isn't anyone." He turned restlessly on the bed. "I asked you before if you'd do a service for my daughter."

"You haven't told me what it is."

"Would you be willing to take care of her for a bit, maybe take her on a little trip?"

"I'd have to think about it."

"There's no time to think about it. I'm talking about right now, this morning. I can provide you with a jet and pilot, and I'll pay you well."

"Where do you want me to take her?"

"Out of the country. Central America would probably be best—we have connections down there."

"It isn't a good idea," I said. "If Laurel killed Bagley, it's better for her to stay here and face her day in court. Given the circumstances, and her emotional condition, she isn't likely to be convicted of murder."

"What will they do to her?"

"I can't predict that. With the kind of lawyers and doctors you can afford, you should be able to get the charge reduced, maybe have her put on probation in her husband's custody."

"Would her husband take that kind of responsibility?"

"I think he would. He loves her."

"But wouldn't everything have to come out in the papers?"

"Everything will anyway. Especially if you try to fly Laurel out of the country."

Lennox was silent for a long minute. "You're right, that wouldn't be a good idea. But there's still something I want you to do for me. For Laurel, I want you to go and look after her, starting now. I can't make it myself, and Laurel and Marian aren't on good terms. They haven't been since Laurel was a teen-ager and started living a life of her own. Will you take over from Marian for me?"

"I'll do my best."

On my way out through the hospital lobby, I met Sylvia Lennox coming in. She looked like the survivor of an almost fatal illness. Her face was carved thin and her eyes were very bright.

"You haven't found Laurel?"

"Not yet."

"How is Jack?"

"He seems much stronger," I said.

"My husband, William Lennox, was killed this morning; did you know that?"

"Yes. I'm sorry."

"I'm sorry, too, which rather surprises me. I've been full of malice towards him, wishing him dead."

"He wasn't killed by a wish."

"I know that, Mr. Archer. I'm not losing my mind, though I may have given that impression yesterday afternoon." She drew in her breath. "Yesterday I seemed to have reached the end of my life, the end of my nature. But just now I've discovered that I haven't. I'm sorry about William's death. I can even feel some compassion for the woman."

"Why don't you tell her that?"

"I don't feel that much compassion," she said dryly.

"Why are you telling me?"

"Because you're a witness. You saw me at my dead end yesterday. I wanted you to know that I'm not going to spend the rest of my life in that state." She moved closer to me and lowered her voice: "But I can't get over what happened to Tony Lashman. Why do you think he was killed?"

"To keep him quiet. He was a witness, too. Now if you'll excuse me, Mrs. Lennox, I should be on my way."

There was one more thing to witness.

XLII

I parked on the road near Jack Lennox's mailbox. Before I approached the house, I got the .38 out of the trunk of my car, loaded it, and put it in my pocket. I moved down the driveway cautiously, studying the lay of the land. It was the first I'd seen of it by daylight.

The house was low, built into the rim of the cliff and partly cantilevered over it. Extending from the house on the right was the patio with the wall over which Bagley had fallen to his death.

A dead grebe covered with oil lay on the patio. Beyond it was an empty field which had been plowed to keep the weeds down. Shore birds driven off the beaches were foraging in the dirt.

Workboats moved back and forth on the water, spraying the unshrinking edges of the oil slick with chemicals and straw. Smoke hung in the sky above them like a dark reflection of the oil on the sea. When I moved closer to the rim of the cliff, I could see the multiple sources of the smoke. Up and down the shoreline great fires were crackling, fed by oil-soaked straw which dozens of men were raking up from the black stony beach.

I envied the men on the boats and on the beaches. I

envied anyone who didn't have my errand to perform.

I knocked on the front door. Marian Lennox must have been watching me from inside the house. She spoke through the door:

"Go away. My husband told me not to let anyone in."

"Your husband sent me here. You remember me, Mrs. Lennox. My name is Archer."

"Why?" she said in a high thin voice. "Why did he send you here?"

"He wants me to look after Laurel."

"I'm perfectly competent—" She caught herself. "Laurel isn't here."

"Your husband says she is. You might as well let me in, Mrs. Lennox. We have some things to discuss."

Abruptly she opened the door. The morning light fell harshly on her face. Her hair was ragged and streaked with white, as if time had run his ashy fingers through it.

The gun with the telescopic sight was standing in the corner of the hallway. I moved past Mrs. Lennox and took possession of it. She didn't try to stop me but simply stood and looked at me with eyes in which the long night still persisted. I disarmed the gun and set it back in the corner.

"Where's Laurel?"

"In her room. I gave her some sleeping pills, and she went to sleep."

"What happened to the sleeping pills she had? The Nembutals?"

"She flushed them down the toilet in the Somervilles' garage. She told me she was on the point of taking all of them. But then she decided to live." The woman's eyes were bright and watchful. "It was a brave decision."

"To go on living?"

"I think so. She has so much to face up to. Didn't my husband tell you what she did?" Her long face lengthened. I thought she was going to cry, but only words came out of her downturned mouth: "She killed a man last night—no, the night before last. She pushed him off our patio and he fell down on the rocks. But you know that."

"How do you happen to know it, Mrs. Lennox?"

"I saw her do it. She ran at him and pushed him with all her force. He went flying over the wall."

She mimicked the action she was describing, pushing her hands out violently in front of her. But the expression on her face, widemouthed and horrified, seemed to be that of the man falling.

"Why did Laurel kill him?"

"I don't know. There have been a lot of things I don't understand."

"Did she remember Bagley from the old days, when she was a little girl?"

"Yes, I believe she did." She picked up the idea. "As a matter of fact, he murdered her baby-sitter when she was three. He shot and killed her."

"And Laurel saw this happen?"

"Maybe she did. She was in the house at the time. She was supposed to be sleeping, and so was little Tom, but maybe she did."

"How do you know these things, Mrs. Lennox?"

"I have my ways of knowing. People try to keep things from me, but I find out."

"Were you in the Russo house the night Allie was shot?"

She nodded. "I went there to bring Laurel home. That was all I did. Jack was supposed to meet me at the club but he didn't come and he didn't come, so I went and brought Laurel home."

"Was Allie dead when you went there?"

"I don't know. I didn't look in the bedroom. I didn't know about her death until I saw it in the paper."

"When was this?"

"Several days later. Little Tom was alone with her all that time. But I didn't know it. I swear I didn't know it."

"I believe you, Mrs. Lennox. Nobody but a ghoul would leave a child alone with his mother's body."

"I'm not a ghoul." She was appalled by the name. "Anyway, he wasn't my child. He belonged to that filthy woman."

"Why do you call her that?"

"Because she was. She was no better than a prostitute. But Jack chose to spend his last night ashore with her. He went to drop off Laurel at her house and never came back. I went there and found him lying drunk in her—"

She clapped a hand to her face. It incompletely masked her widened eyes and mouth.

"Did you shoot her, Mrs. Lennox?"

She spoke after a silence. "If I did, I had good reason."

"Did you, though?"

"I'm not going to answer that," she said behind her hand. "I have a right not to answer. Besides, we know that Nelson Bagley shot her."

"How do you know that?"

"It came out in the *News*. The neighbors saw him sneaking around the house that night, and they gave his description to the police."

"All this was printed in the *News?*"

"It certainly was. I still have the clipping somewhere if you want to see it."

"Did you have more than one copy of the clipping?"

"As a matter of fact, I did. I thought it was important."

"What did you do with the other copies?"

"I sent them to certain people who would be interested."

"Like your husband and your brother-in-law?"

"Yes. I wanted them to know."

"You wanted them to know what you had done, but not that you had done it."

She breathed profoundly, as if she had been holding her breath all night. The walls of the hallway seemed to be closing in. Once again, it reminded me of a cell where prisoners were held without hope of release.

She said, "Why should I be the only one to suffer? You men have all the fun. And then you leave the women alone to suffer."

"Is that what your husband did to you?"

"Again and again," she said. "I told you, he even spent his last night ashore with her."

"So you shot her."

"I'm not admitting anything."

"You admitted that you sent your husband the clipping from the *News*."

"That was no crime. They can't do anything to me for sending him a clipping. It seemed to me he had a right to know about her death." She spoke with a kind of remembered grief, but her grief had long since turned malign. "I used to imagine the look on his face when he opened that envelope with the clipping in it and found out she was dead."

"Why did you send one to Somerville?"

"She was his girl first. He passed her on to Jack." She looked at me with loathing. "You men are dirty creatures, all of you. I'm glad all this has come out. I've been sick of this filthy pretense of a marriage for years."

"Why did you push Nelson Bagley over the cliff?"

"He remembered me. He saw me at the woman's house that night. He was the one who phoned me and told me my husband was with her."

"And you went there and shot her?"

"I'm not admitting anything," she said.

But she looked at me with the realization that there was hardly anything left to admit.

"Did Laurel see you push him over the cliff?"

"Yes. She ran away. But she came back last night."

"Did she speak to you about it?"

"Yes, she did. She said I ought to call the police and make a full confession."

"Are you willing to do that?"

"I don't know. I'm afraid. What will they do to me? I've killed three people." Her face opened as if she was falling again.

"I can understand why you killed Allie Russo," I said, "and Nelson Bagley. But why did Tony Lashman have to die?"

"He knew that Nelson Bagley had come here to the house. He tried to get money from me. He wanted a hundred dollars a day for life."

Her voice was cold and resentful. She had suffered so much that she was immune to anyone else's suffering. I was growing weary of her, and I asked her to take me to Laurel.

We went to a bedroom at the front of the house. The wall that faced the sea was made of glass, but it was heavily draped against the morning. At one end, a glass door opened onto a railed balcony.

Laurel lay asleep on the bed, a pillow under her dark head and an afghan over her. There was a telephone on the bedside table. Before I used it, I bent over Laurel and touched her warm forehead with my mouth. I could hardly believe that she was alive.

Behind me, the door to the balcony opened and closed. Marian Lennox was climbing awkwardly over the railing.

I moved toward her. "Marian, come back."

She paid no attention to me. She stepped off into air and fell in silence until the black boulders stopped her. Smoke swirled over her body like the smoke from funeral pyres.

I went back to Laurel. She stirred and half awakened, as if my concern for her had reached down palpably into her sleeping mind. She was alive.

I picked up the phone and started to make the necessary calls.

ABOUT THE AUTHOR

ROSS MACDONALD was born near San Francisco in 1915. He was educated in Canadian schools, traveled widely in Europe, and acquired advanced degrees and a Phi Beta Kappa key at the University of Michigan. In 1938 he married a Canadian girl who is now well known as the novelist Margaret Millar. Mr. Macdonald (Kenneth Millar in private life) taught school and later college, and served as communications officer aboard an escort carrier in the Pacific. For over twenty years he lived in Santa Barbara and wrote mystery novels about the fascinating and changing society of his native state. Among his leading interests were conservation and politics. He was a past president of the Mystery Writers of America. In 1964 his novel *The Chill* was given a Silver Dagger award by the Crime Writers' Association of Great Britain. Mr. Macdonald's *The Far Side of the Dollar* was named the best crime novel of 1965 by the same organization. Recently, he was presented with the Mystery Writers of America's Grand Master Award. *The Moving Target* was made into the highly successful movie *Harper* in 1966. *The Goodbye Look* (1969), *The Underground Man* (1971), *Sleeping Beauty* (1973) and *The Blue Hammer* (1976) were all national bestsellers. Ross Macdonald died in 1983.

THE THRILLING AND MASTERFUL NOVELS OF ROSS MACDONALD

Winner of the Mystery Writers of America Grand Master Award, Ross Macdonald is acknowledged around the world as one of the greatest mystery writers of our time. *The New York Times* has called his books featuring private investigator Lew Archer "the finest series of detective novels ever written by an American."

Now, Bantam Books is reissuing Macdonald's finest work in handsome new paperback editions. Look for these books (a new title will be published every month) wherever paperbacks are sold or use the handy coupon below for ordering:

NERO WOLFE

He's not much to look at and he'll never win the hundred yard dash but for sheer genius at unraveling the tangled skeins of crime he has no peer. His outlandish adventures make for some of the best mystery reading in paperback. He's the hero of these superb suspense stories.

BY REX STOUT